FIR
FLOOD

'Kalki' is the pen name of Ramaswamy Krishnamurthy (1899–1954), whose career in writing and journalism began as activism during the struggle for Indian independence. He served as editor of the popular Tamil magazine *Ananda Vikatan* before launching *Kalki*. The magazine—and eventually its founder—was named for the mythological tenth avatar of Vishnu to symbolise a vision to 'destroy regressive regimes, express radical thoughts, take readers into new directions, and create a new era'. Kalki wrote several novels, including *Parthiban Kanavu* and *Sivakamiyin Sabadam*, as well as political essays, film reviews, dance and music critiques, and scholarly work.

Nandini Krishnan is the author of *Hitched: The Modern Woman and Arranged Marriage* and *Invisible Men: Inside India's Transmasculine Networks*. She has translated two of Perumal Murugan's works into English: *Estuary* and *Four Strokes of Luck*. She was shortlisted for the PEN Presents translation prize 2022 and the Ali Jawad Zaidi Memorial Prize for translation from Urdu 2022. She is an alumna of the Writer's Bloc playwrights' workshop by the Royal Court Theatre, London. Her novel-in-manuscript was a winner of the Caravan Writers of India Festival contest and showcased at the Writers of the World Festival, Paris, 2014.

PONNIYIN SELVAN BOOK 1

FIRST FLOOD

KALKI

TRANSLATED BY
NANDINI KRISHNAN

eka

eka

First published in Tamil as *Ponniyin Selvan*

Published in English in 2023 by Eka, an imprint of Westland Books, a division of Nasadiya Technologies Private Limited

No. 269/2B, First Floor, 'Irai Arul', Vimalraj Street, Nethaji Nagar, Alapakkam Main Road, Maduravoyal, Chennai 600095

Westland, the Westland logo, Eka and the Eka logo are the trademarks of Nasadiya Technologies Private Limited, or its affiliates.

Translation Copyright © Nandini Krishnan, 2023

ISBN: 9789357762823

10 9 8 7 6 5 4 3 2 1

Typeset by SŪRYA, New Delhi
Printed at Nutech Print Services-India

CONTENTS

1

AADI TIRUNAAL[1]

In the flood of time with no beginning and no end, in the flow of a tale with no rest and no restraint, we ask that our readers embark on the boat of our imagination and journey with us for a little while. Let's set ourselves the speed of a century a second, and go back nine hundred and eighty-two years.[2]

Lying in the southern part of the land of Tirumunaippaadi, which is situated between Thondai Naadu and Chozha Naadu, about two kaadhams[3] to the west of Tillai Chitrambalam, is a lake as large as an ocean. It goes by the name of Veeranarayana Eri. It measures one-and-a-half kaadhams from south to north, and half a kaadham from east to west. Over time, its name has been corrupted to Veeranaathu Eri. Not one soul who chanced upon the lake in the months of Aadi and Aavani, when the first flood of the year had swept its waters right up to the brim where they foamed and frothed and boiled and bubbled, could be exempt from marvelling at the incredible achievements of our Tamil ancestors. Did our forefathers limit themselves to catering to the well-being of their contemporaries alone? It was keeping in mind the future children of this motherland of theirs, generation after generation of descendants sprouting like plantain trees at the feet of their forebears over thousands of years, that they carried out their engineering feats, was it not?

On the eighteenth day of Aadi, in the early hours of the evening, when the waters of the Veeranarayana Lake were gushing in waves quite like the ocean, a young warrior cantered along the banks on his horse. He was a scion of the Vaanar clan, whose bravery has been etched into the annals of Tamil history. His name was Vallavarayan Vandiyadevan. His horse, exhausted from its long journey, had slowed to a walk. He didn't mind, enraptured as he was by the dimensions of the lake and the sights of the day.

It was the norm for all the rivers of Chozha Naadu to overflow with the waters of the first flood on the eighteenth day of Aadi, called the Aadi Perukku, as it was for the lakes that fed from these rivers to be filled with those swirling waters right up to their edges. The waters that coursed from the river called Vada Kaveri by devotees and Kollidam by the commonfolk, through the Vadavaaru River, had leapt into the Veeranarayana Lake and turned it into a churning ocean. The water then irrigated the surrounding lands through the seventy-four canals that were predecessors of the sluice gates of our time. For as far as the eye could see, farmsteads were engaged in agricultural activity that made the most of the water—the men were ploughing the fields, and the women were planting seeds. They kept their fatigue at bay by singing cheerful folk songs.

Vandiyadevan didn't spur his tired horse on. He enjoyed the sights and sounds instead. It had occurred to him to verify whether the lake truly supplied seventy-four irrigation canals. He estimated he had travelled a kaadham and a half along the shore and counted seventy thus far.

Aha! What a gigantic lake this was! How long! How wide! The lakes dug by the kings of the Pallava era in Thondai Naadu would be reduced to little ponds in comparison. How incredible that it had occurred to Prince Rajadityar, the son of Madurai Konda Parantakar, to craft this vast lake so that the waters of the Vada Kaveri would not be wasted! He had not only conceived of such an audacious idea, but had gone on to put thought into action. What a genius he must have been! He had no equal in valour either. He had personally led the vanguard into battle at Takkolam, seated on his elephant, hadn't he? He had lost his life to an enemy's spear embedded in his chest, hadn't he? He had earned the title of 'Yaanai Mel Thunjiya Devar'—He Who Rode His Elephant to the Heavens—in death, hadn't he?

The kings of the Chozha clan were truly awe-inspiring. As was their courage, so was their sense of justice; as was their sense of justice, so was their devotion to God. In contemplating that he had a claim to friendship with the kings of such a clan, Vandiyadevan's shoulders grew broader. His heart swelled with pride in quite the same fashion as the Veeranarayana Lake swelled with its waters when the westerly wind swept across the surface with a 'virrrr'.

Vandiyadevan arrived at the southern end of the Veeranarayana Lake, his mind occupied with such thoughts, and was treated to the sight of the Vadavaaru breaking off from Vada Kaveri to empty itself into the lake. The bed of the lake stretched some distance beyond the water's surface into the shore. In order to prevent damage to the shore during the floods, the residents of this region had planted karuvela and vila trees into the soil. Wild sugarcane bushes made their sturdy way through the banks. To watch from a distance as the waters of the first flood threw themselves into the lake, lined by greenery on either side, was to see a stunning painting come to life.

There were other sights that further enhanced the beauty of this remarkable picture.

It was the auspicious day of the Aadi Perukku, wasn't it? Crowds upon crowds of people from nearby villages had assembled on the shores, dragging along sapparams they had fashioned from the ivory-coloured fronds of coconuts. Men and women and children and even some of the elderly had outfitted themselves in their very finest clothes and ornaments for the occasion. The womenfolk had decorated their hair with kothu upon kothu of thaazhampoo, sevandhipoo, malligai, mullai, iruvaatchi and shenbagam. Families had brought along kootaanjoru—a spicy rice mixture—and ate from areca plates and cups as they strolled along the banks. The thrill-seekers walked across the water to the inlets in the north bank and ate as they watched the water gush in. Some of the children threw their used areca plates into the canals, and laughed and clapped as the water ferried them along the furrows. Young men with a taste for mischief plucked the flowers off their beloveds' hair and threw them into the canals, delighting in watching them re-emerge on the opposite bank.

Vandiyadevan stood at the shore, taking in all this. He could hear the sweet voices of the women as they sang boat songs and flood songs and kummi and sindhu[4].

Vadavaaru pongi varudhu
Vandhu paarungal, palliyare[5]!
Vallaaru viraindhu varudhu,
Vedikkai paarungal, thozhiyare[6]!
Kaveri parandu varudhu,
Kaana vaarungal, pangiyare[7]!

The Vaduvaaru is frothing towards us,
Come and look, palliyare!
The Vallaaru is speeding towards us,
Take in the sight, thozhiyare!

The Kaveri flies towards us,
Come to see it, pangiyare!

There were some girls who were singing songs of praise for the kings of the Chozha clan. Women sang of Vijayalaya Chozhar, a veteran of thirty-two wars that had tattooed ninety-six scars into his flesh, which he proudly displayed as ornaments. His son, Aditya Chozhan, too found a place in the songs, and one girl sang particularly mellifluously of his valour and dedication to Lord Shiva, for whom he had erected sixty-four temples from the origin point of the Kaveri to the estuary where the river merged into the ocean. Another sang of Adityan's son, Parantaka Chozha Maharaja, who had defeated the Pandiyas and Pallavas and Cheras and sent an army to conquer Lanka, and flown the flag of his clan in that land. She drew a crowd, which sighed 'Ah! Ah!' every now and again by way of applause.

As Vandiyadevan listened to them from his perch on the horse, an elderly woman looked at him and called, 'Thambi[8]! You seem to have travelled a long distance. You're tired! Get down from your horse and have some kootaanjoru, won't you?'

Her voice caught the attention of a crowd of young women, who turned at once to look at our young traveller. They whispered among themselves and giggled. Vandiyadevan felt both shy and thrilled by this reception. He wondered, for an instant, whether he should do as the old woman asked and dismount from his horse to eat the kootaanjoru. But if he did, the young women would mob him and tease him mercilessly. So what if they did? It was no mean feat to see such a lot of beautiful girls all in one place, let alone be surrounded and teased by them. Even if they were to ridicule him, the sound of their laughter would be devagaanam, divine music. To Vandiyadevan's eager young eyes, every one of the women appeared to be a Rambha or Menaka, the celestial apsaras.

At the very moment he was weighing his options, he was distracted by a sight from the southwestern part of the Vadavaaru. Seven or eight large boats, their brilliant white sails making them look like enormous swans that had spread their wings as they sluiced through the water, were speeding towards the shore.

The people, who had been caught up in their various celebratory activities, turned as one to admire the oncoming fleet.

One among the boats broke off to rush to the north bank of the lake. Soldiers, with sharp spears that shimmered in the sunlight, dismounted and ran to the shore, yelling, 'Go! Go! Move from here! Move!' at the revellers. The crowd dispersed almost before the soldiers could chase them off.

Vandiyadevan couldn't make any sense of this. Who were these soldiers? Whom were the boats with their white sails bearing? From where were they arriving? Were they members of the royal family?

Vandiyadevan approached an elderly man who was leaning against his staff and watching the proceedings.

'Aiya[9],' he said. 'In whose employ are these soldiers? Whose boats are those that skim across the water like a flock of swans? Why are they chasing away the public? And why does anyone obey them?'

'Thambi! Do you not know or what? Look at the flag fluttering on the boat at the centre of the fleet. What do you see there?' the elderly man asked.

'It seems to have a palm tree on it.'

'Yes, it is indeed a palm tree! Don't you know that the palm tree is the emblem of Pazhuvettaraiyar's flag?'

'Is it the great warrior Pazhuvettaraiyar?' gasped Vandiyadevan.

'It must be. Who else could raise the palm tree flag?' his interlocutor said.

Vandiyadevan's eyes had widened in the incredulity of the moment. They turned to watch the approach of the boats. He had heard ever so much about Pazhuvettaraiyar. Who wouldn't have heard of him? The brothers Periya[10] Pazhuvettaraiyar and Chinna[11] Pazhuvettaraiyar were famous throughout the lands stretching from Eezham in the south to Kalinga in the north. They hailed from Pazhuvoor, situated near Uraiyur on the northern bank of the Vada Kaveri. Their clan had been known for its courage right from the times of Vijayalaya Chozhan. The family had forged its alliances with the Chozha kings through marriages.

This, along with their renowned valour, had endowed them with privileges quite equal to that of the royal family, as well as with the right to fly their own flag.

The older of the two Pazhuvettaraiyars of the day was a veteran of twenty-four battles. It was said he had no equal in daring in the entire Chozha kingdom in his heyday. He was over fifty years old now, and no longer an active participant in battle. Yet, he had been given several crucial responsibilities in the running of the Chozha kingdom and held the exalted position of being the dhanadhikari, the head of the treasury, as well as the dhanyadhikari, the head of the granaries. The kingdom's finances and agriculture were both within his purview. It was his prerogative to decide how much tax must be imposed on the subjects of the kingdom. He could order any of the petty kingdoms, landholdings or large farmsteads to pay a certain tax, and no one could question his authority. It might be said that he was the most powerful man in the kingdom after Sundara Chozha Maharaja.

Vandiyadevan could barely contain his desire to meet such a great warrior, who wielded such boundless power. But then he remembered the confidential words that had been spoken to him by Prince Aditya Karikalan, in the halls of the new Golden Palace of Kanchi.

'Vandiyadeva! I know bravery flows in your every vein; and trusting that you have the brains to go with such brawn, I place a great responsibility upon your shoulders. Of the two olai scrolls I have here, one is to be delivered to my father, the king, and the other to my sister, Ilaya Piraatti. I've heard all sorts of things about even the most important officials in the court at Thanjavur. And so, no one should know of the news I send. Whatever the stature of anyone you may meet, or his position in court, he should never know that you carry these scrolls from me. You must not get into any fight with anyone en route. It won't do if you resist getting into fights yourself. You must desist even when someone challenges you to one. I know of your valour, and you have proven it over and over again. So, remember that there is no shame in avoiding a fight. It will have no bearing on your reputation. Most importantly, you must be particularly prudent around the Pazhuvettaraiyar brothers and my uncle, Madurantakar. They should not even know who you are! And they must never know what your mission is!'

Those were the words of Aditya Karikalan, crown prince of the Chozha Empire and the general of the northern army. He had emphasised over and over again what Vandiyadevan's conduct should be throughout the journey. As these things came to mind, Vandiyadevan stemmed his aching desire to meet and introduce himself to Pazhuvettaraiyar. He tried to spur his horse into a swifter pace. But the horse was too tired to be moved by spurs. Vandiyadevan decided he would spend the night at the palace of Kadambur Sambuvarayar, and leave the next morning with a fresh horse.

2

AZHVARKADIYAAN NAMBI

As Vandiyadevan guided his horse down from the banks of the lake and headed towards the south, his heart danced with delight, quite like the boats that floated and frolicked as they swayed across the waves of Veeranarayana Lake. A latent sense of joy burst through his consciousness. His instinct told him he was about to experience incredible things no one else ever had. If the border regions of Chozha Naadu could inspire such headiness, what awaited him beyond the Kollidam? What would the land's storied bounty of water and lushness of field do to him? What would the people and their women be like? How many rivers would he pass? How many ponds? How many sparkling streams with water so clear one could see down to their beds? What would his first sighting of the Ponni River, enshrined in ancient poetry and the great epics, stir in him? How beautiful the flowering punnai and konnai and kadamba trees on its banks would look!

The kuvalai and kumudam flowers would call out to him with their petals unfurled and the red lotus would greet him with a blossoming smile—what a sweet sight that would be! How wonderful the intricately carved temples that had been erected by generation after generation of Chozha kings, renowned Shiva bhakts, along either bank of the Kaveri would look!

Aha! Pazhaiyarai Nagar! The capital city of the Chozha kings! In comparison to Pazhaiyarai, Poompuhar and Uraiyur might be dismissed as hamlets. The imposing palaces, dizzying gopurams, army camps, marketplaces, Shaivite stone temples and Vaishnavaite vinnagarams of the city were legendary. Vandiyadevan had heard that the tender voices of the great musicians who sang the Devaram and Tiruvaaimozhi verses in those temples left the listeners in swirls of ecstasy. And soon, he would count among those blessed listeners.

Was that all? In a matter of days, he would meet people whom he hadn't dared dream of ever encountering. He would see the king, Parantaka Sundara Chozhan, the equal of Velan in valour and Manmadhan in appearance, in the flesh. Was that all? No, he would see the king's dear daughter, the unparalleled Kundavai Piraatti[1] too!

However, he must get to his destination without obstacle. Well, so what if there was an obstacle in his path? He had a spear in hand, a sword in his scabbard, armour over his chest and courage in his heart. But the Mahatanda Nayakar, Prince Aditya Karikalan, had thrown a spanner in the works by stipulating that he must not get into any fight before his mission was complete. That was a tall order. Well, he'd managed thus far. He had only a couple of days to go before his journey ended. He would simply have to be patient until then.

He had planned to reach Kadambur before sunset, and found himself at the Veeranarayanapura Vinnagara temple before long. With Aadi Tirumanjana Tiruvizha[2] falling on the day, devotees thronged the groves around the temple.

People selling jackfruit arils, bananas, sugarcane and various kinds of sweet and savoury snacks had set up shop. Some stalls sold flowers for the womenfolk, while others sold puja items such as lotus buds. Coconut, tender coconut water, sandalwood, betel leaves, jaggery, puffed rice and akhil—eaglewood—were all being sold. And then there were the entertainers. There was no dearth of astrologers, palmists, seers and sorcerers who swore they could cure snakebite and other illnesses.

As Vandiyadevan took in all this, he was distracted by a large crowd gathered around what appeared to be a heated debate being carried out in stentorian tones. Curious, he brought his horse to a halt by the side of the path and dismounted. He patted the horse, silently instructing his ride to stay put, and shoved his way into the crowd.

It came as a surprise that the argument had only

three protagonists. However, each had his supporters in the stands, which is why there had been such a ruckus. He went closer and listened so he might divine the subject that had divided the house.

Of the three debaters, one had smeared sandalwood markings all over his body, which cemented his allegiance to Vaishnavism, and wore a topknot. He carried a staff too. He was short and stocky, with skin that shimmered like the surface of a diamond. Another had branded his body liberally with the three horizontal lines of tiruneer—the sacred ash—that proclaimed his adherence to Shaivism. The third sported a saffron cloth and a bald head. He was neither a Vaishnavite nor a Shaivite, but had transcended both to profess Advaita Vedanta.

The Shaivite said, 'O, Azhvarkadiyaan Nambiye! Give me the answer to this: Is it true or is it not that Brahma sought to seek the tresses of Shiva and Tirumaal[3] his feet? Did they or did they not give up on determining the proportions of Shiva Peruman's infinite body and surrender at his feet? How can you then proclaim that your God is greater than Shiva Peruman?'

Azhvarkadiyaan Nambi shook his staff and said, 'Oh, right. Veera Shaiva Paadatooli Bhattare! Put an end to your tirade! Your Shiva gave boons to the Lankan king, the ten-headed Ravana, didn't he? And all those boons were reduced to dust in the face of our Tirumaal's avataram Ramapiran's kodanda bow, weren't they? How can you possibly claim that your Shiva is greater than our Tirumaal?'

At this point, the Advaita sanyasi in his saffron costume interrupted. 'Why are the two of you engaged in such pointless debate? However long you go on and on about whether Shiva is greater or Vishnu, there will be no resolution. It is Vedanta that has the answer to your question. For as long as you follow the lower Bhakti margam, you will continue to have this Shiva–Vishnu argument. Above the Bhakti margam is the Gnana margam. And above Gnana is such a thing as the Gnasa margam. Once you have reached that stage, you will realise there is no Shiva and no Vishnu. *Sarvam Brahmamayam Jagat.* Shri Shankara Bhagavatpada says in his *Brahma Sutra Bhashyam* that ...'

Azhvarkaadiyan Nambi cut in with, 'O, give it a rest now, won't you? Do you know what conclusion your Shankaracharya arrived at, after writing all his bhashyams on the Upanishads and Bhagavad Gita and *Brahma Sutras*? What did he say?

Bhaja govindam, Bhaja govindam,
Bhaja govindam, moodhamathe!

'And he said it thrice. It was dimwits like you to whom he referred when he said "moodhamathe"!'

At that, the crowd broke into shouts of 'Aha!' and there was applause and cheers and jeers.

But the sanyasi was unfazed. 'Ade! Munkudumi[4] Nambi! You're right in calling me a "moodhamathi".

You, with a thadi in your hand, are a thadiyan.[5] What could a man who has sought to speak with a thadiyan like you be but a moodhamathi?'

'Oi, swamigale! This that I hold in my hand is not simply a thadi. When called upon to do so, it has the power to break the chrome dome on your shoulders, you see!' Azhvarkaadiyan said, raising the staff in his hand. His supporters yelled, 'O-ho!' in anticipation.

In response, the Advaita Swamigal said, 'Appane![6] Get a hold of yourself. Let the thadi stay safely in your hands. But even if you were to use it on me, I wouldn't be angry. And I won't challenge you to a fight either. That which deals the blow is Brahmam; and that which receives the blow is Brahmam too. If you were to hit me, you would essentially be hitting your own self.'

Azhvarkadiyaan Nambi said, 'Oh, everyone, look at this here! Parabrahmam is going to deal a holy blow to Brahmam. I'm going to assault myself with my thadi!' With that, he began to whirl his staff and make towards the Advaita Swamigal.

Vandiyadevan, who was observing all of this, was tempted for an instant to grab the staff from the topknot-sporting Nambi and deal him four of his 'holy blows' with it.

But suddenly there was a development. The Swamigal was missing! He had disappeared into the crowd. The Vaishnavite fan section was further excited by this, and began to yell and cheer.

Azhvarkadiyaan Nambi then turned to the Veera Shaivar and said, 'Oi, Paadatooli Bhattare! What do you have to say? Would you like to resume the debate? Or would you like to take a leaf out of the Swamiyar's book and run for your life?'

'What, I? I won't run away like that Vedanti of verbosity. Did you think I was like your Kannan?[7] Your Kannan had the distinction of stealing butter from the houses of gopis, gorging on it and then getting beaten by the churning sticks, didn't he? He ...'

Before Paadatooli Bhattar could finish, Azhvarkadiyaan interjected, 'Listen, have you forgotten that your Paramashiva took a flogging on his back while carrying mud so he could eat puttu?'[8] and began to march towards the Shaivite, his staff raised.

Azhvarkadiyaan Nambi's body was all fat and blubber. Veerashaiva Paadatooli Bhattar was of a much slimmer build. The crowd that had been encouraging their argument was now tremendously excited at the prospect of a fistfight.

Vandiyadevan felt compelled to put a stop to this imbecility.

He took a small step forward and said, 'Why are you fighting, aiya? Don't you have anything else to do? If you're spoiling for battle, why not head to Eezham? There's a grand war on there, don't you know?'

Nambi swung round to look at him and said, 'Who is this, who's landed up and cast himself in the role of judge and jury?'

Vandiyadevan's handsome countenance and warrior's bearing had found favour with some sections of the crowd. 'You tell them, thambi! Give these querulous men a lesson in justice and logic. We're with you, don't worry!'

'I'll give you the justice and logic I know. It doesn't appear to me that Shiva Peruman and Narayana Murthy are fighting with each other. They seem to be on rather friendly terms, really. Under these circumstances, why should the Nambi and the Bhattar fight on their behalf?'

Several members of the crowd broke into laughter at Vandiyadevan's quip.

'This boy seems rather smart,' Veerashaiva Bhattar acknowledged. 'But these empty assertions won't resolve the argument, will they? Let him answer the question directly: Is Shiva Peruman a greater God than Tirumaal or not?'

'Shiva is a great God; so is Tirumaal. The two of them are on equal footing in the hierarchy of godliness. Pray to whichever of them you like; why fight?' Vandiyadevan said.

'How can you say that? What is your evidence that Shiva and Vishnu are on equal footing?' demanded Azhvarkadiyaan.

'Evidence? Why, I'll give you evidence! Last evening, I'd gone to Vaikundam.[9] Paramashiva happened to visit at the same time. The two of them sat on thrones of equal grandeur. They were of the same height. Even so, just so there would be no doubt,

I used my arms to measure each of their heights in muzhams[10] and ...'

'Ada pillaai[11]! You're being funny, are you?' Azhvarkadiyaan roared.

'Tell him, thambi, tell him!' the crowd shouted.

'I found, upon measuring them, that they were indeed of the same height. Not leaving it at that, I asked Shiva and Tirumaal to their face. Do you know what they said?

Ariyum[12] Shivanum onnu
Ariyaadavar[13] vaayile mannu

Hari and Shiva are one
Mud in the mouths of those ignorant of this

'And having said this, they gave me this pidi of mud to stuff into the mouths of those who quarrelled over their relative greatness,' Vandiyadevan said, and opened his balled left fist to show them the mud inside. He threw it up in the air.

Inspired by this, members of the crowd fell over each other to grab fistfuls of mud, which they then proceeded to aim at the heads of Nambi and Bhattar. A few tried to stop this sacrilegious act.

'Ade! Doordargalaa?[14] Naastigargalaa?[15]' Nambi cried, and began to brandish his staff at the crowd.

It appeared all hell would break loose, when good fortune sent a commotion their way from some distance.

'Sooradi Soorar,[16] Veerapratapar,[17] the Vetrivel udaiyaar who uprooted the Marapandiyan Army, bearer of sixty-four scars from twenty-four battles, the Dhanadhikari of Chozha Naadu, and the Dhanya Pandaara Nayakar, Devar who determines taxes, Periya Pazhuvettaraiyar makes his entrance! Paraak! Paraak! Make way!' came the thundering cries from the bellmen.

First in the procession were the town criers, followed by the drummers. Then came the flag-bearers with the palm tree standard. They were followed by a line of warriors striding down the street holding their spears aloft. Seated atop the ornamented elephant that brought up the rear was an ajanubahu[18] with dark skin. To watch the warrior approach on the stud elephant was to envision a dark cloud raising its head proudly over the precipice of a grand mountain.

As the crowd parted and melted into the sides of the streets, Vandiyadevan looked at the warrior. The elephant rider must be Pazhuvettaraiyar himself.

Right behind the elephant was a delicate palanquin with silk screens across its doors. Before Vandiyadevan could wonder who its occupant might be, an arm so white it was nearly pink where it wasn't hidden by bangles and bracelets made its way outside the palanquin and parted the silk drapes ever so little. A face of stunning beauty shone from the interior of the palanquin, quite like the light of a full moon hidden behind grey skies that bursts onto earth when the cloud cover parts.

Vandiyadevan possessed eyes that delighted in feminine beauty. And yet, although the woman's glowing face could rival the full moon, the sight did not inspire joy. He felt, instead, an indefinable terror and revulsion.

At that very moment, the woman's eyes narrowed as she squinted at something she had spotted close to where Vandiyadevan stood. The next moment, a screech was heard in a petrified female voice, and the palanquin's silk screen fell back into place.

Vandiyadevan looked about himself. His instinct told him it was something or someone nearby that had inspired the woman's unearthly screech. His eyes fell on Azhvarkadiyaan Nambi, leaning against a tamarind tree, not far behind him. Veera Vaishnava Nambi's face had undergone an incredible change, and was entirely distorted. Inexplicably, Vandiyadevan felt dazed and repelled by the sight.

3

THE VINNAGARA TEMPLE

At times, tremendous events are sparked off by trivial incidents. One such trivial incident was unfolding in Vandiyadevan's life. I was telling you how Vandiyadevan was standing by the road and watching Pazhuvettaraiyar's entourage pass, wasn't I? Not far away from where he stood was his horse.

The horse caught the attention of some of the men who brought up the rear of the procession.

'Ade! Look at that kuruthai!'[1] one of them said.

'Don't say "kuruthai", da! Say "kuthirai",' said another.

'Put your ilakkona aaraaichi[2] aside for now, and figure out whether that's a horse or a donkey first!' said yet another, who liked his jokes.

'Let's find that out too!' said one of the men, and made for the horse. He tried to leap on to the animal's back, but the horse knew the aspiring rider wasn't his master and refused to let the man mount.

'This is a rogue of a horse! I mustn't mount it, I believe! It is only a rider of royal lineage who can mount it, it seems. In that case, Thanjavur Muththarayan will have to come back from the dead himself and mount it!' the man said. His wit amused the other soldiers, who broke into laughter. The Thanjavur Muththarayar clan had been crushed over a century ago. The tiger flag of the Chozhas flew from the edifices of Thanjavur.

'The horse might have its own ideas. But it is my belief that the dead Thanjavur Muththurayan is inferior to the living Thaandavaraayan!' another soldier said.

'Thaandavaraaya! Make sure the horse that won't let you mount is a real, living-and-breathing horse! It could be a poikkaal kuthirai[3] that's been brought here for the temple festivities!' another joker said.

'I'll put that to the test too,' Thaandavaraayan said, as he tried to mount the horse and twisted the animal's tail. The horse, who had his ego, kicked his hind legs several times and ran away from them.

'The kuruthai is running! It is a real kuruthai after all!' the soldiers howled, yelled 'Ui! Ui!' and chased after the running horse.

The horse hurtled into the crowd, which scattered to avoid being trampled. Even so, several of them were kicked to the ground. The horse was half-crazed and entirely dazed.

All this had happened right in front of Vandiyadevan's nose, so fast he hadn't had a chance to react. Azhvarkadiyaan Nambi gleaned from his expression that the horse was his.

'Did you see, thambi, the job those Pazhuvoor louts have gone and done? Why don't you show them some of the attitude you showed me, eh?' he said, not without snark.

Vandiyadevan was fuming. But he had to grit his teeth and hold his temper. The Pazhuvoor soldiers were too numerous for him to take on by himself. They weren't standing around waiting for him to take them on either. Having laughed at the horse in flight, they sped along on their way.

Vandiyadevan set off in the direction his horse had taken. He knew the animal would stop by himself after running for a while. So, he wasn't overly concerned about that. He ached to teach the arrogant footmen of Pazhuvettaraiyar a lesson.

The horse had come to a stop on the other side of the tamarind grove, which was deserted. He was the very image of sorrow. As Vandiyadevan reached him, the horse neighed in protest. *Why did you leave me all by myself, and make me vulnerable to this predicament?* the animal seemed to ask him. Vandiyadevan stroked the horse's back to calm him down and reassure him he was now safe. He then led his ride back to the street.

Several among the crowd chastised him. 'Why did you bring this wild horse into the crowd? How many people it has kicked and shoved!' they said.

'What could this boy do? For that matter, what could the horse do? It was Pazhuvettaraiyar's rogues who are to blame, wasn't it?' some of the kinder souls stepped in to defend them.

Azhvarkadiyaan was waiting by the side of the road.

What on earth, it appears the saniyan[4] *won't let me be!* thought Vandiyadevan, his face distorted with irritation.

'Thambi! Which way are you headed?' asked Azhvarkadiyaan Nambi.

'Who, I? Some distance to the west, and then a turn to the south, and then a curve towards the east, and then southwest,' Vandiyadevan said.

'I'm not interested in all that. I want to know where you will stay tonight.'

'Why is that of interest to you?'

'If you are, by chance, staying at the Kadambur Sambuvarayar Palace, I have a task at hand.'

'Are you some sort of mantra–tantra expert? How did you know I was going to the Kadambur Palace?'

'Why should that be a surprise? A whole lot of guests from a host of towns will be arriving at the palace tonight. Pazhuvettaraiyar and his entourage are headed there too.'

'Really?' Vandiyadevan asked in surprise.

'Really. Didn't you know this? The elephant, horse, palanquin, the guard of honour, they all belong to the Kadambur Palace. They're escorting Pazhuvettaraiyar there. Everywhere he goes, this show of pomp and ceremony must be organised.'

Vandiyadevan's brain whirred silently. He might have a once-in-a-lifetime opportunity to share a roof with Pazhuvettaraiyar. Why, he might even be able to make the acquaintance of the great warrior. But then, his encounter with that warrior's uncouth retinue had left a bitter taste in his mouth.

'Thambi! Will you do me a favour?' Azhvarkadiyaan asked in a beseeching voice.

'What favour could I possibly do you? I'm new to this place.'

'I won't ask anything of you that is not within your powers. Take me to Kadambur Palace with you tonight.'

'Whatever for? Is some Veerashaivar going to be there? Are you going to have a grand debate over whether Shiva or Tirumaal is the greater god?'

'No, no. There's no call for you to think I live to argue. There will be a grand feast at Kadambur Palace tonight. After the feast, there will be a cultural extravaganza, featuring kaliyaattam, saamiyaattam, kuravai koothu and a whole lot of other programmes. I've always wanted to see the kuravai koothu.'

'That's as may be. But how could I possibly take you along?'

'You could say I'm your servant.'

Vandiyadevan's earlier suspicions grew stronger. 'You'll need to find someone else to run this charade for you. I don't need a servant like you. And no one would believe you're my servant either. Also, after everything you've told me, I'm not sure they'll give me a bed in the palace tonight.'

'Oh, so that means you haven't been invited to the palace!'

'I do have an invitation, in a sense. Sambuvarayar's son, Kandamaaravel is a close friend. He has often told me I should stay at their palace if I was ever in this neck of the woods.'

'Is that all? Then you're going to have a tough time of it yourself, let alone with me in tow!'

The two of them walked on in silence for some time.

'Why are you following me?' Vandiyadevan asked.

'I could ask you the same thing. Why are you following me? Why don't you go your way?'

'My only crime is that I don't know the way. Nambi! Where are you headed? To Kadambur, perhaps?'

'No. You've refused to take me along, haven't you? I'm going to Vinnagara temple.'

'To Veeranarayana Perumaal sannidhi[5]?'

'Yes.'

'I'd like to come along, and pray to Perumaal too.'

'I thought perhaps you might not come to a Vishnu temple. It is a temple one must see, a sannidhi at which one must worship. Here, a bhattar called Eeshwara Munigal does kaingaryam.[6] He's a great mahaan.'

'I've heard of him. Look at the crowd! Is there a special utsavam today?'

'Yes. Today is the Andal Tirunatchatiram.[7] With the Aadi Padinettaam Perukku and Andal's birth star falling on the same day, there's bound to be a crowd. Thambi! Have you heard any of Andal's pasurams?'[8]

'I haven't.'

'Don't! Don't ever let that sound into your ears!'

'Why such venom?'

'Not venom, not animosity either. I'm saying this for your own good. If you were to hear Andal's beautiful pasurams, you would throw away your sword and spear and, like me, fall in love with Kannan and set off on a Vinnagara yatra.'

'Do you know any Andal pasurams? Do you sing them?'

'I know a handful. I know a few pasurams by Nammazhvar, who translated the vedas into Tamil. I'm going to sing them at Perumaal sannidhi. You're welcome to listen. Here we are, the temple is before us.'

They had already reached Veeranarayana temple.

~*~

Vijayalaya Chozhan's grandson, Parantaka Chozhan I had earned the title of 'Maduraiyum Eezhamum Konda Kopparakesari'.[9] It was he who laid the foundations of the Chozha Empire. He has gone down in history for building a golden façade for the Tillai Chitrambalam. Along with the titles of 'Chozha Sigaamani' and 'Soora Sigaamani', he was also known as 'Veeranarayanan'.

In his time, the Rashtrakuta kings of the two mandalas to the north of the Chozha kingdom were extremely powerful. Parantaka, expecting an army to leave the cantonment of the Rashtrakuta capital Manyakhetu to challenge the Chozhas to war, stationed his eldest son, Prince Rajadityan, at Tirumunaippaadi with a large army at his disposal. Noticing that the hundreds of thousands of soldiers who made up the army had nothing to do but wait for war, Rajadityan drew up plans for a project that would be of great service to the public. The waters of the Vada Kaveri River or Kollidam emptied into the sea without having served much purpose to the kingdom. He commissioned his soldiers to dig a lake that would be as large as an ocean, so he could put some of these waters to use. He christened it 'Veeranarayana Eri' in honour of his father. He established the town of Veeranarayanapuram on its shores, and built a Vinnagara temple there too. 'Vinnagaram' was the Tamil corruption of 'Vishnu Griham'.

Sriman Narayana Murthy is the god who stretches out on his snake-bed in the water, isn't he? And so, it was a custom back in the day to erect temples for Sriman Narayana on the banks of lakes, so that he would protect the people from flood and drought. Rajadityan had a vinnagaram dedicated to Veeranarayana Perumaal at Veeranarayanapuram.

It was to that temple that Vandiyadevan and Azhvarkadiyaan went. Once they had reached the sannidhi, Azhvarkadiyaan began to sing. He started with some of Andal's pasurams, and then sang pasurams from Nammazhvar's Tamil vedam.

Poliga poliga poliga
Poyittru valluyir saabam,
Naliyum naragamum naindha
Namanukkingu yaadhumillai
Kaliyum kedum kandu kolmin
Kadal vannan boodhangal[10] *mann mel*
Maliya pugundhu isaipaadi
Aadi uzhi tara kandom

Long live, long live, long live,
For the curses that have grasped
Our lives by the throat are gone.
Yaman who rules hell and torments souls
Has no work in this sacred place.
Kaliyugam, which is to blame for all these ills,
Will fade away, as you will see,
For the worshippers of he who is the colour of the ocean
Have descended in large numbers,
And we watch as they sing and dance and rejoice.

Kandom kandom kandom
Kannukinayana kandom
Thondeer elleerum vaareer
Thozhudhu thozhudhu ninraarththum
Vandaar thannandhuzhaayaan
Madhavan boodhangal mann mel
Pandaan paadi ninraadi
Parandhu thiriginranave!

We saw, we saw, we saw,
We saw sweet sights where

Devotees, all of you come here,
So we may pray, pray so that
The wearer of tulasi on which beetles rest,
Madhavan's worshippers sing and dance
And float and fly across the earth.

As he sang the lines, Azhvarkadiyaan's eyes welled up, and tears coursed in streams down his cheeks. Vandiyadevan listened carefully to the words. Although he had no urge to sob, his heart yielded to the lyrics and melted. His opinion of Azhvarkadiyaan underwent a change too. *He is an avid devotee*, he thought to himself.

There were others who were paying as close attention to the pasurams as Vandiyadevan. The temple authorities listened; the archaka Eeshwara Bhattar stood with tears pouring from his eyes as he listened. By him stood his young son, a child whose cheeks still smelled of milk.

Having sung ten pasurams, Azhvarkadiyaan finished with:

Kali vayal thennai kurugoor
Kaari maaran sadagopan
Oli pugazh aayiraththu ippaththum
Ullaththai maasarukkume.

These thousand and ten songs
In praise of the lord's glory,
Composed by Kaari Maaran, Sadagopan

Of Kurugoor with its bountiful fields
Will remove all toxicity from one's heart.

The bhattar's son turned to his father and said
something. Wiping his tears gently, the bhattar said,
'Aiya! Nammazhvar, who is known by the name
Kurugoor Sadagopan, is said to have composed over
a thousand songs. Do you know them all?'

'I don't have that good fortune, I'm afraid. I only
know a few dozen,' Azhvarkadiyaan said.

'You must teach this boy what you know,'
Eeshwara Munigal said.

Over the years, this city would be spoken of with
great reverence. The child who stood with his innocent
face glowing as he heard Nammazhvar's pasurams
would grow up to become Nadamunigal, the first of
the acharyas in the Vaishnavite tradition. He would
go to the Azhvar tirunagaram known as Kurugoor,
and search out and compile the over one thousand
pasurams Nammazhvar had composed. His disciples
would sing these pasurams throughout the land and
spread their divine message.

Nadamunigal's grandson-to-be, Alavandaar, would
do great wonders too.

One day, Sri Ramanujar himself, known as
Udayar,[11] would journey to this city, to see the
birthplace of these two great Vaishnavite seers. He
would be amazed at the sight of Veeranarayana Lake
and its seventy-four canals. It occurred to him that,

in order to symbolise the analogy between the canals
feeding the fields and allowing the people to live and
the flood of compassion and blessing that Narayana
showers on mortals sustaining their souls, seventy-
four acharya peethams must be constructed along the
banks of the lake. These peethams would function as
centres of Vaishnavite learning and produce seventy-
four acharyas known as 'simmaasana adipatigal', who
would transmit their education to their disciples.

All these wondrous events have been recounted in
the *Vaishnava Guru Parampara Charitram*, and so let us
leave them to it and get back to our Vandiyadevan.

No sooner had they finished praying to the deity
and stepped out of the temple than he turned to
Azhvarkadiyaan Nambi and, using the respectful
second-person plural for the first time, addressed him.
'Nambigale! The fact that you were such an exemplary
devotee and iconic scholar had completely escaped me.
Please do forgive any offence I may have caused.'

'I will forgive you. Thambi! But will you do me a
favour now, please?'

'I told you I wouldn't be able to do you the favour
you asked of me, didn't I? And you accepted my
response, didn't you?'

'This has to do with something else. I'll give you a
little note. If you stay at Kadambur Palace, you must
find an appropriate moment to hand it to someone.'

'To whom?'

'You remember the woman who journeyed in a

covered palanquin after Pazhuvettaraiyar's elephant? To her.'

'Nambigale! Who did you take me for? Am I the only one you could find of whom to ask for favours like these? If anyone other than you had dared to say so much as one word of what you ...'

'Thambi! There's no call for such fervour. If you can't do this, please go your royal way. But if only you had done me this favour, I might have at some point proven myself useful to you. Never mind. Carry on!'

Vandiyadevan didn't linger for a moment. He leapt on to his horse and galloped towards Kadambur.

4

THE KADAMBUR PALACE

Vandiyadevan's horse, having rested all this while, had regained his energy; he bounded towards Kadambur Palace and had reached the entrance within a naazhigai.[1] Sengannar Sambuvarayar was the head of one of the most illustrious families of Chozha Naadu in that era. The entrance to the palace could have passed for the portal of a grand walled city. The boundary wall rose high into the air.

Elephants and horses and bulls and their handlers and those assigned to feed them, and the torchbearers and those who had to refill the oil in those torches, all contributed to a heaving crowd. Vandiyadevan, observing all this, felt some hesitation and trepidation creep into his chest.

This appears to be a huge occasion. Perhaps not the best time for me to have landed up here, he thought to himself. He was eager to find out what the occasion was, though. The doors to the palace were open.

However, they were being guarded by men with spears in hand. They looked exactly as he had imagined Yama's dwarapalakas[2] would.

Our young warrior figured it would be most expedient to charge in confidently on his horse; if he dithered, he would be stopped and questioned. He put the thought into action right away. But what a disappointment! No sooner had the horse approached the entrance than two guards crossed their spears and blocked his way. Four others marched up and caught the horse's reins. One of them studied Vandiyadevan's countenance. Another brought the torch almost to his face.

Vandiyadevan, red with rage, snarled, 'Is this the custom of your city? To stop guests at the door?'

'Who are you, thambi, so quick to anger? Which is your hometown?' one of the guards asked.

'You ask me my name and that of my hometown? My hometown is Tiruvallam of Vanagapadi Naadu. Once upon a time, the warriors of your city would brand their chests with the names of my ancestors and swell with pride. My name is Vallavarayan Vandiyadevan! Do you recognise me now?' he demanded.

'All you're missing is a town crier in your entourage,' one of the guards said drily, and the others laughed.

'Whoever you are, you can't enter now. All the guests who were expected today have already arrived. Ejamaan—master—has ordered us not to let anyone else in,' the head of the guards said.

The altercation had drawn the attention of some soldiers further inside the fort, and they came closer.

'Ade! This horse looks like the one we shooed away at the Tiruvizha, da!' one of them cried.

'Call it a donkey, not a horse,' another said.

'Look at the poise of the rider of the donkey,' yet another laughed.

These words were spoken within Vandiyadevan's earshot.

Why invite a fight? Should I go back? he wondered. *Or, should I show them Aditya Karikalan's emblem with his seal on it?* The seal of the prince who commanded the northern army would guarantee his welcome anywhere between Vadapennai and Kumarimunai, wouldn't it? It was when he was weighing these options that he heard Pazhuvettaraiyar's men mock him and his horse. He decided on a course of action right away.

'Let my horse go; I'm going back,' he said.

The soldiers let go of the reins and stepped back.

Vandiyadevan pressed his feet against the horse's underbelly, and reached for the sword in his scabbard at the same time. As he flashed his sword, and it reflected the blinding light of the torch, you might have mistaken him for Tirumaal wielding his chakra. The horse galloped into the fort. The soldiers in his path tumbled as the horse charged through their ranks. The spears clattered against each other as they fell. The horse then pushed through the Pazhuvoor squadron. Entirely unprepared for this lightning strike, the men scattered.

Several other things had occurred by this time. The gates of the fortress had been shut with a 'thadaal-thadaal'. High-pitched cries of 'Pidi! Pidi!'—Catch him! Catch him!—rent the air. The 'clang-clang' of swords and spears was compounded by the 'dadam-dadam' of the murasu drum that sounded out a warning of sudden and extreme danger.

The soldiers swarmed around Vandiyadevan's horse. Twenty, thirty, fifty, perhaps more. Vandiyadevan leapt off the horse and landed on the ground. Swishing his sword, he yelled at the top of his voice, 'Kandamaara! Kandamaara! Your men are killing me!'

His words startled the soldiers surrounding him into backing off by a step.

A voice from the balcony on the highest floor of the palace thundered down, 'What is that commotion? Stop it!'

Seven or eight faces peered down from the balcony.

'Ejamaan! A stranger has broken through the cordon of guards and entered the fort. He has been throwing Chinna Ejamaan's[2] name about!' one of the soldiers called.

'Kandamaara! Go and see what the fuss is about!' said the same stentorian voice they had heard from the balcony. Vandiyadevan surmised that the possessor of that voice was Sengannar Sambuvarayar.

He and the men surrounding him stood frozen in motion for a while.

'What is this scene?' a young voice asked. The

soldiers made way, so the youth who had spoken could reach the centre of the drama. He gazed in astonishment at the man who was flashing his sword as if he were enacting the soorasamharam of Subramanian.[3]

'Vallava, my dear, dear friend!' he cried the very next moment, and ran to Vandiyadevan and embraced him.

'Kandamaara! I came to visit your home because you've asked me so often. And here I'm given this hero's welcome!'

'Chi! Fools! Get lost now! You have all the brains of pulverised saplings!'[4] Kandamaaran said, glaring at the soldiers.

Linking arms with Vandiyadevan, Kandamaaran dragged him off, so excited his feet all but floated over the ground. His heart was leaping with joy. What greater luck could a young man have than finding a true childhood friend? Well, yes, sure, there is love. But then the happiness and thrill that love brings is subsumed by the far larger quantity of grief and pain that accompany the sentiment. Childhood friendship, however, is never marred by so much as a shadow of sorrow. It only ever brings joy to the heart.

As they walked side by side, Vandiyadevan said, 'Kandamaara! What has occasioned such strict security today?'

'I'll tell you all about that later. Remember, back when we were at the army camp on the shores of Pennai River, you used to go on about how you wanted to meet Pazhuvettaraiyar and Mazhuvarayar, and this hero and that hero? All your heroes and sheroes and zeroes have assembled right here!' Kandamaaran said.

He escorted Vandiyadevan to the highest floor of the palace where the guests had assembled, to present him to his father, Sambuvarayar.

'Appa! I have often spoken to you of my friend Vandiyadevan of the Vaanar clan, haven't I? Here he is!' he said.

Vandiyadevan brought his palms together and bowed low to greet the older man.

His friend's father didn't seem particularly pleased.

'Is that so? So, he is the gentleman who caused such commotion at the entrance, is he?'

'The fault wasn't my friend's. It was that of the fools we have hired to guard the entrance!' Kandamaaravel said.

'Even so, there was no call for him to choose this day to land up after dark and enter with such high drama,' Sambuvarayar said.

Kandamaaravel's face fell. He didn't want to extend the argument with his father. He led Vandiyadevan away. He took him to Pazhuvettaraiyar, who was holding court in a high seat that towered over the assembly, and said, 'Mama! This is my dear friend Vandiyadevan, of the clan of Vaanar kings. We were part of the contingent guarding the borders at the army camp by the Pennai River. He would go on and on about how he wanted to meet the greatest among warriors, Pazhuvettaraiyar. He would ask if it was true that Pazhuvettaraiyar's skin bore sixty-four scars. I would tell him he could count them himself someday.'

Pazhvettaraiyar looked at them, and then said, 'Is that so, thambi? You must count my scars yourself in order to believe it is no exaggeration, is it? Are you so very suspicious, then? Or is it your belief that the Vaanar clan has a monopoly over courage?'

The two young men were startled. They hadn't expected him to take Kandamaaran's words so literally.

Vandiyadevan was irritated by the sarcasm. But he hid it, and said with great humility, 'Aiya! The courage of the Pazhuvettaraiyar clan is renowned from Kumarimunai to the Himalayas. Who am I to harbour suspicions?'

'A fitting retort! A clever boy!' Pazhuvettaraiyar said.

The young men made their escape.

Sambuvarayar called for his son and whispered, 'Get your friend dinner soon and make him lie down somewhere away from everyone else. He's exhausted from his journey.'

Kandamaaravel nodded, glowering.

He then led Vandiyadevan to the antapuram, where the women of the palace stayed. Vandiyadevan paid his respects to his friend's mother. He surmised that the girl squirming shyly behind her must be Kandamaaran's sister. Kandamaaran had spoken often of his sister, and Vandiyadevan had harboured all sorts of notions about her. He had to concede she was something of a disappointment.

His eyes scanned the group of women for the lady who had travelled in the palanquin.

5

THE KURAVAI KOOTHU

As the two friends were leaving the antapuram, a female voice called urgently from inside, 'Kandamaara! Kandamaara!'

'Amma is calling me,' Kandamaaran said. 'You wait right here. I'll be back.'

He headed back into the antapuram. Vandiyadevan could hear several excited women's voices speaking at once, piling question upon question, to which Kandamaaran stammered answers. Then, the girls giggled.

The 'gala-gala' of their laughter irked Vandiyadevan. He had a feeling they were mocking him. It was embarrassing and irritating.

Kandamaaran stepped out, linked arms with Vandiyadevan and said, 'Come, let's give you a tour of the palace!'

Even as Kandamaaran showed him the beautiful balconies, wide verandas, trellised terraces, music halls, full granaries, marble domes, maada gopurams, grand stupas, clean barns and spacious stables of Kadambur Palace, Vandiyadevan stopped him to ask, 'Kandamaara! When you went back into the antapuram, there seemed to be quite a riot of laughter and joking. What was that about? Were they so very thrilled by the sight of your friend?'

'They were happy enough at the sight of you. Amma and everyone else quite took to you. But you were not the subject of our discussion.'

'What, then?'

'You know Pazhuvettaraiyar, right? At this age, he has married a young girl. He carts her about wherever he goes, in a closed palanquin. He's brought her here too, but instead of sending her to the antapuram, he has locked her up in his own quarters. A girl who spied this new wife has told them all about how beautiful she is. That's what amused them so much. They're gossiping about whether she might be a Sinhala woman, or a Kalinga woman, or a woman from Chera Naadu. You know Pazhuvettaraiyar's ancestors came to Tamizhagam from Chera Naadu, don't you?'

'I've heard tell. Why, it was you who told me. But leave that aside, Kandamaara. How long ago did Pazhuvettaraiyar marry this mysterious beauty?'

'Can't be much longer than two years. But he has never left her side since the wedding. His muse must accompany him wherever he goes, in the palanquin, of course. People across the country joke about it.

Vandiyadeva! It doesn't quite befit one's dignity to be so obsessed with a woman at this age, does it? That's the thing that has made him something of a laughingstock.'

'Oh, that's not the reason at all. Shall I tell you the honest reason? All women tend to nurse some amount of envy. I don't mean to criticise the women of your household. This is a universal truth. The women of your family are dusky beauties. Pazhuvettaraiyar's muse is white as the moonlight. That's why they're jealous, and have been rumour-mongering.'

'Ade! What is this twist now? How do you know of her skin tone? Have you seen her? Where? How? If Pazhuvettaraiyar were to come to know, your life would no longer be yours to hold!'

'Kandamaara! You know I have little fear of confrontation. And I haven't done anything improper or unbefitting of who I am. I was part of the crowd at Veeranarayanapuram when Pazhuvettaraiyar passed by in a procession. The elephant, horses, palanquin, parivattam,[1] all that was your show of respect, wasn't it?'

'Yes, it was we who organised the procession. What of it?'

'What of it? Nothing. I was just comparing your welcome of Pazhuvettaraiyar to the reception you gave me, nothing else.'

'We gave him the welcome due to an official who imposes taxes. We gave you the reception due to a war hero. Perhaps one day, by the grace of Muruga, if you were to become a son-in-law of this house, we'd give you a bridegroom's welcome, eh?' Kandamaaran said with a hint of laughter. Then, he continued, 'You were about to say something else. We meandered our way to other subjects. Oh, yes, you were speaking about the fair skin of Pazhuvettaraiyar's muse. How did you know?'

'Pazhuvettaraiyar was seated on Kadambur Palace's enormous black bull elephant, looking for all the world like Yama on his buffalo. I was entirely focused on him, and dreaming of the day I would be given this sort of ceremonious welcome, when a closed palanquin passed me by. I was wondering who might be travelling in it when a hand parted the curtain of the palanquin and a face peeped out. Both the hand and the face were as white as the moon. That was all I saw. From what you said, I deduced that the possessor of those must be Pazhuvettaraiyar's muse.'

'Vandiyadeva! You're a lucky man. They say no man has ever seen the Pazhuvoor rani. You had, at least, a glimpse of her face and hand, didn't you? Tell me, which land do you think this beauty might be from?'

'I gave it no thought at the time. But now that you ask, perhaps she is from Kashmir. Or she might be from beyond the seas, from Java or Quedah or Greece or Egypt or Arabia. Perhaps Arabia. They say the women of that region live hidden under veils from birth to death!'

At this moment, the sounds of musical instruments began to beat through the air from somewhere nearby. The salli, karadi, parai, udukku and flute all merged into a rhythm.

'What kind of call is that?' Vandiyadevan asked.

'The kuravai koothu is about to begin! This is the call for everyone to assemble to watch. Would you like to see it? Or would you rather dine early and retire for the night?'

What Azhvarkadiyaan had said about the kuravai koothu came to Vandiyadevan's mind.

'I've never seen the kuravai koothu,' he said, 'and so I wouldn't miss it for the world.'

A few steps on, the friends turned a corner and the grand stage that had been erected for the kuravai koothu emerged before their eyes. People had begun to gather in front of it.

The stage stood between the ramparts of the fort and the walls of the palace, in a spacious courtyard strewn with white sand. Roosters, peacocks and swans had been painted on the stage. It had been decorated with puffed rice made from roasted red grain, turmeric-coated thinai rice, flowers of various colours and kunri beads. The kuthuvilakkus and flame torches did their best to chase away the darkness of night. But the intoxicating fragrance of akhil mixed with the smell of smoke from the torches and made their own mist, dimming the lights. Musicians played with gusto on either side of the stage, and on the ground before it too. The scent of flowers and akhil and the sound of the drums had a vertiginous effect on Vandiyadevan.

Once the most important guests had assembled, the nine women who were to dance the kuravai koothu made their way to the stage. Their costumes and jewellery hugged their frames, and anklets tinkled at their feet. Kanni, kadambam, kaandal, kurinji and sevvalari flowers, all believed to be favoured by Lord Muruga, ornamented their hair. A garland of kadambam flowers was wound around the girls, linking them and making them a unit. Some delicately held toy parrots fashioned from sandalwood and painted bright green.

They bowed low to the assembly, and then began to sing and dance. Their songs were in praise of Lord Muruga and his heroic deeds. They sang of the wielder of the spear who had destroyed fearsome demons such as Soorapadman and Gajamugan. They sang of the victorious warrior who had drained the oceans. They sang of the son of Shiva who, even as celestial maidens yearned to marry him, came down into this world of mortals and courted and married the daughter of the chieftain of a hill tribe from the land of the Tamils. They sang of his compassion. The beats and the rhythmic steps of the dancers had whipped the audience into a frenzy.

Pasiyum piniyum pagayum azhiga!
Mazhaiyum valamum dhananmum peruga!

> *May hunger and disease and enmity be destroyed among us!*
> *May rain and prosperity and wealth shower down on us!*

With those lines, the kuravai koothu ended, and the women left the stage.

Next was the Velanaattam, which would be performed by the Devaraalan and Devaraatti. They wore clothes the colour of blood, and garlands of sevvalari flowers, also of the same colour; they had smeared blood-red kumkumam on their foreheads, and their lips were stained the hue of blood from chewing betel leaves. The veins in their eyes blazed red.

The dance began calmly enough. The two danced alone, and they danced together, and they spun away, and they circled back to each other. As the minutes passed, the pace built gradually. The Devaraatti ran to the spear which had been leaning in a corner of the stage and held it aloft; the Devaraalan tried to prise it away from her; she stopped him. The combat went on until the Devaraalan let out a chilling scream that shook the earth, leapt high into the air and grabbed the spear from the Devaraatti's hand. The Devaraatti made as if she was terrified of the weapon and him, and jumped off the stage.

The Devaraalan stood alone on stage, spear in hand, and began to dance to the beat of the drums. He moved faster and faster, as if in a trance. It was the dance of death. Muruga was on stage, reliving the annihilation of asuras. Sooran and his clan were pulverised. Sooran's head was lopped off over and over again, only to grow back. Every time a new head sprouted, Muruga's fury doubled, and his eyes spat fire. He charged at the demon and killed him. As Soorapadman fell, the spear fell too.

All the musical instruments save for the udukku were silenced. The pujari stood close to the stage, beating the udukku with all his energy. Every atom of the Devaraalan's body shook.

'The sannadam has come,' people in the audience whispered amongst themselves. The spirit of the god had entered the Devaraalan's body; he was in a trance.

After a while, the pujari addressed the Devaraalan, who was flying across the stage, spinning faster and faster, and said, 'Vela! Muruga! Devasenapati! Kanda! Soorasamhara! You must speak to your devotees! You must tell us the word of god!'

'Ask, da! I'll tell you! Whatever you want to know, ask!' yelled the man who was possessed by the sannadam.

'Will the rain pour? Will the floods swell? Will the country flourish? Will all we wish for come to pass?' the pujari asked.

'The rain will pour! The floods will swell! The country will flourish! All you wish for will come to pass! But you haven't done a puja for my mother! Durga asks for a sacrifice. Bhadrakali asks for a sacrifice. Chandikeshwari, the vanquisher of Mahishasura, asks for a sacrifice!' screamed the sannadakaran.

'What sacrifice does she want?' the pujari asked.

'Will you give it to her if I tell you?' asked the possessed man.

'Yes, we will, we certainly will!' the pujari said.

'She asks for the blood of the ruling clan. She asks for the blood of the clan that has ruled for a thousand years!' the sannadakaran thundered.

The men who were seated at the very front of the stage—Pazhuvettaraiyar, Sambuvarayar, Mazhavarayar and the other elite—exchanged glances. Their bloodshot eyes reflected the suspicion in each other's.

Sambuvarayar looked at the pujari and made a subtle sign with his head. The pujari stopped hitting the udukku. The Devaraalan who had been dancing as a possessed man fell like a rootless tree. The Devaraatti ran up to the stage, gathered his limp body and carried him away.

The assembly dispersed in silence; far away, the howling of jackals rent the air.

Vandiyadevan, rattled by all that he had heard and seen that evening, turned in the direction of the howling. There, on the fortress walls, he could see a head. It was the head of Azhvarkadiyaan! For a moment, Vandiyadevan was subject to a terrible emotion. He had a vision of Azhvarkadiyaan's head having been severed and propped up on the wall. He blinked and looked again, but the head was nowhere to be seen. He felt embarrassed for having had such an awful hallucination. His heart was in turmoil from various other emotions he had never experienced before.

6

MIDNIGHT CONFERENCE

The kuravai koothu and the Devaraalan's possessed dance and trance were followed by a grand feast for the invitees. However, Vandiyadevan found little joy in eating. His body was tired, and his mind troubled. Yet, he had no choice but to contend with his friend Kandamaara who sat by him and excitedly gave him a who's who of the guest list.

Aside from Pazhuvettaraiyar and Sambuvarayar, Mazhapaadi Thennavan Mazhuvarayar had joined the gathering; Kunrathoor Perunilakizhaar was there, as were Mummudi Pallavarayar, Thanthongi Kalingarayar, Anjaada Singamutharayar, Irattai Kudai Rajaliyar, Kollimalai Perunila Velaar and several other important men. Kandamaara whispered into his friend's ear, pointing each one out so discreetly that none of the other guests could tell. These were no ordinary men; it wasn't easy to catch them all together, either. Each was a minor king in his own right, or had grown to command the respect due to a minor king because of his exploits on the battlefield. The words 'raja' and 'arasar' had given rise to the corruption 'arayar'. The title meant they were either regional kings or the equivalent of regional kings. It was customary to refer to them by 'arayar' suffixed to the name of their dominions.

Back in the day, royal titles were not the exclusive privilege of those born in palaces and raised in luxury. Men who had proven their valour in battle could lay claim to the rights of a king. Most of the invitees sported a praiseworthy number of battle scars on their bodies. All these kings had sworn their allegiance to Pazhaiyarai Sundara Chozha Chakravarti, and exercised some autonomy over their own territories. Some held important posts in the Chozha court.

Vandiyadevan ought to have been thrilled and energised by the sight of the glitterati. But his heart allowed no such emotion.

Why have all these men assembled here? he wondered often. Vague suspicions and formless misgivings assailed his mind.

It was in this mood that he went to bed. The proliferation of guests necessitated that Vandiyadevan be consigned to an open mandapam in a corner of one of the terraces of that immense palace.

'You seem exhausted. Lie down and rest well. I'll see to the other guests, and then join you here for the night,' Kandamaaran said before he left.

Vandiyadevan's eyes were drowsy with sleep. Nidra Devi[1] claimed him right away. But what was the point? There is such a thing as the mind, which cannot be subdued even by Nidra Devi. His body was motionless and his eyes closed, but his innermost thoughts manifested themselves as dreams. As we know, in the world of dreams, meaningless sequences of events entirely disconnected from logic, and incidents and experiences beyond all imagining, tend to occur.

He heard the sound of a jackal howling from afar. One jackal turned into ten, then a hundred and then a thousand, and they all howled. Still howling, they came closer and closer to Vandiyadevan. In the darkness of the night, their eyes glowed like embers as they stared him down. He turned to run away, but in the other direction were ten, a hundred, a thousand vicious dogs barking madly as they bounded towards him. The hounds' eyes shot sparks at him.

What would become of him, stuck between a pack of dogs and a skulk of jackals? Vandiyadevan shuddered. Thankfully, he could see a temple before him. He ran as fast as his legs would carry him, rushed inside the open entrance, slammed the doors shut and drew the bolt across. When he turned, he realised it was a Kali temple. From behind the statue of Kali sticking out her tongue in terrifying bloodthirst emerged a pujari with an enormous sickle in his hands.

'Ah, you're here! Come!' he said, moving closer

and closer to Vandiyadevan. 'What is the history of your clan? How long have your ancestors been ruling? Tell me the truth.'

'The Vallavarayars of the Vaanar clan have been ruling for three hundred years. In my father's time, we lost our kingdom because of the Vaidumbarayars,' Vandiyadevan said.

'Then you are no fit sacrifice! Get lost!' the pujari said.

All of a sudden, Kannan appeared in the place that had just been occupied by Kalimata. In his sannidhi, two girls carrying flower garlands sang Andal pasurams and danced. The sight brought joy to Vandiyadevan, only for him to be startled by a voice behind him saying, 'Kandom, kandom, kandom, kannukkiniyana kandom.' He sprang around and looked. It was Azhvarkadiyaan who had sung those lines. No! Azhvarkadiyaan's head had sung those lines. The head alone had been placed upon the sacrificial slab, the bali peetham.

Unable to bear the sight, Vandiyadevan turned without looking, and ended up banging his head hard against a pillar. The dream dissolved. His eyes opened. But he was to witness a sight that would merge dream with reality.

Right across from his bed, atop the ramparts of the wall, a head emerged. It was the head of Azhvarkadiyaan Nambi. But this time it was clear that he wasn't dreaming or hallucinating. He knew this because, however long he stared, the head remained there. Besides, it wasn't a disembodied head. One could discern a body attached to it. Azhvarkadiyaan's hands clung to the edge of the wall.

Azhvarkadiyaan was staring keenly at something inside the walls. What was he looking at in there? There must be some evil plot afoot. He had come here as an enemy, with malicious intent. It was Vandiyadevan's obligation as Kandamaaran's dear friend to stop him, wasn't it? Could he expose to harm the hosts who had given him a meal and a bed?

He leapt up, pulled the scabbard he had cast off before lying down, and strapped it to his waist. He headed in the direction of the wall.

Having been assigned a mandapam in a corner of one of the terraces of the palace, he had to run something of an obstacle course before he reached the wall. There were balconies, corridors, terraces, statues, carved seats, pillars, arenas and crevices to cross, jump over, skirt around or crawl through. He was on his way when the sound of a human voice made him stop in caution. He hid behind a pillar and peeped in the direction of the voice. Below him was a hidden courtyard, with high walls rising on three sides. He could see a dozen people seated there. The light of the half-moon was obstructed by the walls. But the flames from a wall-torch made of cast iron allowed him to get a look at their faces.

They were all guests from the dinner—minor kings and officials of the Chozha court. This midnight conference must be owed to a matter of great importance. So, this was what Azhvarkadiyaan Nambi had been looking at, and presumably listening to— what they were doing and what they were saying. There was no doubting his cunning—he had chosen a spot from which he could observe without being observed. But his cunning couldn't save him from Vandiyadevan of the Vaanar clan! He would catch hold of that veshadaari[2] Vaishnavite, drag him here and … but, wait. He couldn't reach the wall without appearing before the gathering. And that might invite danger.

There was no call for him to choose this day to land up, he heard Sambuvarayar say.

It was obvious this was no casual conference. Clearly, they wanted the meeting, and all that was spoken during its course, to remain secret. If they were to catch sight of him under these circumstances, wouldn't it arouse their suspicions? Azhvarkadiyaan Nambi would jump off the wall and bolt before he could explain what had prompted him to leave his bed. He would have no answer if they asked him why he had woken from sleep and made his way here. To make it worse, he would land Kandamaaran in an awkward situation. Aha! There sat Kandamaaran, on the fringes of the gathering. So he was part of the conference! All Vandiyadevan would have to do is wait until morning, and ask him what this had been about.

His eyes happened to fall on a closed palanquin

that lay to a side of the gathering. Ah! This was the palanquin that had followed Pazhuvettaraiyar's elephant, wasn't it? The woman who had been ensconced inside, the woman who had parted the curtain to look out for a moment ... where was she sleeping now? This old man hadn't even sent her to the antapuram! This was the inevitable outcome of a marriage between an aging man and a nubile beauty. The husbands would be haunted by suspicion, and couldn't bear to be separated from their young consorts for so much as a minute. Could she perhaps be inside it at this very moment? Aha! One must feel for this great warrior—he had been fated to suffer the torment of becoming slave to a young woman. For all this, she was no Rathi, Menaka or Rambha! Vandiyadevan vividly remembered the sense of revulsion he had felt when he had seen her face. Why would a man of Pazhuvettaraiyar's mettle be obsessed with a woman like that?

What was even more surprising was Azhvarkadiyaan's madness. Perhaps he had mounted the wall because the palanquin was here? What could his ties to the woman be? She might be his sister, or even his lover. Perhaps Pazhuvettaraiyar had married her by force? He wasn't incapable of it. And Azhvarkadiyaan had been searching for an opportunity to meet her, whatever it took. Well, what did all this drama matter to him, anyway? He ought to get back to bed.

The young man was just turning to go when

he heard himself being spoken of in the gathering downstairs. He listened carefully.

'That boy who arrived here, claiming to be your son's friend, where has he been allocated a bed? Nothing of our discussions must reach his ears under any circumstances. We must remember that he works for the commander of the northern armed forces. Until our plan is finalised and set in motion, let no one know of it. If there is the slightest suspicion that he has got wind of it, we must ensure he doesn't leave the fort. It would be most prudent, really, to see that he is silenced forever right away.'

I leave it to you, readers, to imagine the effect this must have had on Vandiyadevan. But he stood rooted to the spot. He was determined to hear every word that was spoken in the gathering.

Who was the commander of the northern armed forces? The Vadadisai Mahatanda Nayagar? Sundara Chozha Chakravarti's oldest son. The crown prince who was due to ascend the throne after his father. Why did they have a problem with Vandiyadevan working for him? What were they going to say that should not reach the crown prince's ears?

Kandamaaran rose in defence of his friend.

'Vandiyadevan is fast asleep in the corner mandapam of the terrace. He isn't going to hear us speak. He is not the kind of man who pokes his nose into things that do not concern him, either. And even if he were to come to know of something, your plans will not be affected. I will take full responsibility for that,' he said.

'I'm glad you have such faith in him. But none of us knows him, which is why I ask that we exercise caution. What we are about to discuss concerns the ascension to the throne of a great empire. If a single syllable of this were to slip in a moment of carelessness, there will be terrible consequences. You must all remember this,' said Pazhuvettaraiyar.

7

RIDICULE AND RAGE

The moment he heard Pazhuvettaraiyar speak of discussing the ascension to the throne, Vandiyadevan made a decision. He would have to stay right there. Why was the succession up for discussion? The heir had already been announced. And who were they, anyway? What right did they have to convene a conference on this? He must find out what was afoot. Azhvarkadiyaan could do whatever the hell he wanted. It was of no concern to Vandiyadevan.

Vandiyadevan had had a premonition that some surreptitious plot was about to unfold on this day in this place. Azhvarkadiyaan's bizarre request, the manner in which the palace guards had treated him, Sambuvarayar's half-hearted reception, the words of the Devaraalan, had all aroused a series of suspicions. He had a god-given opportunity to resolve those suspicions and find out the truth. Why would he let that slip? Aha! Even his dear friend Kandamaaran had hidden the truth from him. He had seen Vandiyadevan to bed, and then arrived to join this midnight conference. He would have to confront him the next day.

Pazhuvettaraiyar had launched into a speech. Vandiyadevan listened carefully.

'It is to let you all know of something crucial that I have come here. It is for that very purpose that Sambuvarayar has organised this gathering. Sundara Chozha Maharaja's health is of grave concern. I've made discreet enquiries of the royal physicians. They have told me there is no place for hope. His days are numbered. And so, we must think about what happens next.'

'What do the astrologers say?' asked one of the others.

'Why would anyone ask them? We have seen a shooting star in the sky for days on end. Isn't that omen enough?' another said.

Pazhuvettaraiyar responded. 'The astrologers have been consulted too. They simply postpone the inevitable. That's all. We must discuss who will succeed the king.'

'What is the point of discussing that now? Aditya Karikalan has been named crown prince. It happened more than two years ago,' a hoarse voice said.

'True enough, but I'd like to know whether any of us was consulted before the announcement was made. Each of us gathered here belongs to a family that has served the Chozha Empire for at least four generations and over a hundred years. My great-grandfather lost his life in the Tiruppurambiyam war. My grandfather lost his in the war in Velur. My father sacrificed his life in Takkolam. Every one of you has several ancestors who have given their lives to the cause of expansion of Chozha Naadu. Every one of us belongs to a family whose young men have died in war. Even today, in Eezham, boys from our clans, from our families, are on the battlefield. Yet, the Maharaja did not see fit to ask our opinions on who his successor should be. Even King Dasharatha called a council to decide whether Rama would be crown prince. He asked his ministers and courtiers and generals and vassals what they thought. Yet, Sundara Chozha Maharaja did not deem it necessary to ask anyone's opinion. ...'

'It is true he did not ask *our* opinions. But the lord who levies taxes errs in saying that he did not deem it necessary to ask *anyone's* opinion. Periya Piraatti[1] Sembiyan Mahadevi's and Ilaiya Piraatti Kundavai Devi's opinions were sought. Can Pazhuvettaiyar contest this?' said a sardonic voice.

Some broke into laughter at the sarcasm.

'Aha! You laugh! I cannot fathom how you are able to laugh. As I mull this over and over, my insides feel like they are on fire. My blood boils. I wonder why I must hold on to my life when I live so shamelessly. This evening, the Devaraalan said Durga asked for a sacrifice. He said the sacrifice must belong to a royal lineage dating back a millennium.

Choose me for the sacrifice. My clan goes back more
than a thousand years. Each of you slash my throat
with your dagger, and make me the sacrifice. Mother
Durga will be pleased, and my soul will know peace,'
Pazhuvettaraiyar spoke in a thundering voice that was
reminiscent of the possessed Devaraalan's.

There was an immediate hush.

The 'virrrr' of the westerly wind and the 'marmara'
of the trees outside the fort swaying in that wind were
the only sounds that punctuated the silence.

'The King of Pazhuvoor must grace us with his
forgiveness for the thoughtless wisecrack that has
troubled him so. You are our peerless leader. Every
one of us here is bound to follow your orders. We
will walk the path your footsteps carve. We beseech
you to pardon us,' said Sambuvarayar, overcome with
emotion.

'I, too, am guilty of having lost my patience.
For this, I ask the forgiveness of those assembled
here. Consider this: Today marks the centenary of
Vijayalaya Chozha's routing of the Muththarayars to
capture Thanjavur. In the war at Tiruppurambiyam,
he joined ranks with the Pallava Army and decimated
the army of Madurai Pandiyan. Since that time, the
Chozha Empire has grown and expanded day after
day. Not even in the times of Karikaal Valavar, who
tamed the Kaveri,[2] did the Chozha Empire encompass
the vast swathes of land it does now. Today, the
Chozha Empire stretches from Kumarimunai in the

south to Tunghabhadra–Krishna in the north. Pandiya
Naadu, Naanjil Naadu, Chera Naadu, which has never
bent the knee to anyone before, Thondai Mandalam,
Paagi Naadu, Kangapadi, Nulambapadi, Vaidumbar
Naadu, Cheetpuli Naadu, Perumbanapaadi, Kudagu
Naadu where the Ponni River originates, are all paying
their tributes to Chozha Naadu to acknowledge our
supremacy. Our Chozha Naadu's tiger flag flies over all
these lands. Eezham to the south and Irattai Mandalam
and Vengi to the north ought rightly to have submitted
to us by now. I need hardly tell you why that hasn't
come to pass. You are all aware of the reasons.'

'Yes, we are all aware. Eezham and Irattaippaadi
and Vengi and Kalinga have not submitted to us for
two reasons. One is the commander of the northern
armed forces, the Mahatanda Nayagar Prince Aditya
Karikalar; the other is the general of the southern
army, his younger brother Arulmozhi Varmar.'

'I am in agreement with Mazhuvarayar. Over the
last century, this Chozha Naadu followed a different
tradition of choosing the commanders and generals of
armies from what currently prevails. They were the
greatest of warriors, having experienced several wars
in which they had fought bravely. But what has come
to pass now? The elder prince is the commander of
the northern armed forces. And what does he do?
He doesn't lay siege to Irattai Mandalam and Vengi
Naadu. He sits back in Kanchipuram and starts building
a golden palace. I ask you, greatest of warriors, born

in families steeped in heroism. Has any king of the Tamil lands built a golden palace to live in? Not even Parantaka Chakravarti, who won renown throughout the world, who conquered Madurai and Eezham, who now resides in his heavenly abode of Kailasam, did such a thing. He endowed the Tillai Chitrambalam temple with a golden roof. But Price Aditya Karikalar is building a golden palace in Kanchipuram for his royal self to reside in! The palaces in which Pallava emperors lived, the palaces from which they ruled, generation after generation, won't do for his royal highness. Only a golden palace, with precious stones inlaid into the walls, will suffice. He hasn't sent so much as a copper coin to the royal treasury from his successful campaigns at Kangapadi, Nulambapadi and Kudagu.'

'So the golden palace has been built?'

'Yes, I learnt from my spies that it is now complete. And letters have been arriving for Sundara Chozha Maharaja from his treasured eldest son, asking that the emperor grace the newly built golden palace with a sojourn.'

'The Maharaja is going to Kanchi?' asked a worried voice.

'You need have no fear of that. I am here to ensure nothing of the sort happens. And my brother stands as protector of the Thanjavur fortress. No one can slip into the fort without the permission of Chinna Pazhuvettaraiyan. And no one can seek an audience with the Maharaja without my knowledge, or hand him an olai.³ I have intercepted two or three such olais.'

This was greeted by shouts of praise, such as:

'Long live Pazhuvettaraiyrar!'

'Long live the Chanakya tantram[4] of the King of Pazhuvoor!'

'Long live his valour!'

'There's more. The crown prince's antics are far less bizarre than those of Prince Arulmozhi Varmar, who has gone to Lanka to wage war. What have we learnt from our elders about warfare? What is the strategy for an invasion? What code of conduct do we follow? What have our ancestors followed through centuries, as the tradition set by their forebears? When we invade another land, we must earn the food we need to sustain our armies from there. We must pay our soldiers with the goods we capture from there. The bulk of the bounty we seize must be sent to the royal treasury in the capital of the kingdom. But do you know what Prince Arulmozhi is doing? I believe food must be shipped from here to feed our soldiers in Eezham! For the last year, I have sent ten batches of ships with food for our soldiers ...'

At once, the voices rose:

'Ludicrous!'

'Atrocious!'

'Ridiculous!'

'I've never heard of such a thing!'

'This injustice cannot be borne!'

'You must listen to the rationale Prince Arulmozhi Varmar presents for this astounding practice. If we are to earn our food from the land we invade, we will create discontent among the people. So we must not seize their food, I believe! He says our fight is with the royals of Eezham, and not with the commoners. And, therefore, we must not inconvenience them in any manner, it seems! Once we have won in battle against the army of the land, we must rule over the people with their wholehearted wishes and blessings, it seems. And, therefore, food and money must be sent from here, I believe!'

Someone in the group said, 'We must ask nothing of the people whose land we have invaded; we must fall at their feet and worship them—none of us has heard of this code of conduct in warfare!'

'I have not yet spoken of the consequences of this. Thanks to the two princes, the treasury as well as the granaries of Thanjavur Palace have been stripped bare. I am forced to impose heavier taxes on all of you to make up the loss. If only I did not put the needs of Chozha Naadu above all, I would have resigned this cursed post a long time ago.'

'Ah! Never! Our one comfort is that you are the one holding this post and protecting us. Have you not tried to speak to the Maharaja about these aberrations from custom?'

'Would I not! I have spoken of them many, many times. Every time, the response I get is: 'Ask Periya Piraatti; ask Ilaiya Piraatti!' As I said before, our Maharaja has lost the ability to think for himself. And he doesn't consult us on important matters either. It is his Periannai[5] Sembiyan Mahadevi whose word he considers vedavaakku;[6] and then, he tells me to ask his beloved daughter, Kundavai Piraatti, for her opinion. So all of us who have grown grey in the service of the crown must go to that little girl, that girl who has never been north of Kollidam, that girl who has never been south of Kudamurutti, and ask her for her opinion on matters of the state. Can you believe this? Since the very inception of the Chozha rule, there has been no record of women poking their noses into governance. How much longer can we bear such humiliation? The other option is that you vote unanimously for me to resign from my post and this task of imposing taxes so that I can go back to my hometown and ...'

'No! No! Never! Pazhuvoor Devar must not wash his hands of us like this. Or this Chozha Empire, to build which four generations of our forebears have sacrificed their lives and shed and spilled blood, will disappear as dust,' Sambuvarayar said.

'In that case, it is all of you who must come to a consensus and tell me what we must do. It is you who must tell me the cure for this female monarchy that has become even more disgusting than the Alli Rajyam,'[7] said the King of Pazhuvoor.

8

WHO IS IN THE PALANQUIN?

For a while, the group broke into discussion and debate, with several of its members talking simultaneously. Vandiyadevan couldn't make out a word as the men tried to outshout each other.

Sambuvarayar finally raised his voice and said, 'Don't we owe an answer to the King of Pazhuvoor? What is the point of everyone voicing a different opinion? The night has entered its third jaamam, and look—there's the moon.'

'There is a doubt plaguing my mind. I do believe I'm not the only one troubled by this. If the Pazhuvoor Devar will assure me he won't fly into a rage, I would like to ask a question,' said the hoarse voice that had spoken earlier.

'It is Vanangaamudiyaar who speaks now, isn't it? Would he care to stand up and show his face in the light?' Pazhuvettaraiyar said.

'Yes, it is I. And here, I've shown my face in the light.'

'I tend to reserve my rage for the battlefield; I tend to take it out on my enemies. I won't fly into a rage with my friends. And so, whatever it is, please do ask without hesitation.'

'In that case, I will. The criticism that Pazuvettaraiyar levels at Sundara Chozha Maharaja has also been levelled by some at Pazhuvettaraiyar himself. Although I don't believe them, I would like to clarify the issue here, at this time,' said Vanangaamudiyaar.

'What is that? How? Would you care to explain?'

'Everyone is aware that Pazhuvoor Devar married a woman two years ago. ...'

At this, Sambuvarayar's angry voice interrupted with, 'We object to Vanangaamudiyaar's bringing up this issue. To ask our great leader, our chief guest here, such an inappropriate question is absolutely ...'

'I beg of Sambuvarayar to keep a hold on his temper. Please let Vanangaamudiyaar finish his question. It is far better to put one's doubts out there, however much pain they may cause, than to let them fester in one's mind. Yes, it is true that I married a woman after I had crossed the ripe old age of fifty-five. I don't refute this. But I have never claimed to be the Rama avataram of the Kali yugam. Neither have I claimed to be a one-woman man. I fell in love with that woman; she loved me too. We got married in line with our Tamil tradition and custom. In what manner have I erred?'

'None at all!' several voices rose at once.

'I did not say it was wrong to marry the woman. Who among us can claim to be a one-woman man? But ... but ...'

'But what! Ask what is on your mind without hesitation, and be done with it!'

'There are those who say the newly wedded Ilaiya Rani is consulted on all matters by Pazhuvettaraiyar, even matters of the state and governance. They say you take the Ilaiya Rani with you everywhere you go.'

A chuckle was heard.

Sambuvarayar leapt up and snarled, 'Who was it who laughed? Come forward right away and explain what prompted the laughter!' And with this, he pulled his dagger from its sheath and held it aloft.

'It was I who laughed. There is no need for frenzy,' Pazhuvettaraiyar said, and then continued, 'Vanangaamudiyaare! Is it a crime to take my lawfully wedded wife with me everywhere I go? It is true that I do take her along to several places. But it is a malicious rumour that I ask Ilaiya Rani's opinion on matters of the state and governance. I have never ever done that.'

'In that case, I beseech the Pazhuvoor Devar to dispel one last doubt. Why has the palanquin that ought rightly to have been in the antapuram found its way to this confidential conference? Is there anyone inside, or not? If not, where did the light cough that was heard a short while ago, and the tinkle of bangles, come from?'

An awkward silence ensued. The same doubts and questions had arisen in the minds of several of those assembled, and so none could jump in to oppose Vanangaamudiyaar. Sambuvarayar's lips mumbled something indistinct, but he did not step forward either.

Tearing the silence to shreds, Pazhuvettaraiyar said in a booming voice, 'A legitimate question, and one I am bound to answer. I promise to dispel your doubts before this gathering disperses. But you can afford me another half a naazhigai, surely? You do have that much faith in me, surely?'

'Yes, we do, yes, we do, we have absolute faith in Pazhuvettaraiyar,' came a chorus.

'There is no call for one to believe I have less faith in, or respect for, Pazhuvettaraiyar than anyone else. It was because he asked me to speak without hesitation that I asked what I did. This takes nothing away from the fact that I am prepared to obey his every command, and that I would lay down my life for him!' said Vanangaamudi Munaiarayar.

'I am aware of Vanangaamudiyaar's sentiments. I am aware of the faith each one of you has in me. And so, let us make a decision on the issue over which we have called this conference. May Sundara

Chozha Maharaja live long in this world, and rule over the Chozha Empire! But if something were to happen to him, if the physicians' predictions were to come true, if the ill omens we have been observing for the last few days are indeed portents of the worst, we must decide who is entitled to the throne after him.'

'We ask that you give us your opinion on this matter. There is no one here who will voice a contrary one to yours.'

'That is not right. It is crucial that everyone here put forward his point of view. I wish to remind you of certain incidents from the past. The great warrior, the great scholar and the paragon of virtue, Kandaraditya Devar passed away most unexpectedly twenty-four years ago. At the time, his son, Madurantaka Devar, was a one-year-old infant. And so, the king's last words were that his younger brother, Arinjaya Devar, succeed him. It was his wife and reigning queen, Sembiyan Mahadevi, who revealed this to us. We did as the late king had wished. But Arinjaya Devar was not fated to sit on the throne for longer than a year. His eldest son, Parantaka Sundara Chozhar, was a strapping young man of twenty at the time. Keeping the well-being of the kingdom in mind, we ministers and courtiers and kings of smaller dominions and leaders of various persuasions decided he would succeed his father. No one can take issue with this. Until two years ago, Sundara Chozha Maharaja ruled the country in line with custom. He accorded us due respect and consulted us on matters of importance. Chozha Naadu reaped the benefits, knowing greater growth and prosperity than ever before. Now, his health has begun to decline. Under the circumstances, who should be crowned king after him? Kandaraditya Devar's son, Madurantakar, has now come of age, and is fit to rule a kingdom. His intelligence, education, nature and piety speak to the suitability of his candidature. A year younger than Madurantakar is Aditya Karikalar, son of Sundara Chozhar, serving as the commander of the northern armed forces from Kanchi. Which of the two is the rightful heir to the kingdom? What is the tradition of this clan? What does Manu Needhi[1] say? What are the ancient customs of this Tamil land? Is it right for the elder king's son, Madurantakar, to come to power? Or for the younger king's grandson to take the title? Each one of you must say, without hesitation, what you think.'

'It is the son of the elder brother Kandaraditya Devar who is the rightful heir. That is justice, that is tradition, that is custom,' said Sambuvarayar.

'I concur with that', 'My opinion is the same', 'That is my point of view too', 'I've reached the same conclusion', said various voices in the group.

'I share your opinions that Madurantakar is the rightful heir. But is every one of us ready to give one's all in the effort for him to claim that right? Are we willing to pledge our bodies and possessions and souls to fight for it? Are we ready, at this very moment, to swear on Durga Devi that we shall stand by him?' asked Pazhuvettaraiyar, his voice trembling with a passion they had never heard before.

The group was silent for some time.

Then, Sambuvarayar said, 'As God is our witness, we will swear to stand by him. But before we do so, you must clarify one issue for us. What is Prince Madurantakar's stance? Is he ready to mount the throne? We've heard that the son of Kandaraditya Devar has cast off all worldly trappings and immersed himself in the worship of Shiva, that he has no interest in ruling or governance. We have also heard that his mother, Sembiyan Mahadevi, is entirely opposed to her son inheriting the title of king. We wish to learn the truth from you.'

'An apt question, voiced at the appropriate time. I am bound to clarify the issue to which you have alluded. I should have done so before I was asked. Do forgive me for my slip,' Pazhuvettaraiyar said, as an elaborate preamble for the short speech that was to follow. 'All of Chozha Naadu is aware that Sembiyan Mahadevi threw her efforts into diverting her only son's interest from governance to God. But the reason for this remains unknown to Chozha Naadu as well as its people. The reason is simply this—Periya Piraatti was worried that if he were to show any interest in the throne, his very life could be in danger.'

'Aha!'

'Is that so?'

'Is this true?'

'Yes. Isn't it obvious that a mother would much rather her one child stay alive than sit on the throne? Madurantakar, who considers his mother's word a manifestation of divine order, set himself on the path of ascetism. He immersed himself in the worship of Shiva. However, for some time now, he has been undergoing a slow change of heart. The notion that the Chozha Empire is his, and that it is his duty to look after this land, has taken root in his mind. If all of you are in favour of his ascension to the throne, he is willing to reveal himself to you and tell you in person that this is his wish.'

'What evidence do we have for this?'

'I will give you evidence that will satisfy all of you. If I do so, are you willing to take the oath we spoke of?'

'Yes!'

'We are!'

'Of course!'

'Does anyone else have any other doubt niggling at him?'

'No!'

'None!'

'Not at all!'

'In that case, let me present you the evidence. I will also dispel Vanangaamudi Munaiaraiyar's doubt right away,' said Pazhuvettaraiyar, getting up from his seat. He marched up to the closed palanquin and stood before it.

'My prince! You must part the curtain of the palanquin and grace us with your presence. You must give these great warriors, who are ready to pledge their bodies and possessions and souls to your cause, a darshan of your face!' he said, in his humblest tone.

Vandiyadevan, who was hanging on to every word from his hiding place behind the pillar on the terrace, now carefully peeked into the courtyard. Just as he had seen that afternoon, an arm so white it was nearly pink made its way outside the palanquin and parted the silk drapes ever so little. But then he realised that what he had mistaken for a set of bangles or bracelets were the kanganam that princes wore. The next moment, a face of stunning beauty shone from the interior of the palanquin, bringing to mind the full moon. A beautiful form, that might have belonged to Manmadha[2], stepped out of the palanquin and smiled at the gathering. Aha! This was the son of Kandaraditya Devar, Prince Madurantakar! Vandiyadevan had assumed the occupant was a woman because it hadn't occurred to him that a man might travel in a palanquin. Azhvarkadiyaan Nambi must have made the same mistake. He looked across at the wall, searching for Azhvarkadiyaan Nambi's head. But that section of the wall was hidden by the shadows of the trees, and he couldn't see much because of the surrounding darkness.

By this time, frenzied cries of 'Long live Madurantaka Devar!', 'Long live the crown prince!', 'Vetri Vel, Veera Vel!'[3] were rising from the courtyard.

The assembled warriors pulled out their swords and spears and held them aloft.

Vandiyadevan decided it would be imprudent to linger on. He made his way back to the mandapam to which he had been shown, and lay down.

9

A CHAT EN ROUTE

Having spent most of his life in the arid lands north of the Paalaar, Vandiyadevan had never learnt to swim in the currents of a river. Once, when he was manning the border on the shores of the Vada Pennai, he had decided to bathe in the river. He found himself swept into a whirlpool. It tossed him about and made him swirl in circles, even as it dragged him further down towards the riverbed. It sucked his strength away in seconds, and it wasn't long before Vandiyadevan went limp, thinking, *There is no way I can get out of this alive, I'm going to die in a whirlpool*. By some miracle, he was released from his watery trap, and the current carried him to the banks of the river and saved his life.

That night, as he lay in bed, Vandiyadevan felt he was being pulled into a whirlpool yet again. Against his will, he had been trapped in the currents of a royal conspiracy. Could he escape this as he had escaped the whirlpool? Would God save him a second time?

He had been stunned by all that he had learnt from the midnight conference. It had only been a few years since the Chozha Empire had rid itself of its external enemies. Prince Aditya Karikalan, fearless warrior, expert war strategist and a Chanakya in politics that he was, had used his formidable brain and the considerable brawn of the Chozha Army to uproot Irattai Mandalam's King Krishna from Thondai Mandalam. The external foes had been extinguished. And at this time, plots and conspiracies had begun to churn in the innermost circles of the court. What ramifications could this internal turbulence, so much more dangerous than enemies from without, have?

The key conspirators were among the most highly regarded warriors, ministers, leaders and officials of the Chozha Empire. Pazhuvettaraiyar and his brother were forces to be reckoned with. Their strength and influence were unrivalled, as were their reputation and splendour. The other men who had attended the meeting were not far behind. They had their own armies and ruled over vast territories. Could this be the first time they were meeting? How many other such conferences had Pazhuvettaraiyar presided over, carting Madurantakar around in the palanquin and revealing him in this dramatic fashion? Adada! Marrying a young woman in old age had proven to be rather fortuitous for him, hadn't it?

There had been no doubt in Vandiyadevan's mind that the heir to the throne was Prince Aditya Karikalar.

He had never dreamt that there would be a challenge to the claim. He had heard of Kandaraditya Devar's son Madurantakar. It was said that the son, like his father, was steeped in Shiva bhakti. It had never occurred to Vandiyadevan that Madurantakar might be a prospective heir to the throne, or that he would fight for it.

But what would be truly just? Who was the rightful heir to the throne? Aditya Karikalar? Or Madurantakar? The more thought Vandiyadevan gave it, the more it seemed to him that each had a legitimate claim. If there were to be a dispute over it, which of the two would be victorious? Where did his own duty lie? Aha! He had built castles in the air en route from Kanchi to this place, hadn't he? He had hoped that his deference and loyalty to Prince Aditya Karikalar would guarantee him a position of great influence in the court once the prince became king, hadn't he? He had even nursed ambitions of eventually winning back the kingdom that had been wrested from the Vaanar clan, hadn't he? He had believed he'd chosen a puliyankombu, a tamarind tree branch whose slenderness belies its strength, to climb on. And it seemed that this puliyankombu was about to break off.

These thoughts haunted Vandiyadevan and drove away his sleep. It was well into the fourth jaamam of the night when he finally dozed off.

Not even the stinging heat of the overhead sun's scorching rays woke Vandiyadevan the next morning.

It was only when Kandamaaran shook him awake that he got up with a start.

'Did you sleep well last night?' Kandamaaran asked, playing the good host. Then, he added, 'I came to look in on you after I'd escorted the other guests to their rooms. You were paying tribute to Kumbhakarna.'[1]

Vandiyadevan, suppressing the memories that flooded his mind and swallowing the words that threatened to rise from his throat, said, 'All I remember is watching the kuravai koothu and then coming here to lie down. I woke up just now. Adada! It's so late! This must be the second jaamam after sunrise. I must leave right away. Kandamaara! Order your servants to get my horse ready!'

'Very nice! You're leaving already? What's the rush? You must stay for at least ten days before you leave,' Kandamaaran said.

'Oh, dear god, no! My uncle in Thanjavur is very ill. I've had news that he is unlikely to survive. I should go see him as soon as I can. I'll have to leave right away,' Vandiyadevan piled lie upon lie.

'In that case, you must set aside a few days to stay here on your return at least.'

'Of course, we'll see about all that later. Now, give me leave to start from here!'

'Don't be in such a hurry! You can start after breakfast. I'll accompany you up to the Kollidam River.'

'How could you possibly do that? All sorts of important guests have landed up at your place. You can't abandon them and ...'

'There is no guest who is more important than you as far as I'm concerned!' said Kandan Maaravel, and then paused. 'Yes, the guests are people of great prominence. But they have my father and the palace officials to dance attendance on them. I didn't even get to talk to you for long last night. Unless I spend some time catching up with you en route to the river, my mind won't be at peace. I insist on accompanying you to the banks of the Kollidam!'

'I have no objection. It's your wish, and your call,' Vandiyadevan said.

Within a naazhigai, the two friends had mounted their horses and left Sambuvarayar's palace. The horses trotted along at an easy pace. The journey was pleasant. The friends barely noticed the dirt from the road that the wind dusted on their faces every now and again. They were lost in their reminiscences of the good old days.

In some time, Vandiyadevan said, 'Kandamaara! I only got to spend a single night at your house, and yet I couldn't have asked for greater comfort. But I do feel betrayed on one count. You would speak about your sister all the time when we were stationed on the banks of the Vada Pennai River. I didn't even get to see her properly. When she peeped out, hidden behind your mother, I caught barely an eighth of her face! Your sister has more than her fair share of the shyness and naiveté desirable in women.'

Kandamaaran's lips made as if to speak, his mouth as if to open—but no words left them.

'It's all right, there's no cause for regret. You've asked me to stay for a few days on my way back. I'll have plenty of time to meet her and speak to her. And perhaps some of your sister's bashfulness will abate by then. Kandamaara! What did you say your sister's name was?'

'Manimeghalai!'

'Adada! What a lovely name! If only her beauty and nature were to live up to that name. ...'

Kandamaaran cut in, 'My friend! I beg of you. Forget my sister; forget everything I have ever said about her. Don't speak about her ever again!'

'What is this, Kandamaara! It's taken all of one day for you to do an about turn. Just last night, you were speaking about the prospect of my receiving a bridegroom's reception in your home!'

'Yes, it's true that I said those things. But the circumstances have changed since then. My parents have decided to marry my sister off elsewhere; Manimeghalai has consented too!'

Good for Manimeghalai, Vandiyadevan said to himself. It wasn't hard to guess who the bridegroom was. They must have fixed an alliance with Prince Madurantakar, who had emerged from the palanquin. It appeared Madurantakar's allies were leaving no stone unturned to bolster the strength of their faction. Pazhuvettaraiyar was some strategist!

'Aha! I suppose you've plotted to make one of the rich guests from last night the bridegroom! Kandamaara! This doesn't come as a surprise; I don't feel let down either. It is, in a way, expected. ...'

'Expected? How is that?'

'Who would want a poor orphan like me for a son-in-law? Which woman would want to marry a man who has nothing to call his own, no title, no land? What does my ancestral glory, and the fact that my forebears were kings, count for now?'

'My friend! That's enough now! Don't degrade me and my family in this manner! Those are not the reasons at all. There's a far more compelling reason for what happened. If only you knew, you would understand. But I can't speak about that now. You'll learn of it yourself when the time is right!'

'Kandamaara! What is this sudden penchant for cryptic speech?'

'Forgive me. The circumstances are such that I can't take even you into confidence. However things turn out, our friendship will never be affected. Please believe me. The moment I'm allowed to speak, you're the first person I'll run to, to fill in on what is under way. Until then, trust me. Trust that I will never let you down! I won't abandon you! You can rely on me!'

'My heartfelt gratitude for this promise. But then I don't understand what circumstances might lead you to possibly let me down or abandon me. And I'm not the kind who relies on anyone else either, Kandamaara! The sword in my scabbard and the spear in my hand are all I rely on!'

'You might have the opportunity to wield that sword and spear soon. And then, we will fight for the same side, standing shoulder to shoulder. Your ambitions will be fulfilled too. ...'

'What is this talk? Do you expect war to break out sometime soon? Or, do you plan to go join the war in Eezham?'

'Eezham? You'd be shocked if you heard the wonderful manner in which that war is being conducted! It seems grains and food must be supplied from Chozha Naadu for our soldiers fighting there! What a shame! No, I don't plan to join that war ... I'm talking about something else. Please bear with me. I'll tell you all when the time is right. Don't probe me now, for god's sake!'

'All right, all right! You don't have to say anything you don't want to. You don't even have to open your mouth again. There, Kollidam approaches!' Vandiyadevan said.

They could see the foam from the grand river in the distance. The friends had reached the shore in minutes.

The first flood of Aadi had swept down the river, pushing its banks apart. The trees on the far side looked like little plants. The waters of the first flood stirred whirlpools, drew kolams, set off drumrolls, tried to break the banks and screamed 'Ho!' as they rushed and gushed and pushed towards the ocean. The sight left Vandiyadevan mesmerised.

A lone boat floated in the harbour. The two boatmen held long oars. A passenger was already ensconced inside. He appeared to be a paragon of Shiva bhakti.

Looking at the friends approach the river, one of the boatmen called out, 'Saami! Are you going to get on the boat?'

'Yes! He's coming. Hold on!' Kandamaaran called.

The friends dismounted from their horses.

'I should have thought this through! What do I do with my horse? Will he fit into the boat?' Vandiyadevan asked.

'There's no need for that. There are two men following right behind us. One will ride your horse back to Kadambur. The other will accompany you on the boat and procure you a horse on the other bank,' Kandamaaran said.

'Aha! What foresight! You're a true friend!' Vandiyadevan said.

'You must have thought the Kollidam was like the Paalaar or Pennai. How would you know you couldn't ride a horse through the river?'

'Yes, do forgive me for insulting your Chozha Naadu's river with my ignorance! What sort of river is this! What sort of flood! It swells like the ocean!'

The two friends hugged long and hard before they parted ways.

Vandiyadevan made his way to the boat.

One of the men who had followed from the palace got on it too.

The boat was all ready to leave, and the boatmen dipped their oars into the water.

All of a sudden, a voice called from a distance, 'Stop! Stop! Stop the boat!'

The boatmen hesitated.

The man who was shouting reached the bank in no time. Vandiyadevan recognised him right away. Who should it be but Azhvarkadiyaan Nambi?

Realising the man was a Vaishnavite, the Shaivite in the boat said, 'Go! Row away! I won't sit in the same boat as that heretic! Let him take the next boat!'

But Vandiyadevan addressed the boatmen and said, 'Hold on. Let him join us. There is plenty of space on the boat. Let's take him along.'

There was much he wished to ask Azhvarkadiyaan Nambi about the events of the previous night.

10

THE ASTROLOGER OF KUDANDAI

When Ponni, born and bred in Kudagu Naadu, had reached maidenhood, she wished to leave for the home of her bridegroom, Samudra Raja, the king of the ocean. She crossed forests and hills, flowed over stones and slopes, negotiated pits and precipices, and ran as fast as she could towards him. As she drew closer and closer to Samudra Raja, the thrill of meeting her beloved coursed through her body. Soon, she grew two arms to throw around him and, spreading them wide, leapt and skipped through the path that would lead her to Samudra Raja. Two arms, she felt, wouldn't do justice to the anticipation and joy in her heart. And so they multiplied into ten, into twenty, into a hundred. She threw them all out as she neared his home.

And what did the foster mothers of Chozha Naadu do to ornament the bride who was dashing towards her cherished husband? Adada! What beautiful green sarees they draped around her! What riotous colours of flowers they weaved through her hair! What rare fragrances they sprayed on her! Aha! How can one hope to describe the sight of the punnai and kadamba trees on either bank raining ruby flowers down on her? Not even the celestial blossoms the devas threw down from the skies could rival them!

Oh, Ponni! Which young maiden wouldn't lose herself in delight at the sight of you? Which woman's heart wouldn't brim over with contentment watching you dance along in your bridal finery? It is but natural for a bride to be surrounded by her unmarried bridesmaids, isn't it?

Among the elegant arms Ponni had thrown out to caress her husband was one called Arisilaru. This beautiful river flowed just south of the Kaveri. No one could tell of her presence from a distance. She was hidden behind a thick canopy of lush green trees. Arisilaru was a royal maiden who had never left the safety of the antapuram since birth. The beauty of this graceful river could find no parallel on this earth.

Right. If the readers would tear themselves away from the thoughts triggered by the word 'antapuram' and accompany us to the Arisilaru, bend under the branches of the thicket of trees and get past them … adada! What is this beautiful sight? It is as if beauty itself were being beautified, nectar itself being sweetened!

Who are these lovely ladies seated in a luxurious boat carved in the likeness of a swan? They could be versions of Goddess Saraswati herself! And who is this jewel among women seated in their midst, like a full moon glowing among the stars, like a queen born to rule the seven worlds? And who is this serene beauty sitting by her side, holding a veena, the perfect foil to her vivacity? They might be Gandharva women, their melodious voices stirring notes of music into the song of the river. One of them was meenalochani, with eyes like pools where fish danced; another was neelalochani, her eyes bringing to mind the deep blue of the ocean. One had a face like a tender lotus, another lips like the petals of a lotus in full bloom. As for the girl who was playing the veena, one cannot stop staring at her delicate fingers, long and slim as the petals of the kanthal flower, as they dance over the frets of the instrument.

And what of the song they are singing? Even the river has subdued her currents so she can listen to their voices, hasn't she? The parrots and koels that live on the trees by the banks have slipped into silence! It should come as little surprise that humans, blessed with ears and the ability to hear, are moved by the intoxicating music from the boat. Let us listen:

Marungu vandu sirandhu aarpa
Manippu aadai adhuporthu
Karungayarkan vizhithu olgi
Nadandhai vaazhi! Kaveri!
Karungayarkan vizhithu olgi
Nadanda ellam ninkanavan

Tirundu sengol valaiyamai
Arinden vaazhi! Kaveri!
Poovar solai mayilada
Purindu kuyilgal isaippaada
Kaamar maalaiarugasaiya
Nadandai vaazhi! Kaveri!
Kaamar maalaiarugasaiya
Nadanda ellam ninkanavan
Naama velin tirangande
Arinden vaazhi! Kaveri!

As bees buzz on either side,
Wearing your fabric of flowers,
Your dark, fish-like eyes wide open,
You walk by. Long live, Kaveri!
Your dark, fish-like eyes wide open,
Your husband's sceptre stays unbent,
I hear. Long live, Kaveri!
As peacocks dance among bowers of flowers,
And koels sing in time to their feet,
Bearing swaying garlands of flowers,
You walk by. Long live, Kaveri!
Bearing swaying garlands of flowers,
You walk, and I see
Your husband's skill with the spear,
Long live, Kaveri!

We have heard these divinely beautiful lines somewhere, haven't we? Yes, they are from the *Silappadikaram*.[1] They come alive as never before in the voices of these lovely maidens, and draw the listener in. They must be the closest confidantes of the Ponni, for no one else could sing with such energy and such emotion of her beauty! Adada! The music, lyrics and passion of those lines swell into a flood of nectar as they sing. What's the point of this dissection and analysis of music and lyrics and songs and tunes? It has nothing to do with any of that. This is some sort of illusory magic, a spell that intoxicates the singer and listener alike and drives one mad.

The boat gently floats to a halt in a cove, where the trees have afforded a gap for a little harbour. Two women disembark; of them, one has the bearing of a queen born to rule the seven worlds. The other is the maiden who drew out such melodious notes from the veena.

They were both ravishing beauties, but the loveliness of each belonged to a different genre. One had the dignified grace of the pink lotus, the other the fragile tenderness of the kumuda flower. If one was the full moon, the other was the golden crescent of dawn. One was a dancing peacock, the other a koel in song. One was Indrani, queen of devas, the other Manmadha's beloved Rathi. One was the gushing Ganga, the other the blushing Kaveri.

Let us no longer keep the readers in suspense; let us reveal the identities of the two women. The one with an air of authority was Sundara Chozha's daughter, Kundavai, sister of Arulmozhi Varman who would go down in history as Rajaraja Chozha. Beloved of the people, and titled Ilaiya Piraatti, she would be the very foundation of the great empire in the days to come. She would raise her nephew, the son of Rajaraja Chozha, to become the greatest of warriors and the highest of kings. The other was the daughter of the king of Kodumbalur, a maiden who had sought the honour of being Kundavai's companion. She who would eventually earn honours that would make history was now the embodiment of self-restraint, sweetness and serenity.

As the two women got on to the shore, Kundavai turned to the others and said, 'You stay right here. We'll be back within a naazhigai.'

The other occupants of the boat were princesses too, daughters of minor kings as was the Kodambalur princess. Each had come to the palace of Pazhaiyarai hoping to be Kundavai's favoured companion. As they watched her walk away with a lone friend, instructing the rest to stay where they were, one could see the betrayal and envy in their eyes.

A chariot fitted with horses was waiting for the two women.

'Vanathi! Get up on the chariot!' Kundavai said, and followed her friend onto it. The chariot set off as fast as the horses could carry it.

'Akka! Where are we going? Won't you tell me?' Vanathi asked.

'Why not? We're going to the house of the astrologer of Kudandai,' said Kundavai.

'Why are we going to visit the astrologer, Akka? About what do you want to consult him?'

'What else? You, of course. For a few months now, you've been walking around in a daze. You look emaciated. I'm going to ask when the daze will lift, and when your health will return!'

'Akka! For god's sake, my health is fine. There's no need to ask him about me, let's go back!'

'No, di, amma,² no! I'm not going to ask about you. I'm going to ask about myself.'

'What are you going to ask him about yourself?'

'Will I get married? Or will I die an old maid?'

'Akka! How does it make any sense to ask this of the astrologer, when you should be asking yourself? All you'd need to do is incline your head slightly, just so, and every king who rules over any land from the Himalayas to Kumarimunai would come running down to throw his hat in the ring. Why, they'd even come from across the seas! I wonder which great king is destined for your hand. It is you who must decide, though, isn't it?'

'Vanathi, even if we assume you're right, there's an obstacle—any king who marries me would want his bride to come back with him to his kingdom. I cannot bear to leave this Chozha Naadu where the Ponni flows. I have sworn I will never leave.'

'That is no obstacle. Any king who marries you will be your slave forever, and do your bidding. If you were to ask him to stay on in Chozha Naadu, he would!'

'Aha! This is like catching a mouse and cuddling it in one's arms. Can you imagine the consequences of uprooting a king from his country?'

'But surely everyone who is born a woman must get married?'

'There is no such rule in any shastra, Vanathi! Look at Avvaiyar. Didn't she live a long, happy, maiden's life, writing poetry?'

'But Avvaiyar became an old woman at a young age thanks to a boon from God. That hasn't happened to you, has it?'

'Well, then, if I'm to marry, I'd have to find an orphan ... one of our soldiers, perhaps. He won't have a kingdom to his name. He won't ask me to accompany him to another country. We will live on in Chozha Naadu.'

'Akka! So you'll never leave our Chozha Naadu?'

'Never! Not even if I'm asked to be the queen of the heavens!'

'My mind is finally at peace today.'

'What is this about, now?'

'If you were to go away to some other country, I'd have to follow you. I cannot live without you. But then, neither can I live away from our lush Chozha Naadu.'

'But if you were to get married, you'd have to go away too, won't you?'

'I will never get married, Akka!'

'Adiye! Where did all that advice you just gave me disappear?'

'Do I have the privileges you do?'

'Adi, kalli! You little vixen! I know everything. You think you can throw sand into my eyes, eh? You're not loathe to leave Chozha Naadu. The Chozha Naadu that you love has now taken off with sword and spear to Eezham, hasn't it? You thought I couldn't read your mind, did you?'

'Akka! Akka! Am I such a fool? Where is the sun? And where is the dewdrop of dawn? What is the point of the dewdrop aspiring to the sun?'

'Yes, well, the dewdrop may be small, and the sun large and bright. But even so, the dewdrop has imprisoned the sun within itself, hasn't it?'

In a voice heavy with excitement and anticipation, Vanathi said, 'Do you really think so? That the dewdrop might one day join the sun?' And then, her heart grew weary again. 'The dewdrop has its desires; it imprisons the sun, yes. But what would be the point? It doesn't take long for the dewdrop to get its just deserts, does it? It dries out in the sun, leaving no trace of its one-time existence.'

'That is incorrect, Vanathi. The sun sees the dewdrop's deepest desires and pulls her into himself. He doesn't want the eyes of any other man to fall on the dewdrop he so loves. And when the night sets in, he releases her again. The dewdrop that disappeared does reappear, doesn't it?'

'Akka! You're just trying to comfort me.'

'In that case, there is something in you that needs

comforting. And all this while you denied it. See, that is why we're visiting the astrologer of Kudandai.'

'If there is something in me that needs comforting, what would be the point of asking the astrologer about it?' sighed Vanathi.

The house of the astrologer was tucked away in a nook of the city, in an isolated spot by the Kali temple. The chariot circled around the town, without entering its gates, and reached the house. The ease with which the charioteer negotiated the way suggested this wasn't the first time he had driven there.

The astrologer was waiting with one of his disciples outside the house. He greeted his guests with great respect.

'Perumaatti! You are the embodiment of Kalaimagal and Tirumagal, Saraswati and Lakshmi in one! Do come in, do come in! This poor man's hut must have earned some goodwill to have you visit again!' he said.

'Josiyare![3] No one will come looking for you now, I hope?' Kundavai asked.

'They won't, thaaye![4] Not many people come looking for me these days. It is when people face problems that they seek out astrologers. Under the rule of your great father, Tiru Sundara Chozhar, people have forgotten what trouble feels like. They have health and wealth, peace and prosperity. Who will come looking for me?' the astrologer said.

'So you're suggesting I must be plagued by some problem to come looking for you.'

'No, Perumaatti! Not at all! One would have to be blind to think the daughter of the king of Pazhaiyarai, blessed with the navanidhi—the nine treasures of Kubera—must be plagued by any problem! Even as the troubles of everyone else have disappeared, this poor astrologer finds himself in a bind. He has no patron. And so, you have come as an avatar of Ambika herself to solve his problems. Thaaye! Do grace this hut with your presence. I commit a grave error in stalling you at the entrance!' the astrologer said.

Kundavai turned to the charioteer and said, 'Drive the chariot to the Kali temple, and park it under the shade of the banyan tree.'

Then, she and Vanathi followed the astrologer inside the hut.

'Appane!' the astrologer called to his disciple. 'Stand guard at the entrance. Even if someone were to chance to come this way, don't let him or her in!'

His house had been spruced up so it was fit to receive Ilaiya Piraatti. A painting of Goddess Ambika had been placed in an alcove, decorated with flowers and anointed with sandal paste. Two seats had been appointed for the princesses. The wicks of the kuthuvilakku had been lit, and kolams ornamented the space. Palm leaf manuscripts and wooden planks bearing horoscope charts had been artfully strewn on the floor.

The astrologer waited for the princesses to take their seats before he sat.

'Ammani!⁵ You must tell me what has brought you here.'

'Josiyare! Can't you divine it from the stars?' Kundavai asked.

'As you wish, thaaye,' the astrologer said. Closing his eyes, he moved his mouth in some kind of prayer. When he opened his eyes, he said, 'Komaatti,⁶ you're here to consult me about the horoscope of this maiden here. That is what Goddess Parasakti tells me. Is this true?'

'Aha! Amazing! What can one say of your skill? Yes, josiyare! I'm indeed here to ask about this girl. She came to the Pazhaiyarai Palace a year ago. For the first eight months, she was cheerful and happy, the most ebullient of my companions, laughing and dancing and prancing about. But something has happened to her over the last four months. She seems to be in a daze all the time. She has forgotten how to laugh. Nothing's the matter with her health, she says. If her family were to see her and question me about her well-being, I wouldn't know where to turn my face. ...'

'Thaaye! Isn't she the cherished princess of Kodumbalur? Her name is Vanathi, isn't it?' the astrologer asked.

'Yes. You seem to know everything!'

'I have this royal maiden's horoscope, too, in my collection. Give me a moment,' the astrologer said. Drawing an old wooden box to himself, he spent some time rifling through its contents. He finally pulled out a horoscope from it and stared at it, transfixed.

11

GRAND ENTRANCE

The city which has today found a place even in English dictionaries under the name 'Kumbakonam' went by the name 'Kudamookku', colloquialised 'Kudandai' in the time in which our story is set. Besides being a holy place, with its temples and sites of pilgrimage, it was also famous for its astrologer. Not far from Kudandai, towards the southwest, was the temporary capital of the Chozhas, Pazhaiyarai. It stood proud and majestic, with its palace terraces and temple gopurams caressing the sky.

The astrologer of Kudandai had been collecting the horoscopes of every royal who lived in the Pazhaiyarai Palace. It was among these that he found that of the Kodumbalur princess, Vanathi. Having spent a good while squinting at the horoscope, the astrologer then stared at Vanathi's face. He turned back to the horoscope, and then to her face. His eyes moved from one to the other in rapid succession, but not a word escaped his lips.

'What is this, josiyare! Are you going to say something or not?' Kundavai Devi asked.

'Thaaye! What can I say? How can I say it? I happened to look at this horoscope once before. I couldn't believe it. I thought there must be some mistake, for this couldn't possibly happen. Now, when I examine the horoscope and then this girl's face, I'm ... I'm astounded.'

'Yes, yes, take your time being stunned. Once you're done, tell us whatever you can, in some detail.'

'This is a very lucky horoscope, thaaye! If you won't be offended, I'll tell you—this is a step above your own horoscope. I have never seen such a stupendous horoscope, ever!'

Kundavai smiled. Vanathi, embarrassed, said, 'Akka! He says this unlucky wretch has the luckiest horoscope in the world! This must be what he tells everyone!'

'Amma! What did you say? If what I say proves false, I will quit my vocation,' the astrologer said.

'There's no need for that, josiyare. Don't do all this. Do continue telling people how lucky they are. The reason she's suspicious is that you've waxed poetic about her horoscope, without getting into the specifics.'

'You want specifics? Here they are! Four months ago, something happened that might have been interpreted as inauspicious. There was a slight slip; but in reality, it is not inauspicious at all. It is the spark which will trigger this princess's great fortunes!'

'Vanathi! What did I tell you?' Kundavai Devi said.

'You must have coached him earlier,' Vanathi said.

'Look at her, josiyare, see how this girl talks!'

'Let her talk as she will, thaaye! Let her say whatever she wants! When she marries the king of kings …'

'There we go. The only way to satisfy young women is by telling them of their marriages, isn't it?'

'That's what I'm coming to, thaaye. But I can't start off with talk of marriage right away, can I? It would be poor form. People would say this old man has lost his mind!'

'Where will her husband come from, josiyare? And when? How will we know he is the one? Can you tell this from her horoscope?'

'Aha! Can I not? Of course, I can!' And the astrologer squinted at the horoscope again. We can't tell whether he was really studying it, or making a show of studying it.

Then, he looked up and said, 'Ammani! This princess's husband doesn't need to come from a great distance. He is from these parts; but this great warrior is not in this land at the moment. He has crossed the seas.'

Kundavai turned to Vanathi. Vanathi's face betrayed the joy and thrill that coursed through her heart upon hearing this.

'And then? Who is he? To which clan does he belong? Is there some way we can identify him?'

'Yes, certainly. The lucky man who is destined for this woman will have the sign of the sangu and chakram on his hands—the conch and the discus of Lord Vishnu himself, amma!'

Kundavai turned to Vanathi again. Vanathi was staring at the floor.

'In that case, shouldn't we look at her hands? Surely, she must have a corresponding mark!' Kundavai Piraatti said.

'Thaaye! Have you ever looked at the soles of her feet?'

'What is this, josiyare! What kind of talk is that? You would like me to press her feet, would you?'

'No, I did not say anything of the sort. But one day, hundreds of thousands of royal women, titled ladies, princesses, queens, grand dames, will all line up for the honour of touching the soles of this lady's feet, thaaye!'

'Akka! This old man is having me on! He's mocking me. Is this why you brought me here? Get up, let's go!' said Vanathi, angrily.

'What are you getting all upset about, girl? Let him say what he wants.'

'I'm not saying what I want. I'm only telling you what the horoscope says. Poets sing of "paadataamarai", lotus feet. Ask her to show you the inside of her arch. You will see the outlines of lotus petals for sure!'

'Enough, now! Josiyare, if you say anything more about her, she'll drag me out of here. Tell us about her husband instead. ...'

'Aha! I will! The lucky man who will win her hand is the bravest of the brave! He will lead the vanguard in hundreds upon hundreds of battles and win crown after crown. He will be the king of kings. He will rule as emperor for a very long time, winning the praise of kings.'

'I can't believe this! How will this come to pass?' Kundavai asked, her face playing host to a dance of delight, excitement, doubt and anxiety in turns.

'I don't believe this either. He's just going on about something ... he thinks it will please you to hear this, that's all!' Vanathi said.

'It doesn't matter if you refuse to believe this today. One day, you will. On that day, don't forget this penurious astrologer.'

'Akka! Can we leave?' Vanathi asked again. The corners of her large black eyes were brimming with tears.

'Let me say one last thing. You can leave after you hear that. The great warrior who will marry this girl must face all sorts of dangers and negotiate perilous times; he has hordes of enemies. ...'

'Aiyo!'

'But all those dangers and perilous times will fly away; his enemies will perish. This girl's suitor will overcome all obstacles in his path and reach the heights of fame and greatness ... and there's something far more important than all this, thaaye! I'm an old man, and so I will speak plainly. Take a look at this girl's midriff one day. If you don't see the outlines of a banyan leaf on it, I will give up this vocation!'

'What is so wonderful about a banyan leaf, josiyare?'

'Who is the god who rests his divine body on a banyan leaf, don't you know? This girl's womb will nourish a boy who resembles Mahavishnu in every way. Her husband will have to cross stumbling blocks and overcome obstacles. But her son will know no such thing as an obstacle. Everything he wants will come to him without his doing a thing; all that he touches will turn to gold; everything he fancies will come to pass; every patch of land on which he lays his feet will become his own; every place on which he lays eyes will fly the tiger flag. The armies her son leads will run like the first flood of the Ponni! They will brook nothing in their paths. Goddess Jayalakshmi herself will fold her hands and bow to him and serve him. All three worlds will sing of the greatness of his birthplace. His dynasty will win renown throughout the world. ...'

As the astrologer reeled off his predictions as if in a trance, Kundavai's eyes were focused on his face, her ears on his every word.

'Akka!' said a pleading voice.

Kundavai turned, startled.

'Something ... something is happening to me,' Vanathi said, even more pitifully.

She fell to the floor in a sudden faint.

'Josiyare! Bring some water at once!' Kundavai said, cuddling Vanathi to her lap.

The astrologer brought the water; Kundavai took it and sprinkled some on Vanathi's face.

'Nothing will happen to her, amma! Don't worry!' the astrologer said.

'I'm not one bit worried; she has a tendency to do this. It's happened five or six times before. She will open her eyes in a while. And then she will ask whether we are on earth or have gone to Kailash!' Kundavai said.

Then, she went on in a softer tone, 'Josiyare! I came to ask you about something important. For some time now, people have been saying all sorts of things in the cities of this land. A shooting star has been making its appearance in the skies for a few days. Does this truly have any significance? Does this spell danger for the empire? Will there be some sort of change or confusion?'

'Please don't ask me about this one thing, thaaye! Lands, empires, governance ... these things don't have horoscopes. One can't predict what will happen. This wasn't part of my study. Perhaps scholars, ascetics, yogis and sages will be able to divine something with their special powers. Where the question of empire and rule is concerned, auspicious times and stars and horoscopes and predictions lose all power. ...'

'Josiyare! You speak with great skill and sophistry. There is no need to study the horoscopes of empires. But you can look at the horoscopes of my father and brothers, can't you? Isn't that like looking at the horoscope of this empire?'

'I'll do that at leisure some other day, amma! But I can tell you that these are treacherous times, where danger and confusion will reign supreme. Everyone must exercise caution and be wary. ...'

'Josiyare! Ever since my father, the emperor, left Pazhaiyarai for Thanjavur, I've been rather worried ... something has been gnawing at me. ...'

'I've told you earlier, thaaye! These are perilous times for the Maharaja. Your family will face great danger. But Durga Devi's grace will save you from all this.'

'Akka! Where are we?' said Vanathi's feeble voice. From her resting spot on Kundavai's lap, she fluttered open her eyelashes, bit by bit, like a butterfly's wings.

'Kanmani![1] We're still on earth. The pushpak viman hasn't yet shown up to take us to heaven. Let us go on our earthly chariot with its horses to the palace!' Kundavai said.

Vanathi sat up and asked, 'Did I faint?'

'No, you didn't faint; you just dozed off on your Akka's lap! Didn't you hear me singing a lullaby?'

'Don't be angry, Akka! I just felt lightheaded all of a sudden. ...'

'Of course, you did! If the astrologer had said all that about me, I would have felt lightheaded too!'

'It's not because of that, Akka! Do you think I believed a word of what he said?'

'Whether you did or not, you gave the astrologer a fright! I shouldn't take you anywhere with me again!'

'I told you back then that we shouldn't go to the astrologer's house. It was you who ...'

'Yes, yes, it was all my fault. Now get up. Can you walk the few steps to the threshold or should I carry you on my hip?'

'There's no need for all that. I can walk just fine!'

'Hold on, thaaye! I must give you Devi's prasaadam. Please do take it with you,' said the astrologer, and began to put away the horoscopes.

'Josiyare! You've predicted all sorts of things for me, but you haven't said a thing about Akka?' Vanathi said.

'Amma! I have said everything there is to say about Ilaiya Piraatti. What is left for me to say?'

'The bravest of the brave who will marry Akka ...'

'The warrior who shuns help and singlehandedly defeats foes ...' Kundavai interjected.

'What doubt do you have? He will be a mighty prince, a hero in ...'

'He will have all the thirty-two samudrikaa lakshanams; he will rival Brihaspati for intelligence, Saraswati for education, Manmadha for beauty, Arjuna for skill!'

'Where will that handsome, valiant prince who is befitting of Ilaiya Piraatti's hand come from?'

'He is coming, thaaye! He's coming! He will certainly come; he will make his appearance very soon!'

'How will he come? Riding a horse? Or driving a chariot? On an elephant? Or on foot? Or will he fall from the skies and break through the roof right now?' Kundavai said ironically.

'Akka! I hear hooves!' Vanathi said excitedly.

'Yes, you'll hear things no one else does!'

'No, I'm not joking. Listen!'

They fell silent, and the sound of the hooves of a horse galloping as fast as he could towards them could be heard.

'So what, di? Is it a strange occurrence for horses to run through the streets of Kudandai?' Kundavai said.

'No, it sounds as if it is approaching us!'

'You'll hear all sorts of things. Come, get up, let's go.'

Just then, they could hear some commotion outside the house; they heard voices too.

'This is the house of the astrologer, isn't it?'

'Yes, who are you?'

'Is the astrologer in?'

'You can't go inside!'

'I will!'

'I won't let you!'

'I must see the astrologer.'

'Come later.'

'I can't come later! I'm in a hurry!'

'Ade! Ade! Stop! Stop!'

'Move aside! If you stop me, I'll kill you!'

'Aiya! Aiya! No! Don't! Don't go inside!'

Their voices were drawing closer and closer. Padaar! The door crashed open. And with that stentorian herald, a young man made his grand entrance. Another man was trying valiantly to hold him back by his shoulders. The young man shrugged him off and crossed the threshold. As the readers must have already guessed, our young man was indeed Vandiyadevan. All three occupants of the house turned as one to look at him.

Vandiyadevan, too, looked at them. No, he looked at one among them. No, not that either; he didn't see Kundavai Devi in her entirety; he saw only her lovely face. And if you asked me whether he saw at least her face in its entirety, I'd have to say no, not that either. He saw her lips, the colour of coral stone and slightly parted in surprise; he saw her large eyes, where stateliness, surprise, mischief and amusement contrived to cohabit; he took in her eyelids and dark eyebrows; the pink cheeks with their deep dimples; her neck, smooth and white as a conch. He observed all these aspects one by one; each found its own indelible place in his heart.

All of this took seconds. He turned to the astrologer's disciple right away and said, 'What is this, pa? Why didn't you tell me there were ladies inside? If you had, would I have barged in like this?'

He hurried outside, pushing the disciple ahead of him. But, before he went, he turned back to look at Kundavai Devi once more.

'Ade appa! It's like a cyclone just passed!' Kundavai Piraatti said.

'It hasn't yet passed; listen!' said the princess of Kodumbalur.

They could hear Vandiyadevan arguing with the disciple.

'Josiyare! Who is he?' Kundavai asked.

'I don't know, thaaye. He seems to be from some other town. A bit of a raging bull, I think.'

A sudden thought struck Kundavai, and she broke into peals of laughter.

'Why are you laughing, Akka?'

'Why, you ask? We were discussing whether my suitor would arrive on a horse or elephant or break through the roof, weren't we, just now?'

Vanathi began to laugh too. The notes of her laughter infused themselves into those of Kundavai's, and the sound rose in waves of music. It drowned out the argument outside.

The astrologer conducted himself as if he were speculating intensely about something, as he offered the women kumkumam in silence. The two accepted it and got up. They went outside, accompanied by the astrologer.

Vandiyadevan, who wasn't far from the threshold, saw them, and said, 'Please forgive me. This genius didn't think to tell me there were ladies inside. That is why I rushed in so unceremoniously. Please do forgive me for it.'

Kundavai looked at Vandiyadevan teasingly with her lovely eyes, brimming with cheek. She didn't respond to his apology. She linked arms with Vanathi and walked towards the banyan tree under which the chariot was parked.

'It appears the women of Kudandai aren't given to good manners. When a man has taken the trouble to come up and speak, would it kill them to respond with a kind word?' Vandiyadevan's raised voice fell on their ears.

The charioteer was ready with the horses. As soon as the princesses were seated, he hopped on to his own perch. The chariot sped on its way to the banks of the Arisilaru. Vandiyadevan stood watching until the chariot disappeared.

12

NANDINI

Vandiyadevan, whom we saw into a boat on the banks of the Kollidam, has contrived to land up at the house of the astrologer of Kudandai. We must figure out how this happened, mustn't we?

The Shaivite, who had taken issue with Azhvarkadiyaan Nambi boarding the same vessel as he, turned to Vandiyadevan as soon as they were on their way, and said, 'Thambi! I allowed him to climb aboard on your account. But for as long as he is on the boat, he must not utter that eight-letter name. If he does, I'll have him thrown into the Kollidam. The boatmen are my people!'

'Nambi adigale! Did your blessed ears take that in?' Vandiyadevan asked.

'As long as he doesn't utter the five-letter name, I'm happy not to speak the holy eight-letter name,'[1] Azhvarkadiyaan said.

'Who is he to preclude my saying the five-letter

name, the panchaaksharam, of Shiva Peruman himself?
No, I will not listen to him, I will not!

> *Katroonaippootti kadalir paaichinum*
> *Natrunaiyaavadhu Nama Shivaya ve*
>
> *You could tie me to a stone pillar and throw me in*
>   *the sea,*
> *Staying by my side is Nama Shivaya, and he alone.*

Azhvarkadiyaan retorted with:

> *Naadinen naadi naan kandu kondein*
> *Narayana ennum naamam*
>
> *I searched, I searched and found*
> *The name Narayana*

'Shiva-shiva Shivaa!' said the Shaivite, plunging his
index fingers into his ears.

Once Azhvarkadiyaan stopped singing, the Shaivite
released his fingers from those orifices.

Azhvarkadiyaan turned to Vandiyadevan and said,
'Thambi! Listen to this Veera Shaivar go on. It is such
great torment to him to hear the name of Tirumaal …
and yet this Kollidam River reaches us after washing
the feet of the lord who rests in Srirangam. It is
knowing that waters that have washed Perumaal's
feet have been purified by those divine soles that
Shiva Peruman immerses himself in those waters at
Tiruvanaikaval and prays to Vishnu, isn't it?'

He had barely finished the sentence when the Shaivite leapt on him. The two of them tumbled over in a jumble of arms and legs in one corner of the boat, which rocked madly. Vandiyadevan and the oarsmen intervened to pull them apart.

'Paragons of bhakti! It appears you both intend to attain moksham in this Kollidam River. But I have a whole lot of things to settle in this world before I go,' Vandiyadevan said.

One of the boatmen said, 'We can't be certain that falling into the Kollidam will help one attain moksham. But we *can* be certain that it will help one attain the stomach of a crocodile. Look, there!'

They looked in the direction in which he was pointing, and saw a crocodile open its enormous jaws.

'I'm not one bit scared of crocodiles. Narayanamurthy who saved Gajendra from the jaws of the crocodile hasn't gone anywhere, has he?' Azhvarkadiyaan said.

'Hasn't gone anywhere?! He's probably gone to hide in the saris of the gopis in Brindavan!' the Shaivite said.

'Or, Shiva might have got himself into some trouble like he did by granting all sorts of boons to Bhasmasura, and come running to plead Tirumaal for help, and Tirumaal might have gone off to his rescue,' Nambi said.

'The Vaishavite seems to have forgotten how Tirumaal was put in his place when it was Shiva who had to step in and annihilate the three worlds—the Tripura Samhaaram,' the Shaivite said.

'Swamigale! I don't understand why you must go on and on like this! Why don't you simply worship whichever god you like and go your way?' Vandiyadevan said.

Why, indeed, did the Shaivite and Azhvarkadiyaan speak with such vitriol? Why did an argument of this very nature break out in Veeranarayanapuram? This might be a good opportunity to enlighten the readers.

In ancient times, the Tamil-speaking lands were largely dominated by Buddhism and Jainism for about six hundred years. The influence of these religions proved fortuitous for the land. Sculpture, painting, poetry and literature of all kinds found great patronage. Then, it was the era of the Azhvars and the Nayanmars. They wrote beautiful pasurams in Tamil, sweeter than nectar, and spread Vaishnavism and Shaivism through their devotion and discourse.

Their methodology of proselytism proved powerful; they put sculpture and music to effective use in their efforts to popularise their faiths. The pasurams of the Azhvars and the Devara Pann of the Moovar[2] were set to music that could rival that of the devas. Listening to these divine tunes would galvanise one's heart and sow the seeds of faith where there had been none. They lent renown, grace and purity to the Vishnu and Shiva temples in which they were sung. Where they were once built using bricks and wood, temples were now being constructed in stone. From the time of Vijayalaya Chozha, the Chozha kings and their kin had commissioned the erection of these stone temples.

It was around this time that something very special occurred in Kerala. Kaladi witnessed the birth of a great man, who renounced the world for sanyasa when he was still a child. He mastered the religious treatises in Sanskrit, and using the Vedas, Upanishads, Bhagavad Gita and *Brahma Sutras* as the foundation, he began to preach Advaita Vedanta. His knowledge of the Sanskrit texts enabled him to travel throughout the land preaching his philosophy. He set up eight schools of Advaita, and the disciples of these schools furthered his mission of spreading the religion.

In the Tamil lands of the time in which our story is set, about nine hundred and eighty years ago,[3] there had been great communal turbulence, which had several toxic aspects. Militant Vaishnavites and Shaivites cropped up everywhere and got into raging arguments. These debates also saw the participation of Advaitis. These religious debates sometimes turned into riots.

There is a story that quite wonderfully illustrates the Shaivite–Vaishnavite rivalry.

A Vaishnavite from Srirangam was walking along the outer walls of the Tiruvanaikaval temple. A stone suddenly fell on his head, opening a gash that began to bleed. The Vaishnavite looked up. He saw a crow perched on the gopuram, and realised the bird was the cause of his injury. It had knocked off part of the old gopuram. He forgot his pain at once and cried joyously, 'Vaishnavite crow of Srirangam! Well done! Demolish this Shiva temple stone by stone!'

The reader must know of the extent to which Shaivites and Vaishnavites hated each other in order to understand the nuances of our story as it progresses.

To return to our journey across the river, let us join the men disembarking on the other shore. The Shaivite got off the boat, flung a final curse at Azhvarkadiyaan—'You will come to grief!'—and went on his way.

The soldier from Kadambur who had accompanied Vandiyadevan set off to nearby Tirupanandal to fetch him a horse. Azhvarkadiyaan and Vandiyadevan sat in the shade of a peepul tree by the riverside. The chirps of the hundreds of birds sitting on the branches of the tree reverberated through the air.

Each of the two, Vandiyadevan and Nambi, was hoping to extract information from the other. They beat around the bush for a while.

'Why, thambi! You went to Kadambur Palace leaving me behind, didn't you?'

'Getting in was hard enough for me alone, Nambigale!'

'Really? How did you manage, then? Or did you end up not staying?'

'I stayed, of course, I did. Would I take no for an answer once my mind was made up? The guards at the door stopped me. I charged past them on my horse, and everyone who tried to hinder me ended up sprawled on the floor. Before they could surround me and attack, my friend Kandamaaran showed up and ushered me inside.'

'I thought as much. You're gutsy. And then what happened? Who were the guests?'

'Everyone who is anyone, really. I don't know all their names. Pazhuvettaraiyar was there, with his young wife. Appappa! How does one even begin to describe her beauty?'

'Did you see her, then?'

'Yes, of course. My friend Kandamaaran took me to the antapuram. I saw her there. Pazhuvettaraiyar's Ilaiya Rani stood out among all the women there. Her fair face shone like the full moon, surrounded as it was by the darkness of the other faces. Rambha, Urvashi, Tilottama, Indrani, Chandrani ... she'd best them all!'

'Adeyappa! Such fervent description! What happened next? The kuravai koothu was held?'

'Yes, and it went off very well. I was thinking of you as I watched it.'

'Just my luck. What happened after?'

'The Velanaattam. The Devaraalan and Devaraatti came up on stage and started a frenzied dance.'

'Did the sannadam come? Did they make any predictions?'

'Aha! All you wish for will come to pass! The rain will pour! The country will flourish! And so on ... the sannadakaran went on about it.'

'Was that all?'

'Then he said something about the kings and other royal matters, but I tuned out.'

'Adada! Was that all? You should have paid attention, thambi! You're a young man. You seem to have the makings of a great warrior too; you should keep your ears open when people speak of royal matters.'

'You're right. It struck me this morning that I ought to have.'

'Why this morning?'

'This morning, Kandamaaran and I rode to the Kollidam together. He told me that after I'd slept, the guests gathered for a conference to discuss all sorts of royal affairs.'

'What did they discuss?'

'I have no clue. Kandamaaran spoke in riddles, but didn't go into the specifics. I believe some kind of event will occur soon. He said he would tell me then. He was being all mysterious. Why, Swamigale! Do *you* know something?'

'About?'

'There's talk about the town ... that a shooting star has been spotted in the sky. The king is in some kind of danger. The throne is set to acquire a new occupant. They say all sorts of things. The gossip goes all the way to Thondai Mandalam. Apparently, several big fish have joined hands to put their heads together over who will be the next king. What do you think? Who will inherit the crown?'

'I don't know all that, thambi! What do I have to do with royal matters? I'm a Vaishnavite. I'm a devotee of the disciples of the Azhvars, a servant of servants. I just go from place to place singing the pasurams I know!'

Having said this, Azhvarkadiyaan began to sing:

Tirukanden, ponmeni kanden …

Vandiyadevan interrupted with, 'For god's sake, stop!'

'Adada! Here I am, singing a divine pasuram, and you ask me to stop!'

'Azhvarkadiyaan Nambigale! I have a doubt. May I voice it?'

'Please do.'

'You won't chase me with your staff?'

'You? Do I stand a chance against you?'

'Your Vaishnavism, devoutness, your urdhva pundra[4] marks, singing of pasurams … all this strikes me as a farce.'

'Aiyayo! What kind of talk is this! Sacrilege! Sacrilege!'

'No sacrilege-vacrilege here. You're putting on this farce to disguise your lecherousness. I know your like. They're crazy about women. What is it you all see in them? Any woman I see only invokes my wrath.'

'Thambi! There are those who are crazy about women. But don't count me in that list. I'm no actor. It's wrong of you to suspect that I'm putting on a farce.'

'Then why did you ask me to pass on a letter to the woman who was riding in the palanquin? Is it right to desire another man's wife? It was to see her that you wanted to come to Kadambur Palace, wasn't it? Please don't deny this.'

'I'm not denying it. But your deductions are wrong. My reasons for wanting to meet her are different. But that's a long story.'

'There's no sign of my horse yet. You might as well tell the story. Let's hear it!'

'A story, as in, not a fictional one. This is a story that truly played out. A strange one! One that will stun you! Are you sure you want me to tell you?'

'If you want to!'

'All right, I will. I'm in a bit of a hurry. But I'll tell you the story before I go. I might have to plead another favour from you someday. You won't refuse this time, will you?'

'If there is some justification for it, I won't. You don't have to feel compelled to tell me this story if you don't want to.'

'No, no! I absolutely must tell you. The young wife of this Hiranyasuran, that demon Pazhuvettaraiyar, the one to whom I wanted you to pass on a letter ... her name is Nandini. Her story will astonish you. It would make you seethe that such injustice can exist in this world!' And with this prologue, Azhvarkadiyaan launched into the story of Nandini.

Azhvarkadiyaan was born in a village on the banks

of the Vaigai River in Pandiya Naadu. One day, when his father had gone to the nandavanam—the flower garden—by the river, he had seen an abandoned baby there. It was a girl, a beautiful little child. He brought her home. Her loveliness made her an instant darling with the family. She was given the name 'Nandini', since she was found in the nandavanam. She had been raised as Azhvarkadiyaan's sister.

Her devotion to Lord Vishnu grew with her. People spoke of her as a second Andal. Azhvarkadiyaan believed this firmly. When his father passed away, he took on the responsibility of raising the child. The two of them went from place to place, singing the pasurams of the Azhvars and spreading the Vaishnavite faith. Those who heard Nandini singing the pasurams with all the strength of her devotion, wearing a tulsi garland, found themselves almost intoxicated.

Once, Azhvarkadiyaan had gone on a yatra to Tiruvengadam. His return was delayed. And that's when a terrible thing happened to Nandini.

The Pandiyas and Chozhas were locked in their final, decisive battle near Madurai. The Pandiya Army was routed. Their king, Veerapandiyan, had sustained grievous injuries on the battlefield. Some of his most devoted aides had found him among the bodies and tried to save his life. They ran through the night, and arrived at Nandini's home. Seeing the king in this terrible state, Nandini took pity on him and began to nurse him back to health. But the Chozha warriors closed in on the hideout soon enough. They surrounded the house, broke in and murdered Veerapandiyan. Pazhuvettaraiyar found himself infatuated with Nandini's beauty, and took her captive.

This had occurred three years earlier. Azhvarkadiyaan had not seen Nandini since. He had been trying since then to meet her alone just once, and free her from Pazhuvettaraiyar's clutches if she so wished. He was yet to succeed.

Vandiyadevan's heart melted when he heard the story. For a moment, he considered telling Azhvarkadiyaan Nambi that the occupant of the palanquin hadn't been Nandini but Prince Madurantakan. But something stopped him from saying the words. It struck him that the whole story might have been a figment of Azhvarkadiyaan's imagination. So he kept the secret he had learnt at Kadambur Palace to himself.

The soldier from Kadambur made his appearance in the distance, with a horse in tow.

'Thambi, will you help me?' Azhvarkadiyaan asked.

'How could I possibly help? Pazhuvettaraiyar is powerful enough to send tremors through the Chozha Empire. And I'm a nobody, with no influence of any sort. What could I possible do?' Vandiyadevan said cautiously. Then, he added, 'Nambigale! You said you knew nothing of royal matters. But can't you tell who the heir to the throne is, if something were to happen to Sundara Chozha Maharaja?'

He searched Azhvarkadiyaan's face for a tell-tale sign, but couldn't detect the slightest change.

'What do I know about all that, thambi? The astrologer of Kudandai might be able to tell you!' Nambi said.

'O-ho! So the astrologer of Kudandai really is that clever, is he?'

'Impossibly clever. He knows astrology; he can read minds; he is up to date with current affairs, and can make predictions based on those too!'

Then I must meet him, Vandiyadevan decided.

From the beginning of time, the human species has been keen to know what will come to pass in the future. Kings and mendicants, ascetics and family men, scholars and fools, everyone is curious about the future. So it should come as no surprise that our young warrior, who had crossed the entire land, facing all sorts of danger to fulfil his secret royal mission, was just as curious.

13

THE WAXING MOON

Once the princesses' chariot had disappeared from view, the astrologer showed Vandiyadevan into his home. He sat on his high chair, and invited the young man, who was sizing up the place, to sit too. The astrologer then looked his visitor up and down.

'Thambi! Who are you? What brings you here?' he asked.

Vandiyadevan laughed.

'Ennappa, why do you laugh?'

'No, it's just that an astrologer with as great a reputation as yours should have to ask what brings me here! Doesn't your craft tell you who I am, why I am here, and everything else you may want to know?'

'O-ho! Why not? I could certainly look it up. But if I were to take the trouble to turn to the stars for everything, how will I get paid?'

Vandiyadevan smiled and said, 'Josiyare! Your visitors who just left, who are they?'

'Oh! They? I know whom you're asking after. I know, thambi, I know! You're asking about my visitors on whom you barged in after dragging my disciple from his post, aren't you? The ones who've got on a chariot and are racing away, leaving clouds of dust behind them, yes?' asked the astrologer of Kudandai, avoiding a straight answer.

'Yes, yes! They're the ones I'm asking after. ...'

'Why, feel free to ask. Who said you shouldn't?' Those two visitors of mine are two young women!'

'I could see that for myself, Josiyare! I'm not blind. I can tell the difference between man and woman. I can even make out when a man has disguised himself as a woman.'

'So, what is it you want to know?'

'Right, so they're women. But what I want to know is, who are they, of which jaathi ... and so on.'

'O-ho! So that's what you want to know, eh? Among women, Padmini, Siddhini, Gandharvi and Vidyadari are the four jaathis—the four types. It appears you have some training in the samudrika lakshana shastras. Of these four jaathis, the two women are Padmini and Gandharvi respectively.'

'Kadavule!'—oh, God!

'Why? Appane!'

'I call for God, and *you* ask me why? You're God, are you?'

'Why is that wrong? Haven't you heard that God is sarvaantrayaami—present inside everyone and everything? It appears you don't have much to do with your elders. It is God who is inside me, and God who is inside you. And inside the disciple you dragged into my house, too.'

'Enough, enough, please stop.'

'It was God who commanded that I speak until now, and God who asks that I stop, too.'

'Josiyare! I asked who the two women who just left are—where are they from, which clan, what are their names, that's what I want to know. If you could give me a straight answer, without speaking in riddles ...'

'If I could, what would you give me, appane?'

'My vandanam'—salutations.

'You can keep your vandanam to yourself. If you can give me some pondhanam—wealth in gold—let me know.'

'If I were to give you pondhanam, would you tell me for sure?'

'Only if it is something that can be told, thambi! An astrologer has many visitors. One oughtn't speak about one to another. I won't tell you anything about the women who just left. And if someone else were to ask me something about you, I wouldn't breathe a word either.'

'Aha! Azhvarkadiyaan Nambi was right about you.'

'Azhvarkadiyaar? Who is he?'

'Don't you know? He spoke as if he was a dear friend of yours. Have you not heard of Azhvarkadiyaan Nambi?'

'Perhaps I would recognise him; the name doesn't strike a chord. Could you describe him? That might help.'

'He's short and stout, has a munkudumi, a top-knot. He smears sandalwood paste all over his body. If he chances upon a Shaivite, he gears up for battle. If he chances upon an Advaiti, he grabs his staff. You said a while ago, "You are God, and so am I", didn't you? If Azhvarkadiyaan had heard this, he would have yelled, "God is attacking God!" and begun to chase you around with his staff. ...'

'Thambi! From your description, it appears you're talking about Tirumalaiappan. ...'

'Does he have more than one name?'

'He has a name for every port, that veera Vaishnavar.'

'And a disguise for every interlocutor?'

'Aha! A disguise for every way the wind blows.'

'And his speech is a melange of imagination and lies?'

'Three-quarters and three-and-a-half veesams[1] of imagination and lies; a half-veesam of truth.'

'So a thoroughly wicked character.'

'One can't say that, either. Good to the good, and wicked to the wicked, shall we say?'

'So one can't trust his word, then.'

'It depends on the word.'

'For instance, his telling me it would be a good idea to consult you about the future ...'

'I said there was a half-veesam of truth in what he says, didn't I? This would fall under that.'

'All right, then, give me an astrological consultation. I have to leave soon, aiya!'

'Where do you have to go in such a hurry, appane?'

'Can't you tell from your powers of divination? Where I must go, where I must not, whether my mission will be accomplished ... these are the things about which I wanted to ask you.'

'Well, I need some sort of concrete chart to be able to divine the future. I need a horoscope. Or, at least the date of your birth and your birth star; if not that, at least your name and where you're from. ...'

'My name is Vandiyadevan!'

'Aha! Of the Vaanar clan?'

'Yes.'

'Vallavarayan Vandiyadevan?'

'Yes, the man himself.'

'You could have told me earlier, thambi! Your horoscope is with me. I'll be able to find it if I look around.'

'O-ho! How is that?'

'What other work does an astrologer like me have? We collect the horoscopes of the men and women born into eminent families.'

'I wasn't born into an eminent family, was I?'

'What a thing to say! Is yours an ordinary clan? How many paeans have been sung in praise of the Vaanar clan! You probably haven't heard those.'

'Let me hear one.'
The astrologer began to sing right away:

Vaanan pugazhuraiyaa vaayundo maagadarkon
Vaanan peyarezhudhaa maarbundo; Vaanan
Kodi thaangi nillaadha kombundo undo
Vaanan adi thaangi nillaa arasu

Is there a mouth which does not sing the Vaanan's praise?
Or a chest that doesn't have his name inscribed on it?
Or a kombu[2] that does not bear the Vaanan flag?
Or an arasu[3] that does not bow under his feet?

It was evident he was no songster. But he had set the poem to music, and sang with great clarity and passion.

'How is the poem?' he asked.

'The poem sounds good enough. But unless I tie my flag on to the kombu[4] of some bull, none other will fly it. And the only way an arasu will bow under my feet would be for me to climb the branches of an arasu tree. And I can't say that for sure, either. For all we know, the branch might break under my weight and throw me to the ground.'

'This is your situation today. But who knows how your fortunes might change tomorrow?'

'I assumed you knew, or I wouldn't be here,' Vandiyadevan said.

'What do I know, thambi? I'm just a normal mortal, like everyone else, aren't I? But the planets and stars tell of events yet to come. I simply divine what I can and tell those who ask me, that's all.'

'What do the stars and planets tell of me, josiyare?'

'That you will rise higher and higher by the day.'

'Good news, indeed. My height is already a hindrance. I had to bend under the doorway to enter your home. What good will rising higher do me? Can you get into the specifics, please?'

'If you ask me a specific question, I will.'

'Will the mission which takes me to Thanjavur be successful? Tell me.'

'If it is on your own mission that you're headed to Thanjavur, it will be successful. Your planets are positioned most fortuitously. But if you're acting on behalf of someone else, I will have to look up that person's horoscope!'

With a shake of the head, Vandiyadevan touched his finger to his nose and said, 'Josiyare! I've never met anyone as prudent and clever as you!'

'There's no need for flattery!' the astrologer said.

'All right, fine. Let me put it to you openly. I have to get myself an audience with the king in Thanjavur. Will that come to pass?'

'There are two more powerful astrologers than I in Thanjavur. You'll have to ask them.'

'Who are they?'

'One is Periya Pazhuvettaraiyar. The other is Chinna Pazhuvettaraiyar.'

'They say the emperor's health is in a terrible state. Is that true?'

'Everyone has something to say about everything! Gossip is free, isn't it? Don't listen to all that! And don't speak of it either!'

'If something were to happen to the king, who will inherit his title? Can you tell?'

'Neither you nor I will inherit the title. Why should we give any thought to it?'

'We've been spared that fate!' Vandiyadevan said.

'True enough. It is no ordinary role, to be the incumbent. It is fraught with danger, isn't it?'

'Josiyare ... Prince Aditya Karikalar, you know, who is in Kanchi now ...'

'Yes, he is. You're here on his behalf, aren't you?'

'You've finally guessed. I'm thrilled. Now, what is his fortune like?'

'I don't have his horoscope with me, thambi! I'll have to consult it before I can tell you.'

'How about the fortunes of Prince Madurantakar?'

'His is a strange horoscope. Quite like that of a woman. It suggests he'll always bend to the will of others. ...'

'But they say Chozha Naadu is ruled by women. They say it's even worse than the Alli Rajyam!'

'Where do they say such things, thambi?'

'To the north of Kollidam.'

'Periya Pazhuvettaraiyar. He must be speaking of his new wife, the Ilaiya Rani, to whose will he bends.'

'What I've heard is different.'

'What have you heard?'

'They say it is the emperor's daughter, Kundavai Piraatti, who is running a female monarchy.'

The astrologer searched Vandiyadevan's face for a sign that he might have recognised Kundavai Devi as the last visitor to the house, and that this might have prompted the question. But he could see no hint of that.

'Entirely false, thambi! The Chozha emperor is in Thanjavur. And Kundavai Piraatti in Pazhaiyarai. On top of this ...' he trailed off.

'On top of this ...? Why did you stop speaking?'

'One must be discreet during daytime, thambi. And entirely silent at night. But there is no harm in telling you. What influence does the king have anymore? It is the Pazhuvettaraiyar brothers who exert all the influence in the kingdom, isn't it?' the astrologer said, and studied Vandiyadevan's face again.

'Josiyare! I'm not spying for Pazhuvettaraiyar. There is no call for you to harbour such suspicions. Just now, you spoke of the fragility of royal dynasties. You cited the Vaanar clan into which I was born as an example. I beg of you, tell me the truth. What does the future hold for the Chozha dynasty?'

'I'll tell you the truth; I'll tell you without a smidgen of doubt. Towards the end of the month of Aani, the first flood will sweep through Kaveri and her distributaries. Everyone who lives downriver knows that the flood will increase in intensity day after day. It will grow through the months of Aavani and Purattaasi, and begin to subside in the months of Karthigai and Margazhi. The people who live by the river will know when a flood is subsiding too. The Chozha Empire is like the first flood in the early months. It will grow for centuries. The Chozha kingdom is like the waxing moon, with days to go for Pournami, the full moon. It will reach greater heights of glory in the coming days.'

'You've finally confirmed this, after all the conversation and questions. Vandanam. Now, if you can tell me one more thing, please do. For the longest time, I have wanted to board a ship and cross the oceans. ...'

'This desire will be fulfilled too. Your yogam is Shakata. It is as if your legs were on wheels. You will travel without rest, on foot, by horse, by elephant, by ship. You will cross the oceans very soon.'

'Aiya! The commander of the southern armed forces, who is now leading the war in Eezham, Prince Arulmozhi Varmar ... can you say anything at all about him? How are his stars and planets aligned?'

'Thambi! People who journey on ships tend to use the magnetic compass and lighthouses for guidance. But do you know what is most useful to the traders as they guide their ships through the swilling waters in the middle of nowhere? The Druva Natchathiram, the Northern Star, the pole star. All the other stars— even the Mandala of the Seven Sages—and the planets may change positions and directions, but the Druva Natchathiram alone remains steadfast. The youngest

son of Sundara Chozhar, Arulmozhi Varmar, is like the
Druva Natchathiram. Nothing can shake his resolve.
Sacrifice, discipline and courage are all manifest in
him. He is as street smart as he is scholarly. The sight
of his beautiful, innocent face alone will fill one's heart
and kill one's problems. He is Lady Luck's favoured
son. Just as seafaring traders chart their course with
the Druva Natchathiram as their guide, young men
such as you, trying to negotiate the ocean of life,
would benefit from taking Arulmozhi Varmar as your
pole star.'

'Appappa! How you speak of Prince Arulmozhi
Varmar! One would think a girl was describing the
lover with whom she is besotted, to hear you talk!'

'Thambi! You could ask anyone in Chozha Naadu,
and he would speak exactly as I have.'

'My most sincere vandanams to you, josiyare!
When the time comes, I will follow your advice.'

'I only said what I could divine—that your stars
and planets are in the most favourable position.'

'I'll be on my way, josiyare. Along with my
heartfelt vandanams, I give you what pondhanam I
can afford. I plead that you accept.' And with this, he
set down five gold coins of a kazhanju[5] each.

'The generosity of the Vaanar clan remains
undiminished!' said the astrologer as he accepted the
gold.

14

A CROCODILE ON THE
RIVERBANK

Back in the day, travellers journeying from Kudandai
to Thanjavur would walk along the banks of either the
Arisilaru or the Kaveri up to Tiruvaiyaaru. They would
then turn south for Thanjavur. There were plenty of
ferries available to cross the Kudamurutti, Vettaaru,
Vennaaru and Vadavaaru rivers along the way.

Vandiyadevan made for the Arisilaru after leaving
Kudandai. The scenery that unfolded before him
exceeded the high expectations he had had of Chozha
Naadu from hearsay. A pleasant sight is always
sweeter the first time one comes across it, isn't it?
The lush green fields, boughs of ginger and turmeric,
sugarcane and plantain fields, coconut and areca nut
tree groves, the lakes, streams, reservoirs and ponds
took turns appearing before him. Alli and kuvalai
flowers competed for space in the streams, while
pink and white lotuses and blue and red water lilies

filled the ponds. Flocks of white storks flew overhead. Pink-legged cranes stood in the water with one foot raised, as if they were trying to appease the gods to ask for a boon. The 'gubu-gubu' sound of water flowing through canals that irrigated the fields, and the sight of men ploughing the fields whose soil had already been churned and their womenfolk planting seeds in the ploughed fields, and the chorus of them singing away the stress of labour and the smell of sugarcane stalks being crushed for their juice, which was then boiled to make jaggery, teased the young man's senses.

Huts with thatched roofs of coconut fronds or straw dotted the groves. The villagers had swept their front yards so the floor shone as if it were a mirror. Some had left rice and paddy crop to dry outside their front doors. Hens and roosters that announced their arrival with a 'Kokkarakko!' pecked at the grains. The girls who had been instructed to guard the crop from these predators didn't chase them away. *How much grain would those birds eat after all?* they thought, as they occupied themselves in their sozhi and pallanguzhi games.

The smoke from the wood fires made its way through the roofs of the huts. Mixed with the odour of the coals from the woodstoves was the aroma of grain being milled and sugarcane being boiled and the stench of meat being roasted. Most warriors of the day were meat-eaters. Vandiyadevan was, too; and so, his mouth watered at the smell.

Blacksmiths had set up workshops by the roadside, and the blazing fires from within made a 'thaga-thaga' sound as they heated the iron; the ironworkers, while banging the metal with a 'tanaar-tanaar' beat, crafted them into spades, shovels, crowbars and ploughs for farmers, and spears, lances, daggers, swords and shields for the soldiers. Men from both walks of life waited impatiently for their implements.

Even the smallest of hamlets had little temples to call their own. The temple gongs, nagara drums, chants of the priests and devaram songs sent their music out into the air. The local deities of villages, such as Mariamman, were subject to more rustic methods of worship. They were propitiated by priests dancing with the karagam pot balanced on their heads and beating the udukku drum.

Young cowherds drove their charges, with bells around their necks, to graze on pasture. Some of the cowherds even played the flute!

The men who were working the fields went to rest under the trees when they were tired. For their entertainment, they goaded rams into fighting each other. Peahens perched on rooftops and sang their mating call, to which their male counterparts responded, gathering their peacock trains with great difficulty as they 'jivv'-ed up into the air to join their females. Doves cocked their pretty necks as they flew about the place. Paavam! The parrots and mynahs, imprisoned in their cages, sang sorrowful songs.

Vandiyadevan took all this in, slowing his horse to a walk so he could enjoy the ambience.

His eyes had a fair bit of work to do. His heart was full from everything he saw. And yet, in the innermost recesses of his mind's eye, as if shrouded slightly by mist, a woman's face haunted him. Aha! Couldn't that woman have parted her lovely red lips to speak a few words to him? What would she have lost by making conversation? Who could that woman have been? Whoever she was, shouldn't she have had the manners to respond to him? Did he look so unimportant as to be undeserving of such basic courtesy? That old astrologer had tricked him. He hadn't given away her identity. He was a wily man, impossibly so. How well he could read people and see into their hearts! What vast experience of the world his speech betrayed! He hadn't said anything of import. He had got away with extreme discretion in speaking of royal matters. He had either said nothing, or spoken elaborately of things that were already common knowledge. But he *had* said Vandiyadevan's stars and planets were positioned favourably. For that alone, he deserved to be borne some goodwill.

Vandiyadevan went on his way, preoccupied with these thoughts. Every now and again, the real world pulled him back from his daydreaming. He arrived at the banks of the Arisilaru at long last. As he walked by the riverside, he heard the clinking sound of women's bangles, and the 'gala-gala' of female laughter. The thick foliage hid the women from sight. He searched the gaps in the vegetation, wondering where the women were.

Suddenly, he heard someone screaming, 'Aiyo! Aiyo! Crocodile! Crocodile! I'm scared!'

He directed his horse towards the sound of the panicked voice.

He could see the women through the trees. Many wore terrified expressions on their faces. And wonder of wonders! Two among them were the women who had left the astrologer's house as Vandiyadevan had made his appearance. He noted all this in an instant. And was that all he noted? Under a tree that cast a large shadow was a crocodile, half in the water and half on land, its jaws wide open. He had just seen a crocodile approach with open jaws on the Kollidam River, and heard enough about how dangerous the animal was. Upon seeing this crocodile, his blood froze. The crocodile was very close to the women who had been laughing moments earlier. With its open mouth displaying its ugly teeth and evil intentions, the crocodile was a picture of terror. All it would take was one leap, and the women would be history. The girls were in no state to run and escape through the trees either.

For all the turmoil in his heart, his determination knew no doubt. He didn't hesitate or rethink his course of action. He aimed his spear and threw it into the air. The spear sank into the thick skin of the crocodile's back and pierced through the animal's hide. Our hero then reached for his sword and ran towards the crocodile to finish the job.

As he did, he heard the women break into their 'gala-gala' laughter again. The sound was jarring to Vandiyadevan's ears. Why were they laughing when they were in such peril? He stopped for an instant, and looked at their faces. There was no sign of fear or tension on them. They only seemed amused. He could barely believe it was they who had screamed 'Aiyo! Aiyo!' not so long ago.

One of them—the woman he had seen at the astrologer's house—said in a pleasant voice that was no less commanding for its sweet notes, 'Girls! Keep quiet! Why are you laughing?' He heard her chiding them as if in a dream.

He stood still, his sword raised to strike. He stared at the crocodile, and then looked again at the women. A mortifying doubt rose in his head.

By this time, the woman who had spoken had made her way to the front and stood before the crocodile, as if she were its protector.

'Aiya! Our heartfelt vandanams to you. But you needn't trouble yourself in vain!' she said.

15

VANATHI'S SORCERY

Ilaiya Piraatti Kundavai Devi and the Kodumbalur princess, Vanathi, had mounted the chariot and headed for Kudandai, hadn't they? We must now learn what the women whom they had left behind on the boat spoke among themselves, and what they did after.

'Adiyei, Tarakai! Look at the fortune that's fallen upon this Kodumbalur creature, di! Why is our Ilaiya Piraatti so very fond of her?' one said.

'No fondness-vondness here, Varini! That girl has been behaving like a lunatic for the last four months. She faints at the drop of a hat. Ilaiya Piraatti is worried because this is an orphan girl trusted to her care. That's why she's taken her to the astrologer, to figure out what's happened to her. If she's been possessed by some spirit, they'll have to do some mantra-tantra to chase it out, won't they?' Tarakai said.

'There's no spirit-virit in there, di. Which spirit could possibly possess her? She'd drive a hundred spirits to hell all on her own!' Varini said.

'Those fainting fits of hers are all an act too. Her plan is to enact an elaborate drama and gradually trap the prince in her web!' another said.

'Niravati has it right! And that's not all, is it? Remember how she dropped the plate carrying the lamp that day? That was all a ruse to make him take notice of her! How could a plate one is holding with both hands fall? Is our prince a tiger or a bear to scare someone so much as to cause one's hands to tremble like that?' Varini said.

'The way she collapsed, on cue ... how cunning one must be to pull that off!' Niravati said.

'What's even more ridiculous than her drama is the fact that Kundavai Devi and the prince fell for it!' said Sentiru.

'This is a world for liars and con artists and schemers and sorcerers,' Mandakini said.

'Our prince who was setting off for war turned back to go check on Vanathi, didn't he? What more evidence do we need that her sorcery has reaped its rewards?' Varini said.

'Oh, no such thing. The prince is so very soft-hearted that he wouldn't dream of leaving without checking on a woman who'd fainted right before his eyes. Don't attribute so much significance to that,' Tarakai said.

'You're right about the prince. Where in all the fourteen worlds, the seven higher and the seven lower ones, would you find a man as genuinely good as he? Not in epics, not in fables or folklore would you find such a hero. But I'm talking about something else. This woman—this Vanathi—fainted, didn't she? Do you know why? There was no need to visit the astrologer to figure it out. I would have told them myself!' Varini said.

'Tell us, won't you?' Sentiru said.

Varini whispered into her ear.

'What secret is she telling you? Are we not allowed to hear it?' Niravati demanded.

'Apparently, that was no ordinary fainting fit. It was her libido that triggered it! She fainted from desire!' Sentiru said.

The women broke into peals of laughter, sending the birds in the trees by the shore into panicky flight.

'If our prince returns from Lanka, she'll try her magic dust on him again. We mustn't give her space to do that!' Niravati said.

'If she doesn't go insane before the prince returns, my name isn't Tarakai; I'll change it to Tatakai,'[1] Tarakai said.

'Let all that rest now! Ilaiya Piraatti has set us a task, hasn't she? Come, we must get it done before she returns!' Mandakini said.

Two of the women busied themselves moving a loose plank from the floor of the boat. In the box-like space exposed once the plank had been moved was a huge crocodile! That is to say, a stuffed crocodile.

Cotton and fibre had been expertly used to bring the dead crocodile to life by a taxidermist. The women pulled the crocodile out of its resting place and rowed the boat towards an enormous tree with long roots, some of which bobbed in the river. They carefully arranged the crocodile so that a part of it lay on the tree's roots and the rest in the river current. They secured it with a rope so it wouldn't be washed away, and hid the rope among the roots. It looked like a real, live crocodile once they were done.

'Mandakini, why do you think Ilaiya Piraatti has asked us to tie this stuffed crocodile to the tree?' Tarakai asked.

'Can't you guess? Vanathi is scared of her own shadow, isn't she? Ilaiya Piraatti wants to shock her into acquiring some courage!' Mandakini said.

'It appears Kundavai Devi has already decided to have Vanathi married to the prince,' Niravati said.

'If there's any serious talk of that, I'll poison Vanathi with my own hands, just you wait and see!' said Varini, who was prone to jealousy.

'There's no reason for you to be so angry. Apparently, every king from the Irattai Mandala Chakravarti of Maniya Kedam to the ruler of Vengi Naadu to the emperor of Kalinga to the Chakravarti of Kannosi to the far north is waiting in line to marry his daughter off to our prince. Who cares about Kodumbalur Vanathi with such illustrious alliances on offer?' Mandakini said.

'Sure, all those kings can wait in line! But it is our prince's wish that counts, isn't it? Apparently, he has said that if he ever marries, it will only be to a woman from the Tamil lands. Haven't you heard?' Sentiru said.

'Oh, that's excellent. Then I say each princess among us should try her hand at winning him over. Do you think we can't do what Vanathi has done? Don't we have magic dust at our disposal too?' Tarakai said.

And what was the incident that had spawned this conversation among the girls? The readers should now be apprised of this.

16

ARULMOZHI VARMAR

About nine hundred and eighty years ago,[1] Korajakesari
Varmar Parantaka Sundara Chozhar ruled as a monarch
without equal in the south. He was crowned king
about twenty-four[2] years before our story begins. The
preceding century had been one of immense gain for
the Chozhas, and their strength had grown by the day.
The empire had spread in all four directions. However,
when Sundara Chozhar ascended the throne, their
enemies to the south and north were growing more
powerful. Kandaradityar, his predecessor, had been so
immersed in his Shiva bhakti, even earning the epithet
'Shivagnana Kandaradityar', that he had not put his
mind to the expansion of the realm. Kandaradityar's
successor, his brother Arinjayar, had only ruled for
a year before he lost his life in Aatroor in Thondai
Naadu. These were the circumstances under which his
son, Sundara Chozhar, was handed the sceptre.

Sundara Chozha Chakravarti possessed all the

credentials and character that were desirable in an ideal king. He was an astute warrior who had set off for the south with an army almost right after his coronation. The Chozha and Pandiya armies clashed in a fierce battle at Sevoor. At the time, the Sinhala king Mahindan had sent a large army to aid the king of Madurai, Veerapandiyan. But the Chozhas ripped through both armies. Veerapandiyan, having lost his men, the crown and all support, escaped with only his life in his hands. He was forced to cool his heels in a mountain cave in the middle of nowhere. The Eezham Army had been decimated in the battle of Sevoor. The few soldiers who remained alive left their bravado and dignity on the battlefield, and took to their heels to save their lives.

It had been a long-standing custom for the Sinhala kings to send forces to the aid of the Pandiyas every time they clashed with the Chozhas. Sundara Chozha Chakravarti wished to put an end to this practice once and for all. He decided to dispatch an army to Eezham and teach the Sinhala kings a lesson in their own backyard.

A formidable army was sent to Sinhala under the command of the Kodumbalur royal Parantakan Siriya Velaan. Unfortunately, circumstances prevented the Chozha Army from reaching Lanka as one unit. They did not have enough ships at hand. It would have been prudent for the first regiment that landed on the Sinhala shores to wait for backup. But the regiment was impatient and forged ahead, only for the warriors to find themselves surrounded by the Sinhala Army under the command of its experienced general Sena. A terrible battle followed in which the general of the Chozha Army was killed, leaving behind a legacy of fame and honour, and etching himself into the annals of history as 'Eezhathu Patta Parantaka Siriya Velaan'—Parantaka Siriya Velaan Who Ascended to the Heavens at Eezham.

Once Veerapandiyan, hiding in his cave, got wind of this, he found the courage to clamber out of his hole and put together an army. This time, he would not get away with his life. His army was routed by Sundara Chozhar's oldest son, Aditya Karikalar, whose heroic deeds in the war were capped off with the title 'Veerapandiyan Thalai Konda Kopparakesi'—The Royal Lion Who Claimed Veerapandiyan's Head.

So infuriated were the Chozhas that not only the emperor but also the generals, commanders and soldiers were all united in their determination to quell the Sinhala Army for good. They readied an army larger than any other that had ever set sail for Lanka. All that was left to do was to choose its leader. The crown prince, Aditya Karikalar, was fighting on the northern front. He had driven away the Rashtrakuta armies of Irattai Mandalam, which had been making incursions into Tirumunaippaadi and Thondai Naadu, and set up his base in the ancient city of Kanchi. He was preparing for war on the northern front, to further expand the borders.

Since the obvious choice was now out of the reckoning, the other commanders of the Chozha Army fell over themselves, each trying to prove his worthiness to lead the force into Eezham. It must be noted that back in the day, it was a rare occurrence for one to avoid conscription, or for a soldier to avoid war. They competed to go. This often gave rise to jealousy and enmity among the senior army officials. Now, they couldn't wait to head to Eezham and show Mahindan his place. The issue was settled with finality when Sundara Chozha's younger son, Arulmozhi Varmar, came forward.

'Appa! I've had enough of being coddled at the Pazhaiyarai Palace by my aunts and grandmothers. Make me the Mahatanda Nayagan, the commander of the southern front. I will go to Lanka myself and lead the war at Eezham,' said Prince Arulmozhi Varmar.

He was all of nineteen at the time. He was the last of his father's children, the apple of everyone's eye; the queens of the Pazhaiyarai Palace loved him no more than the commonfolk did.

Sundara Chozhar was considered the epitome of good looks. His father, Arinjayar, had married Kalyani, a princess of the Vaidumbarayar clan—sworn enemies of the Chozha clan—after chancing upon her and finding himself intoxicated by her pulchritude. Their son, Sundara Chozhar, had been given the name 'Parantakar' by his parents. But such was his radiant beauty that he had begun to be called 'Sundara Chozhar' by everyone who saw his face.

All his children had inherited his good looks. But Arulmozhi Varmar had an edge over the rest. His loveliness was ethereal. As he toddled his way about the palace in his infancy, the queens would kiss him so often that his cheeks acquired a permanent red tinge. Of all the women who doted on him, the most ardent was his sister, Kundavai. Although older than her brother by only a couple of years, she had always believed it was her responsibility to raise him right. Arulmozhi, too, was just as devoted to her. If she said the word, it would be obeyed. The holy trinity of Brahma, Vishnu and Shiva could try to change his mind, but Arulmozhi would dismiss them all. To the brother, his sister's wish was divine command.

Kundavai would often examine her brother's features carefully, not only when he was awake but also when he was asleep. She would sit for hours studying his beloved face. *This boy has some divine power! It is I who must bring it to the fore and allow it to shine!* she would think to herself. When her brother was asleep, she would take his hands and look at his palms. It appeared to her that the creases on his palms were formed in the image of the conch and the discus that were Lord Vishnu's marks. *Aha! He was born to unite the whole world under his banner, and bring everyone within the shade of his protection*, she would think.

But there seemed to be no scope for him to ever mount the throne of the Chozha kingdom. There were two older claimants to the title. How could the kingdom be his then? To which throne would he ascend? Who knows what the gods had planned? The world was expansive. There were scores of nations and kingdoms on its surface. We've heard the stories, haven't we, of brave warriors who conquered foreign lands and became kings of those territories? Didn't the prince who was chased away from the Vanga Naadu, that is nurtured by the river Ganga, make his escape to Lanka and establish a kingdom there? Didn't the Sinhala dynasty that rose from him rule for a millennium?

So it was that Kundavai Piraatti made plans upon plans for her brother without a moment's rest. When, at last, the question of choosing a commander for the army that would invade Lanka arose, she decided that Arulmozhi was the man for the job.

'Thambi, Arulmozhi! A moment's separation from you causes me immense anxiety. And yet the time has come for me to ask you to leave for Lanka myself. You're the one who must lead the forces!' she said.

It was with great thrill that the prince consented. His heart had been aching for an escape from the comforts of the palace and the cossetting of the royal women. Now, his beloved sister had asked him to leave! What obstacle could possibly stop him now? Once Kundavai Devi had put her mind to it, there was nothing in the Chozha Empire that would not defer to her plans. Sundara Chozha had such love and faith in his darling daughter.

Prince Arulmozhi Varmar was made the commander of the southern front. He went to Lanka, and waged war for a time as the head of the army. But the war did not end as quickly as they had hoped. There were differences in his manner of conducting war and the custom of others. He asked for everything he needed to be shipped to him from home, rather than seize the goods from Lanka. The arms, equipment and other necessities of war were not sent to him on time. And so, he made a trip to his homeland, met his father, made arrangements for the consignments to arrive seamlessly and prepared to return.

Kundavai Devi had made her own arrangements—a grand send-off for her brother in the most opulent palace of Pazhaiyarai. As Arulmozhi Devar left, the palace courtyard rang with the victory beats of murasu drums, the lusty blowing of conches, the sounds of parai drums and war cries that rent the air and echoed from the skies. All the women of the Chozha clan assembled to bless the palace darling, anoint his forehead with consecrated water and ward off the evil eye.

At the point where the palace exit gave way to the street, Kundavai Devi's companion princesses stood carrying gold plates that bore lit oil lamps. They were royals themselves, and lived in the Pazhaiyarai palace because it was deemed an honour to be chosen for service to Sembiyan Mahadevi, and friendship with Kundavai Piraatti. Among them was the daughter of

Kodumbalur Siriya Velaan, Vanathi. As the prince neared them, the princesses grew feverish with excitement. When he approached, they circled the plates in the air.

Suddenly, Vanathi's entire body began to tremble. The plate she bore slipped from her hands and crashed to the ground with a 'tanaar'.

Adadaa! What is this ominous sign? thought everyone in unison.

But then they noticed that, although the plate had fallen to the ground, the wick of the lamp had remained lit. This was of some comfort to the assembly.

'This is a greatly auspicious sign,' the elders reiterated.

Arulmozhi Varmar flashed a smile at the young woman who had been so rattled for no rhyme or reason, and set off. The moment he left, Vanathi, too, fell down in a faint. So embarrassed was she at what she had done that she collapsed just as the plate had. On Kundavai's command, the other princesses carried her to a room and laid her on the bed. Kundavai, without even waiting to see her brother off, hurried to the chamber and tried to revive Vanathi.

Arulmozhi Varmar, who had seen her fall as he was about to mount his horse, sent a messenger to ask whether she had regained consciousness, before he left.

Kundavai Devi said to the messenger, 'Ask the prince to come here for a bit, and see her.'

The prince, who had never disobeyed his sister's command, returned to the palace. The sight of his sister holding Vanathi to her chest and trying to revive her wrenched his heart.

'Akka! Who is this woman? What is her name?' the prince asked.

'She is the daughter of Kodumbalur Siriya Velaar. Her name is Vanathi. She tends to be scared of her own shadow,' Kundavai said.

'Aha! Now I see why she fainted. Her father was the one who set out for Lanka and never returned; he lost his life in the Eezham wars. She must have relived that time,' the prince said.

'Perhaps. But don't you worry about her. I'll look after her. Go to Lanka and come back victorious soon! Please keep sending me news of the goings-on there,' Ilaiya Piraatti said.

'As you wish. And please do send word if anything of importance occurs here,' the prince said.

At this point, perhaps stirred by the pleasant notes of the prince's voice, Vanathi's consciousness began to return. Her eyelids parted slightly. When she saw the prince sitting across from her, her eyes popped open, widening in shock. And then her face blossomed. The smile that teased apart her coral lips poked dimples into her cheeks. Along with her consciousness, her sense of embarrassment returned, and she sat up in a hurry. She turned and realised Ilaiya Piraatti had all but sat her on her lap. Vanathi was overcome with mortification. Everything that had just passed came rushing back.

Her eyes brimming with tears, she said, 'Akka! What have I gone and done!'

Before Kundavai could reply, the prince said, 'There's no need for you to worry about that, Vanathi! It's quite natural for someone to suffer a slip. And you had reason to respond as you did. I was just telling Ilaiya Piraatti about this.'

Vanathi could barely believe her eyes or her ears. Was the prince, who was reputed to have no time to so much as cast a glance at women, actually speaking to her in this manner? Offering her words of comfort? What had she done to deserve such good fortune? Aha! Her hair stood on end. She thought she might faint again.

'Akka, the armies are waiting, I will have to leave. When you send news from here, please do let me know how this woman's health is too. Take good care of this girl, who has no parents to look out for her,' the prince said, as he left.

Kundavai Devi's other companion princesses were witness to this scene, watching and eavesdropping as they were from the various nooks and balconies of the palace. The flames of jealousy were fanned. From that day forward, Kundavai Devi began to single out Vanathi for special attention and affection. She never let her out of sight. She began to give Vanathi lessons in the arts and sciences in which she herself had been educated. Everywhere she went, she took Vanathi. She often asked the princess to accompany her to the palace garden, where the two of them would whisper together. She told Vanathi of the dreams she had for her brother's future. Vanathi absorbed all this intently.

Vanathi followed this incident up with several further fainting fits. Each time, Kundavai Devi would tend to her and stay until she recovered. Vanathi always came to with wrenching sobs.

'What happened, asadu![3] Why are you crying like this?' Kundavai would ask.

'I don't know, Akka! Forgive me!' Vanathi would reply.

Kundavai would hug her, stroke her hair and console her. As their intimacy grew, so did the jealousy of the other princesses. And, therefore, it was quite natural, don't you think, for them to speak as they had after Kundavai and Vanathi had set off in the chariot for the house of the astrologer of Kudandai?

17

THE HORSE REARED!

Kundavai had all but decided that the most suitable bride for her peerless brother was Vanathi. However, there was a single flaw she wished to remedy in this bride—Vanathi was faint-hearted, she thought. She would be marrying the most courageous of warriors, the man who would bring the entire world under his reign. Would it do for her to swoon at every opportunity? Kundavai intended to alter her personality so that she was the very epitome of stoicism and strength. And, hence, this elaborate charade with the fake crocodile. But the Kodumbalur princess passed the test with flying colours.

Once they had returned from the house of the astrologer of Kudandai, Kundavai and Vanathi boarded the swan-shaped boat. They sailed for a short while. It was their wont to halt the boat at a spot where the thick trees on either side of the bank hid them from the view of passers-by and splash about in the water; they intended to do the same today. Once everyone had disembarked, one of the women began to yell, 'Aiyo! Crocodile!' She pointed behind the tree to which they had secured the boat. 'Crocodile! Crocodile!' she screamed again.

All at once, the others took up the cry too. 'Aiyo! Crocodile! I'm scared! Save me!' and so on they shrieked, as they ran away from the stuffed crocodile.

And yet, the faint-hearted Vanathi remained unfazed. The sudden appearance of the fierce crocodile with its jaws wide open had not unsettled her. The panic of the other women, orchestrated by Kundavai, did not appear to affect her in the least.

'Akka! The crocodile only has its strength when it is in water. It is powerless when it is on land. It can't do anything to us. Ask them not to be scared!' the Kodumbalur princess said.

'Adi, you wicked kalli![1] You knew all this while that the crocodile wasn't real! Someone has given us away!' the other princesses said.

'Even if it had been a real crocodile, I wouldn't have been scared. I'm only scared of lizards and cockroaches,' Vanathi said.

It was at this time that Vandiyadevan arrived to rescue the women from the terrible crocodile. He leapt off his horse in a single, fluent motion and flung his spear at it quickly too.

When the stately young woman stood right before the crocodile and addressed him, Vandiyadevan's hair stood on end. His entire body was aflutter. His angst at her having ignored him at the astrologer's house disappeared. But that the crocodile—the fierce crocodile with its jaws at the ready to devour anyone it chanced upon—was right behind her, for some reason, troubled him. Why had she come and stood before the crocodile? What did her reassurance, that there was no need for him to put himself to trouble, mean? Why had the crocodile not budged, or so much as flinched, in all this time?

The young woman went on speaking. 'Aiya! Back in Kudandai, you apologised for having barged into the astrologer's house. We walked away without even acknowledging that apology. This might have led you to conclude that the women of Chozha Naadu are lacking in manners. Please do not think thus. My friend who had accompanied me had fallen into a sudden faint, and I was flustered. This was why I didn't respond properly to you. ...'

Adada! What an intoxicating voice! Why does my heart swell with joy upon hearing her words? Why does my throat dry up? Not the flute, nor the veena, nor the maddalam, nor the war drums have inspired such frenzy in my soul! I want to cut her short, and yet I find myself unable to interrupt her speech. My tongue is stuck to the roof of my mouth. The very wind has frozen, and I can't breathe. The waters of the Arisilaru are frozen in time. And then this crocodile ... why, it has frozen too!

Even as Vandiyadevan's heart churned with the

turbulence of his emotions, the woman's voice went on, as if in a dream: 'Even now, you have done this deed, believing you were saving a group of hapless women from a crocodile. You flung your spear at the predator. Such lightning reflexes and unerring accuracy are rare qualities in a warrior. ...'

At this, the other women, who had gathered by the trees and were listening in, broke into peals of laughter. And the sound pierced through Vandiyadevan's infatuated, dreamlike trance. The spell with which her lovely voice and careful words had bound him broke.

He stared hard at the crocodile. Ignoring the woman who stood before its body, he went right up to it and examined it. He wrenched out the spear he had aimed at its back. No blood gushed out of the gaping wound the spear had inflicted on the crocodile. What spilled out instead? Banana fibre and cotton!

Those cruel women laughed yet again. This time, they all but cackled. Vandiyadevan's heart, mind, body and soul felt like they would shrivel up. He had never before been thus humiliated. What had he done to deserve to lose face before all these women? Were they even women? No! No! They were rakshasis! He shouldn't so much as stand anywhere near them! He shouldn't so much as look at them!

Chhi! My beloved spear! That such a fate should befall you! That you should be subject to such ignominy! How will I ever make it up to you. ...

These thoughts jostled against each other in a

fraction of a second, in Vandiyadevan's head. If only the assembly of cacklers had been male, the riverbank would have turned into a battlefield. Those who had dared to laugh at him would have paid for it with their lives! Their blood would have run in the currents of the Arisilaru! But these were women! What could he do to them? The only option he had to end the episode was to get away from them as fast as he could.

Without so much as a glance in the direction of the women who had made him want to curl up and die, Vandiyadevan leapt on to the opposite bank of the river. At that precise moment, his horse neighed. It seemed to him that the horse had joined forces with the women and was mocking him too. And so, he turned all his fury on the horse. Jumping on to the saddle, he pulled the reins and gave the animal two sharp whacks with the leather. The horse responded by rearing and galloping away from the riverbank at a mad pace.

For some time, Kundavai stared after the horse. She kept staring until the dust the horse's hooves had raised settled.

Then, she turned to her companions and said, 'Girls! You have no sense of propriety! You shouldn't have laughed as you did. It's one thing to give voice to our mirth when we're by ourselves. But shouldn't you exercise some restraint in the presence of a man we don't know? What impression have you given him about the women of Chozha Naadu?'

18

IDUMBANKAARI

We abandoned Azhvarkadiyaan, also known as
Tirumalai, in the coracle harbour by the banks of
the Kollidam. Let us now turn our attention to that
militant Vaishnavite.

As Vandiyadevan got on his horse and left for
Kudandai, Tirumalai watched after him, and said to
himself: *This young chap is quite something. If I sneak in
through the wooden blinds, he gets one up on me by sneaking
in through the kolam dots. I've failed to figure out whose
man he is, why he's been engaged and where he's headed.
I don't even know if he was part of the conspiring group at
Kadambur Palace. Thank heavens I had the good sense to
tell him about the astrologer of Kudandai. Let's see if the
astrologer is able to divine what I couldn't!*

'What, swami! Are you speaking to the peepul
tree? Or to yourself?'

Tirumalai turned when he heard the voice. It was

the palace employee who had been sent to procure a horse for Vandiyadevan.

'Appane! Was it you who asked? I'm not speaking either to myself or the peepul tree. There's a betaal hanging in this tree. I was chatting him up for a bit,' Tirumalaiyappan said.

'Oho! Is that so? And is that betaal a Shaivite or Vaishnavite?' his interlocutor asked.

'I was asking him that very question. But you landed up and interrupted us. The betaal has now disappeared. Anyway, let it go. What is your name, appane?'

'Why do you ask, swami?'

'It was you who stopped the coracle from capsizing midstream. Shouldn't I ensure I remember such an altruistic soul?'

'My name ... my name ... is ... Idumbankaari, swami!' the man said, dragging out the response.

'Oh! Idumbankaari? That sounds familiar, for some reason!'

Idumbankaari chose that moment to do something quite bizarre. He placed his open palms one over the other, and wiggled his thumbs. Even as he did this, he looked Tirumalaiappan in the eye.

'Appane! What are you trying to signal? I'm afraid I don't understand,' Tirumalai said.

At this, Idumbankaari's dusky face darkened further. He knitted his brows. 'I? I didn't signal anything!' he said.

'You did, you did! I saw it for myself. There is a hasta—a hand gesture—for the first avatar of Tirumaal in the Bharatanatyam Shastra. You seemed to evoke that.'

'What do you mean by the first avatar of Tirumaal? I have no clue, swami!'

'Don't you know Vishnu's first avatar? The matsya avatar?'

'The fish, you mean?'

'Yes, appane, yes!'

'Good god, swami! You seem to have a unique pair of eyes, swami! You see betaals on empty trees. And you see the matsya avatar in my plain hands. Perhaps the swami is partial to fish?'

'Tchah, tchah! Don't say such things, appane. But leave that be. You remember that militant Shaivite who came with us on the coracle? Did you see which way he went?'

'How could I not? He came along with me, going the same way I went to procure a horse. He was cursing you all through ...'

'What did he say about me?'

'That if he were ever to see you again, he'd lop off your topknot and shave your head and ...'

'Oho! So he's a barber too, eh?'

'He would wipe off the naamams you've drawn on your hallowed skin, and smear them with the three lines of ash that symbolise Shiva.'

'In that case, I must make it a point to meet him again. Do you know where he's from?'

'I heard from the horse's mouth that he was from Pullirukkum Velur.'

'I must meet that militant Shaivite before I do anything else. Which way are you headed? Perhaps you're coming that way too?'

'No, no. Why should I go that way? I'm going back to Kadambur. Or my master will have my eyes gouged out.'

'Then, head for the river right away. Look, a boat is about to leave!'

Idumbankaari turned and saw that Azhvarkadiyaan was right—the boat was all set to sail.

'All right, swami! I'll take your leave,' Idumbankaari said, and hurried off towards the harbour.

Halfway through, he glanced back. Azhvarkadiyaan, in the meantime, had done something quite bizarre himself. With one agile leap, he had hidden himself among the thick branches of the peepul tree. And so, when Idumbankaari turned, he was nowhere to be seen.

Idumbankaari reached the coracle harbour. The boatman called, 'Do you want to go to the other bank, appa?'

'No. I'll get on the next boat. You carry on!' Idumbankaari said.

'Ade! Is that all? I halted the boat as I saw you rush down to the harbour, assuming you were in a hurry to go!' the boatman grumbled, as he lowered his oars into the water and navigated his way out of the harbour.

Tirumalai, who had by now climbed halfway up the peepul tree, thought, *Oho! So I had it right. He hasn't got on the boat. He's going to come back this way. I should see where he heads. I'm sure he held the matsya hasta. What could that mean? Fish! Fish! What could fish signify? Ah! It is the emblem of the Pandiya flag, isn't it? Perhaps ... ahaha! Could it be? Well, we'll have to see. We'll have to be patient. The circumspect will rule the world, while the overeager will be left to haunt the forests. That said, it appears that in this era one is better off ruling a forest than the world. Even so ... let's hold on.* And thus he spoke to the formless betaal on the peepul tree.

Soon, things unfolded as he had expected. The boat left without Idumbankaari. Idumbankaari stared hard at the peepul tree from the riverbank. Then, he scanned all four directions to look for Azhvarkadiyaan. Having ascertained that the man was not hanging around, Idumbankaari approached the peepul tree. He carried out another recce of the surroundings, and then sat down in the shade. His eyes roved, looking all about himself, as if he were expecting company. But it didn't occur to him to look up at the tree. Even if he had thought to look, Tirumalai had taken such good care to camouflage himself that Idumbankaari couldn't have possibly spotted him.

About half a naazhigai passed thus. Tirumalai's legs were beginning to go to sleep. He couldn't hold on to his perch for much longer, he thought. Idumbankaari showed no sign of leaving his spot. How was Tirumalai to escape? However careful he was, there was no way he could alight from the tree without making some sound. That would draw Idumbankaari's attention right away, and he would spot Tirumalai. The man had a fearsome sword at his waist. What was the guarantee he wouldn't use it on Tirumalai?

What other option did Tirumalai have? He could let out an otherworldly shriek and jump on Idumbankaari. Chances were that Idumbankaari would think the betaal had got him, and faint from the fear, surely? Or, he might try to escape the betaal. Tirumalai could make his own escape then. Just as he was weighing these options, it appeared his ordeal was at an end.

A man was approaching the tree from the southwest, through the road leading to Kudandai. Tirumalai intuited that this was the man whom Idumbankaari had been expecting all this while.

As soon as he spotted the newcomer, Idumbankaari stood up. The other man made the same sign Idumbankaari had, the matsya hasta. Idumbankaari reciprocated the gesture.

'What is your name?' the man asked.

'I'm Idumbankaari. And you are ...?'

'Soman Saambavan.'

'I've been expecting you.'

'And I've been looking for you.'

'Which way must we go?'

'Westwards.'

'Where to?'

'The enemy's pallipadai.'[1]

'Near Tiruppurambiyam ...?'

'Don't speak so loudly! What if someone overhears?' Soman Saambavan said, scanning the four directions.

'There's no one about. I've already checked.'

'There's no nook anywhere about that someone could slip into?'

'Not a single one.'

'In that case, let's go. I'm not very sure of the way. You go ahead. I'll follow. Just stop now and then to make sure you haven't lost me.'

'As you say. Our path is a tricky one. There are forests and slopes and thorns and stones. You'll need to be careful.'

'All right, all right. You start off now! Even if it's a forest track, if you so much as hear someone else approach, you must hide right away. Do I make myself clear?'

'Yes, yes, I know.'

Idumbankaari set off westwards from the riverbank. Having given him a head start, Soman Saambavan followed in the same path. Azhvarkadiyaan sat on his perch until both men had disappeared. He observed everything with his eyes and ears.

Aha! What times these were! All sorts of unexpected things were underway. By god's grace, he had the opportunity to learn some grand secret! The rest would depend on his presence of mind. He hadn't been able to find out much at the Kadambur

Palace. He must employ more expediency this time. The pallipadai at Tiruppurambiyam ... it must be the Ganga king Prithvipati's. That temple had been built a century ago. It was in a dilapidated state, with the forest encroaching into its premises. It was in the heart of the forest, some distance from the nearest habitation. Why were the two of them going there? If they had something to discuss among themselves, they could have done it right here. There was no call for them to trek a kaadham through the forest. Surely this meant there was to be a larger gathering at the pallipadai? Why, though? One of them had referred to Prithvipati as 'the enemy'. To which kingdom had he been the enemy? Aha! It appeared Tirumalai's surmise had been right. Well, he would ascertain that shortly. They were taking the route by the banks of the Kollidam. He would take the one by the Manni River. True, the forest was denser there, but then that wasn't of much concern to Azhvarkadiyaan. So what if there were forests and slopes and thorns and stones? The landscape ought to be scared of him, not the other way round.

Thinking thus, and muttering all through, Tirumalai got down from the peepul tree and headed south. Once he reached the Manni River, he turned west. Making his way through the deserted forest with its thick undergrowth, he contrived to reach the pallipadai temple by sunset.

19

THE FOREST BATTLEFIELD

In the ancient times, it was a tradition in the Tamil lands to erect monuments to memorialise great heroes who had been martyred on the battlefield. If it was a simple stone monument, it was called 'nadukarkoil'—a temple made of assembled stones. If a deity had been installed and the idol consecrated, it became a temple known as 'pallipadai'.

About half a kaadham to the northwest of Kudandai, on the northern bank of the Manni River, not far from the village Tiruppurambiyam, was one such pallipadai, erected in the memory of the Ganga king Prithvipati.

Those who are well-versed in world history say certain battles, such as those of Waterloo and Panipat and Plassey, changed the course of history. As far as the Tamil lands were concerned, the Battle of Tiruppurambiyam was one such. This battle had occurred about a century before our story opens. It is crucial that Tamil people know of this slice of their history.

About five hundred or six hundred years after the golden era of kings like 'Karikaal Valavan' Perunarkilli, Ilanjet Chenni and Todithot Sembiyan, it was as if Chozha Naadu had fallen in the shadow of a lasting solar eclipse. The Pandiyas to the south and the Pallavas to the north had gathered strength and were crowding out the Chozhas. In the end, the Chozhas were forced to migrate from their capital, Uraiyur, to escape the constant harassment by the Pandiyas, and move to Pazhaiyarai near Kudandai. But they never stopped thinking of Uraiyur as their capital; neither did the kings give up the title of 'Kozhi Vendar', which they drew from that city.

Among the Chozha kings of Pazhaiyarai, Vijayalaya Chozhar's fame was unparalleled. He had led the vanguard in numerous battles and carried ninety-six scars on his body.

In later times, royal poets would sing his praise with verses such as:

Enkonda thonnootrin melumiru moonru
Punkonda vetri puralavan

A total of six over ninety
Scars decorate the victorious protector

Punnooru thanthirumenir poonaga
Thonnoorum aarum sumanthonum

On his hallowed flesh, as ornaments
He bears six and ninety wounds

His son, Aditya Chozhan, lived up to his father's name and fame. He would lead the army to numerous victories on the battlefield too. Vijayalaya Chozhar reached an age when he no longer felt able to rule and, having crowned his son king, retired from his royal duties. At the time, the enmity between the Pandiyas and the Pallavas had come to a head, and there were frequent clashes between the two. The Pandiya king of the time was Varagunavarman. The Pallava king was Aparajitavarman. The battles between them would largely take place on Chozha lands. Chozha Naadu was like a hapless chicken trapped in a clash between elephants. The people of the land suffered. And yet, Vijayalaya Chozhar found a way to use these wars to his advantage. He would go with his tiny army and join either faction. Sometimes they faced defeat, but the martial spirit of the land was enhanced by these constant battles.

Everyone knows that Chozha Naadu was a beneficiary of the lushness wrought by the Kaveri and her distributaries. All those distributaries branched off from the southern side of the Kaveri. There was only one river which branched off from the Kollidam and darted between the Kollidam and the Kaveri. This was known as the Manni River. It was on the north bank of the Manni, near the village of Tiruppurambiyam, that the final war between the Pandiyas and the Pallavas played out. The two armies were quite equally matched. The Ganga king Prithvipati had joined forces with the Pallava king Aparajitavarman. So had Aditya Chozhan.

The Chozha Army was puny in comparison to the Pandiya and Pallava forces. Yet, Adityan knew that if the Pandiyas were to win the war, the Chozha clan would be entirely wiped out. This was why he had chosen to back the Pallavas, bolstering their strength with his small army, just as the Kaveri feeds into the vast ocean.

The war raged on, with the battlefield expanding from kaadham to kaadham. All four sections of the armies—chariots, elephantry, cavalry and infantry—were involved in the clashes. The earth shook as elephants battled like mountains pounding each other. As horses clashed, it was like two tornadoes meeting, while the spears the cavalry troops used against each other blazed like lightning. Chariots dashed into chariots until they were reduced to their broken parts, flung in all four directions. The war cries of the infantry, as sword fought sword and spear fought spear, made the three worlds tremble. In the blood that flowed through the battlefield, the debris of broken chariots floated like the planks of a capsized ship in a whirling sea. Thousands of men died on both sides.

After three days of gory war, the Pallava Army was left with only one regiment standing. Those soldiers were exhausted. The Pandiyas, on the other hand, seemed to have got a boon from the gods to know no fatigue, and their men advanced tirelessly.

Aparajitavarman called a council in his tent. Aparajitan, Prithvipati, Adityan and their highest-ranking commanders took part. They decided it was impossible to withstand the onslaught, and the best course of action would be to retreat to the northern bank of the Kollidam.

It was under these circumstances that the battlefield witnessed a miracle. Tired with old age, bearing ninety-six scars on his body, and with his legs rendered all but useless from the terrible injuries they had endured, Vijayalaya Chozhan somehow contrived to enter the battle arena. Knowing that the consequences of a Pallava retreat to the north of the Kollidam would be disastrous—and long-lasting—for the Chozha dynasty, the elderly lion had decided to fight one last war. Just the sight of the old king on the battlefield rejuvenated the hopes of the allied forces on the Pallava side. This lion's roar fed new life into their bodies.

'An elephant! Give me an elephant!' he said.

'Our entire elephantry has been wiped out. Not a single one survived,' they said.

'A horse, bring me one horse at the very least,' he said.

'Not one horse is left alive,' they said.

'Are at least two brave Chozha warriors alive? If so, step forward!' hollered Vijayalayan.

Two hundred stepped forward instead of two.

'Two men. Two men with strength in their shoulders and steadfastness in their hearts, come forward to carry me. The rest follow in pairs behind us. If the two men bearing me are to fall, they will be replaced by the two behind!' said that bravest of brave warriors.

Two Bheemasenas[1] broke from the group to carry Vijayalayan on their shoulders.

'Go! Go to the battlefront!' he shouted.

The fighting was still on in a corner of the battlefield. The maravas of the south were forcing back the keezhainaattaar from the east. Vijayalayan rode to the battlefront on his human mount. He carried a long sword in each hand and whirled them like the Sudarshan Chakra of Tirumaal's Krishna avataram as he plunged into the melee. No one was able to stop him. Everywhere he went, the bodies of enemies piled up.

Yes, many of the warriors who had retreated advanced again to see what was going on. They stood stunned at first, stupefied by Vijayalayan's superhuman courage. Then, egging each other on, they entered the fray as well. That was all it took for Devi Jayalakshmi to turn the fortune in their favour.

The Pallava Army commanders gave up all intention of retreating to the northern banks of the Kollidam. The three kings came to battle, surrounded by their most trusted lieutenants. It wasn't long before the Pandiya soldiers began to retreat.

The Ganga king Prithvipati carried out a great many heroic deeds on the battlefield that day before he laid down his life and went to the heavens a proud martyr. He was memorialised on the battlefield with a veerakkal, a stone of courage. Later, the pallipadai temple was constructed.

For a while after, those lands that had witnessed such a terrible battle remained barren. People did not venture anywhere near the site of the war. After some time, a forest took root there. The undergrowth grew thick around the pallipadai temple. Foxes began to inhabit the alcoves. Owls and whimbrels made their homes in the canopies. Over time, visitors dwindled to zero. The temple began to wear a neglected look. At the time of our story, it was entirely dilapidated.

Azhvarkadiyaan arrived at this dilapidated temple at dusk. The fierce demons that stood guard on either edge of the temple's mandapam glared down at him to scare him. But could this veera Vaishnava icon be scared away? He leapt on to the mandapam and made a place for himself on one of the branches that intruded into it. He took a good look in all four directions. His eyes had a superpower—they could tear darkness to shreds and scan the surroundings carefully. His ears, too, were so sharp they could hear the softest of rustles.

A naazhigai passed after sunset, and then two. Three, now. The blackness of the night seemed to suffocate him. Occasionally, he could hear a 'sala-sala' among the trees. There, a weasel was climbing the tree! There, an owl was hooting! Here, a whimbrel was whistling! A bird, startled by the weasel, was flapping its wings to fly to a higher branch. The foxes had set up a howl. There was a noise right overhead. He looked up—a squirrel, or a chameleon, or some such rodent or reptile had got on to the branch.

Through the branches, he could spy a piece of the sky. Constellations of stars were blinking at him with a 'munuk-munuk' as they peered down. In the surrounding isolation, it appeared the stars were making friends with him. And so, Azhvarkadiyaan responded softly:

'O stars! It seems to me you're laughing at the ignorance and stupidity of us earthly inhabitants. You have reason to mock us. You've seen the terrible war of a hundred years ago, the war that was fought right here, and the rivers of blood that ran through these lands. You wonder why people foster such bitter enmity against each other. Why must they spill each other's blood until it floods the land, you wonder. This is called "bravado". We're heroes, you see.

'A century has passed since the death of a man whom they call their "enemy". This is the *enemy's* pallipadai, they say. And they're going to have a conference at the pallipadai of this enemy. The name of the dead evoked to plot the destruction of the living! Why wouldn't your eyes twinkle with amusement, dear constellations in the sky? Laugh away!

'Dear god! Has this been a fool's errand? Is the entire night going to pass like this? Are the people I'm expecting never going to arrive? Did I hear them wrong? Was I not paying enough attention? Or have those matsya hasta signallers changed their minds and gone elsewhere? What a letdown this has been! I'll never forgive myself if I've been conned tonight. Ah! I can see a glimmer of light! What is that? It has disappeared. Now, I see it again. There's no doubt. There! Someone's coming this way with a flaming torch. No ... two of them! My wait hasn't been in vain!'

The two men who approached went some distance beyond the pallipadai. They made their way to a clearing and stood waiting. One sat down. The other flashed his torch in all directions and peered into the night. Clearly, he was waiting for someone else. In a short while, two others arrived. They must be familiar with the place, or they could not have found their way through the dark of the night and the denseness of the forest.

The group was speaking among itself. But Azhvarkadiyaan could not hear a thing. Adada! It appeared all the trouble he had gone to, to get there, would be for nothing. He couldn't even make out who these people were.

Two more men arrived, and joined the group in conversation. One of the newcomers carried a bag. He emptied its contents. In the light of the torch, gold coins twinkled brightly.

The man who had poured out the coins laughed like a madman and said, 'Friends! We're going to bring down the Chozha Empire with funds from the Chozha treasury! Isn't that hilarious?' And he laughed even louder.

'Ravidasare! Don't speak so loudly! Let's lower our tones,' one of the men said.

'Aha! What does it matter how loudly we talk here? Only foxes and weasels and owls and whimbrels could eavesdrop on us! Thankfully, they won't go and tell on us!' Ravidasan said.

'All the same, it would be prudent to talk softly, wouldn't it?'

With that, they began to whisper among themselves. It seemed pointless to Azvarkadiyaan to sit on his precarious perch without being able to listen in. He would have to get down and make his way closer to the conference. He would have to handle the danger that would pose. Having made up his mind, Azhvarkadiyaan began to climb down. He brushed against a branch, and there was a rustle.

Two of the men jumped up and yelled, 'Who goes there?'

Azhvarkadiyaan's heart stopped. He had no recourse but to run away from them as fast as he could. And yet, the sound his feet made against the forest floor would give him away! They would catch hold of him. At that very moment, a whimbrel flapped its wings and hooted, 'Oom! Oom!'

20

'THE FIRST ENEMY!'

Azhvarkadiyaan silently sang paeans to the owl that had hooted in the nick of time. The conspirators figured the bird had been the source of the sound that had startled them.

'Ade! That damn owl gave us a fright! Cut the bloody thing into pieces!' one of them said.

'There's no need for that. Reserve your knives for a worthier cause. Sharpen them so we can wipe out our enemies from their very roots. Owls and whimbrels are not our enemies; they're our friends. We are up when people ordinarily sleep. It is these nocturnal birds that keep us company,' said Ravidasan.

Azhvarkadiyaan had tip-toed his way to the vicinity of an enormous Indian laurel tree, even as he listened to their conversation. The tree, over a hundred years old, had spawned roots upon roots that spread in all four directions. There were nooks on the forest floor where these roots overlapped and danced across each other. There were recesses in the barks of the trees themselves, too. It was in one such alcove that Azhvarkadiyaan hid himself, blending in with the bark.

'For as long as the treasury of the Thanjavur rajya is around, we won't be short of resources. We must have the courage and grit to see the plan that we have set in motion through. We must have the strength to guard our secret until the deed is done. We must split ourselves into two groups. One will leave for Lanka at once. The other will head to Thondai Mandalam and await the appropriate time to carry out the task. Both must be done simultaneously, and the groups must finish their respective tasks around the same time. If we allow room for breathing space once we've disposed of one enemy, the other will be on alert. That cannot happen. Do you see? Who among you is eager to leave for Lanka?' Ravidasan asked.

'I'll go!', 'No, I will!', 'Please let me!' cried a chorus of voices all at once.

'We'll take a call on who is to go the next time we gather together in Pandiya Naadu. In the meantime, there are certain preparations that must be undertaken here,' said Ravidasan.

'Which is the best way to get to Eezham?' one of the men asked.

'Kodikkarai is an option. It's easier to cross the sea from there. But reaching Kodikkarai from here will be a tough ask. There are enemies everywhere, and spies dotting the route. So our best bet would be to go to

Sethu, and then cross the sea to land near Mathottam. The members of the Lanka group should know how to row boats, keep catamarans afloat and swim in the sea. How many of you can swim?'

'I can!', 'Me!', 'I know how to!' rose a new chorus.

'First, we must meet the Lankan king Mahindan and speak to him before we get down to business. So, at least one of the contingent that heads to Eezham must be fluent in Sinhala. Ah! Our Soman Saambavan hasn't arrived as yet! Has anyone seen him today?'

'I'm right here!' said a voice, very close to where Azhvarkadiyaan had secreted himself away.

Azhvarkadiyaan drew himself even closer to the tree. Adada! What an inconvenience it was that this bloody body of his had run to fat!

Two newcomers joined the group. Azhvarkadiyaan made so bold as to peep from his nook, so a tiny part of his face made its way outside the shade of the tree. He ascertained that these two were indeed the men who had met under the peepul tree by the banks of the Kollidam.

The moment he spotted them, Ravidasan said, 'Oh, there you are! Join us! I was worried some danger had presented itself on your way here, and perhaps you would not be able to make it. Which way did you come, and from where?'

'We walked alongside the banks of the Kollidam. We saw a skulk of foxes en route. It took us a while to avoid getting caught by that lot, that's why we're late,' said Soman Saambavan.

'Fear of lions and tigers is understandable. But what could people who are afraid of foxes of all creatures hope to achieve?' said one member of the group that had already assembled earlier.

'Don't say that, appane! The fox is far more evil than the lion or the tiger! Lions and tigers hunt alone. One can take on such an enemy. But foxes hunt in packs, and, therefore, make formidable enemies. It was because the foxes of Chozha Naadu came as a huge pack that our peerless king of kings was defeated, that he eventually lost his life, wasn't it? Would such a thing have occurred if they hadn't come in a pack?'

'We will wipe out that clan of foxes! We will lay waste to their very roots!' said Soman Saambavan, who had worked himself up into a rage.

'And here's what we will need in order to get that done!' Ravidasan said, pointing to the heap of gold coins he had poured out earlier.

Soman Saambavan sifted through the coins, took up a few, and examined them. 'Ah! A tiger on one side, and a palm on the other!' he said.

'Chozha gold; Pazhuvettaraiyar's insignia. I did as I promised I would. What news do you have? Our Idumbankaari must have something to share, surely?' Ravidasan said.

'I've done as you instructed, and am in the employ of the Sambuvarayar Palace. All that effort came to

·fruition only yesterday,' Idumbankaari began. 'There was a grand feast at the Sambuvarayar Palace last night. Periya Pazhuvettaraiyar, Vanangaamudi Munaiyaraiyar and Mazhapaadi Mazhuvarayar were among the dignitaries who were being hosted there. The kuravai koothu and Velanaattam were held. The sannadam possessed the Devaraalan who danced the Velanaattam. What he said was in line with what we want people to see; it will come in handy for our goal. Everyone believes Pazhuvettaraiyar's Ilaiya Rani is travelling with him in a closed palanquin. Pazhuvettaraiyar told the gathering that Sundara Chozha Maharaja's health is poor, and he won't live long. Everyone took a unanimous decision that his heir should not be Aditya Karikalar, but Madurantaka Devar. But some wanted to know whether Madurantaka Devar would agree to this. Pazhuvettaraiyar said they could hear it from the horse's mouth, and opened the screen of the palanquin. Madurantaka Devar stepped out! He said he was willing to take on the title and ...'

'So they're going to crown a hero who dresses in drag! Wonderful! Let them go ahead. Everything is unfolding as we expected. This sort of internal conflict flaring up in Chozha Naadu will be immensely useful to us. Whatever happens, however it works out, no one will suspect us now. Idumbankaari! You've brought us some crucial news. How did you learn all this? How did the opportunity present itself?' Ravidasan asked.

'I was deputed to stand guard and ensure no

one came that way when they held their midnight conference. I kept my eyes and ears open.'

'And did you learn anything else from keeping them open?'

'Yes. There was someone else listening in on everything that happened at that midnight gathering—a man who climbed the wall of the fort and saw it all.'

'Aha! Who was that?'

'A Vaishnavite with a topknot ...'

'Aha! It was he, was it? I thought as much! What did you do about this? You didn't drag him to Sambuvarayar?'

'No. I thought he might be one of ours. I figured perhaps you had sent him yourself.'

'You've made a grave error. No, he's not one of us. He's short and stocky, always up for a fight. His name is Tirumalaiappan. He calls himself "Azhvarkadiyaan".'

'That was the very man. I realised my error this afternoon. I learnt he was not one of us.'

'And how did you learn this?'

'Last night, a childhood friend of Kandamaaran came to the Kadambur Palace, too. He had no connection with the secret gathering. He lay down in a corner that was assigned to him, and slept peacefully through the night. This morning, Chinna Ejamaanar Kandamaaran escorted his friend to the banks of the Kollidam. I'd learnt of his plan, and made sure I kept popping up before him. He asked me to accompany them. He turned back at the northern bank of the

Kollidam. He asked me to go with his friend to the southern bank, procure him a horse, and then return. I asked for permission to stop at Kudandai to meet my aunt, and so I have been able to come here without arousing suspicion.'

'Right, right. But how did you learn that the Veera Vaishnavite was not one of ours?'

'The Vaishnavite hurried to the coracle as it was leaving the harbour. His exchange with Kandamaaran's friend made me wonder whether he was on our side after all. He spoke somewhat heatedly. Then, on the southern bank of the Kollidam, he appeared to be waiting for me. I made our secret sign at him. But he didn't understand. So it was evident he wasn't one of us.'

'Now you've made an *extremely* grave error! You shouldn't make our secret sign at absolute strangers! Friends, listen carefully! We have work in Kanchipuram, as well as in Lanka. Our sworn enemies are in both these places. But an even greater enemy than those two, our first enemy is this man Tirumalaiappan who masquerades under the false name "Azhvarkadiyaan". He could ruin us and our plans entirely. He's trying to lure away the devi who is our peerless leader. Here's another thing to keep in mind—if any of you encounters him anywhere, under any circumstances, reach for the nearest weapon at hand and plunge it into his chest, so you kill him. If there is no weapon available to you, strangle him with your bare hands.

Or slip poison into his food. Or push him into the river, so he becomes the dinner of hungry crocodiles. Just as you would exercise no compassion towards a scorpion or a snake and send them to their deaths, send him to meet his maker, too! If you can offer him as sacrifice to Durga Devi or Kannagi Amman, all the better. For as long as he walks the earth, he will be a thorn in our side …'

'Ravidasare! He must have some influence for you to reiterate all this so passionately. Who is he?'

'Who, you ask? He is a tremendously skilled spy!'

'Whose spy?'

'I've had my doubts for a while. I couldn't figure it out for the longest time. I initially suspected he might be Sundara Chozhar's or Aditya Karikalan's man. I realised that was not the case. You know the treacherous hag in Pazhaiyarai, that creature Periya Piraatti? Now, I think he may be her spy.'

'Aha! Is that so? Why does Sembiyan Devi, who is so immersed in Shiva bhakti and her devotional duties at the temple, need a spy?'

'That's all a façade. Her Shiva bhakti is about as genuine as Topknot's militant Vaishnavism. She's a demon who has taken on the role of the enemy to the very son she birthed! This is why her own brother, Mazhuvarayan, fell out with her and joined Pazhuvettaraiyar's gang, isn't it?'

'Ravidasare! Is there anyone else like the topknot-sporting Vaishnavite?'

'There is an astrologer in Kudandai, about whom I have my suspicions. Under the guise of reading horoscopes, he milks his visitors for information. None of you must ever go to his place; if you do, he'll do a number on you.'

'Whose spy do you think the astrologer is?'

'I haven't been able to find out yet. He could be the spy of the fake prince who is now cavorting about in Lanka. But I'm not too worried about the astrologer. No great disaster will be set in motion by him. It is the Vaishnavite who scares me. Wherever you chance upon him, kill him at once as you would a scorpion or snake, with about as much compassion as you would exercise for those creatures!'

Listening to all this from the shelter of the tree, Azhvarkadiyaan found himself trembling. He broke into a sweat from topknot to toe. He wondered whether he would escape with his life from the tree. As if he didn't already have a full plate, a sneeze chose that very moment to tease his nostrils. He tried his best to stifle it, but failed. He stuffed his top cloth into his mouth and let out a muffled 'nachhhhhh'. Right on cue, the wind stopped blowing and the leaves of the forest trees stopped rustling. And so it was that Azhvarkadiyaan's stifled sneeze announced itself to the conspirators.

'I heard a sound from behind that tree. Take a torch and find out what the matter is,' Ravidasan said.

The torchbearer approached the tree. As he got

closer and closer, the surroundings grew brighter. This was it! He was coming round the corner. Once he turned, Azhvarkadiyaan would find himself entirely exposed. What would happen next? If he managed to escape, he'd have to count this as a second lease of life.

Tirumalaiappan's heart beat fast. He looked about himself to try and spot an escape route. There was none. He turned to the other side. He spotted an enormous bat absorbed in its penance, hanging upside down from a branch. In an instant, he reached out, grabbed the bat and threw it at the face of the torchbearer right as he came round the bend. The torch fell to the ground and its flame died.

The man who had taken a blow to the face from the bat's huge wings cried, 'Ei! Ei! What? What!'

The sound of several running feet approached. Azhvarkadiyaan, too, ran as fast as he could and disappeared into the foliage.

'What happened?' 'What is this?' 'What went on here?' chorused several voices.

The torchbearer began to tell the tale of the bat that had assaulted him.

Tirumalaiappan could hear the conversation clearly for some distance.

21

THE SCREEN WENT 'SALA-SALA'

Was it conceivable for two minds to coexist simultaneously within the same man's head? Vandiyadevan's experience that day would teach him that it was.

He was journeying through the lushest parts of the land known as 'Chozha Vala Naadu'—the lush land of the Chozhas. The fresh waters were swirling in the rivers of the kingdom. The waters bubbled with a 'gubu-gubu' through irrigation canals and streams and brooks and fields. Everywhere one turned, water cooled one's eyes. How apt it was that the Chozha land was known as 'Valanaadu' and the king 'Valavan'!

As these thoughts ran through his mind, he was parallelly reminded of the perils ahead for the kingdom and the king. What was his duty under these circumstances? Should he restrict himself to delivering the letter he had been assigned by Aditya Karikalar to the Chakravarti, and consider his job done? Why must he get embroiled in this fevered clash over inheritance and power? What did it matter to him who sat on the throne of Chozha Naadu? Hadn't the Chozhas started out as enemies of his own Vaanar clan? It was the Chozhas and Gangas and Vaidumbas who had snuffed out the Vaanar kingdom and ensured their flag had no pole to fly on. Could Aditya Karikalar's affection make up for the injustice of yore?

Che-che! How could one speak of those old wars as 'injustice'? It was as natural for kings to fight each other, as it was for victory and defeat to take turns visiting a warrior. What was the point in the vanquished fuming against the victors? When his own ancestors had been at their peak, they had brought various other kings to their knees, hadn't they? They had destroyed entire clans, hadn't they?

What was that song? Ah, he remembered it now:

Senai thazhaiyaakki senguruthi neerthekki
Aanai midhitha arunjetril—maanabaran
Paavendar thamvendan vaanan pariththu
Naattan moovendar thangal mudi

In the holy slush of the battlefield,
Beaten to marsh by soldiers' feet,
Irrigated by rivers of blood,
Churned by war elephants,
Our Vaanar king planted
The head of his enemy
That he had plucked
From defeated shoulders

His own ancestors had wrought such heinous deeds on the battlefield, too. The losers in battle were condemned to their own hells. That was the way of the world. Could all kings be as generous in victory, as compassionate, as Rama and Dharmaputra? It was their generosity and compassion that had sent those two kings to exile in forests. Their courage and the company of equally courageous brothers did not save them from suffering. Compassion did not go with kingship. In fact, one must admit the Chozhas had a tendency towards compassion. They had always tried to convert enemies into friends. They had forged marital alliances with other clans to this end. Had Sundara Chozhar's father, Arinjaya Chozhar, not married the daughter of Vaidumbarayan? Wasn't it by dint of being the son of that epitome of beauty Kalyani that Sundara Chozhar and his offspring were quite so handsome?

Ah! The word 'beauty' brought to mind the woman from Kudandai ... the woman by the banks of the Arisilaru. Truth be told, she had never really been dismissed from his mind, or his heart.

Even as his mind was outwardly contemplating the natural lushness and royal conundrums of Chozha Naadu, his inner mind was fixated on that woman. Now, both these parts of his mind channelled themselves towards the same object—that woman. Every manifestation of nature's beauty reminded him of some aspect of hers. Smooth bamboo shoots evoked her shoulders. The kuvalai flowers crowding the ponds were comparable to her lovely eyes. Could the pankaja flower, the lotus, be any match for her glowing complexion? Would drawing a parallel to the buzz of the bees as they hovered over the flowers by the riverside do justice to her dulcet voice?

Nature's bounty may have inspired and informed poetic imagination, but could they truly stand up to her exquisite beauty? The sight of her face had sent tremors through his body. The very thought made his heart beat faster. Flowers and bees didn't draw such a physical response from him, did they?

Che-che! He had forgotten the sage advice of the elders. There is no graver danger than the seductiveness of a woman in this worldly life. A man who hoped to make something of himself must never fall into this trap, or he was done for. Did one need to look any further than the story of Kovalan from *Silappadikaram* to learn just what lust could do to a man? Why even turn to legend, when there was a real-life example in Periya Pazhuvettaraiyar, that bravest of brave warriors who exerted more influence than anyone else in Chozha Naadu, and yet was the subject of snide gossip thanks to his obsession with his wife?

Then again, people didn't know the truth. They didn't know who the occupant of the covered palanquin was. This was why they indulged in such foolish talk. Surely, Madurantaka Devar had no cause to take to such desperate measures and abase himself so much? Must he journey in a closed palanquin, in Pazhuvettaraiyar's wife's stead, from town to town? Was this befitting of manliness? Was this any way to earn support for one's bid for the throne? Could he possibly protect a crown thus earned? He would be forever dependent on the good offices of Pazhuvettaraiyar and his allies, and feel compelled to bow down to their every wish, wouldn't he?

For that matter, Sundara Chozha Chakravarti's conduct in this department wasn't particularly laudable either. He ought not to have conceded so much authority and influence to people like Pazhuvettaraiyar. And that too, when he had two such valorous sons. And a daughter whose intelligence and talent had the entire kingdom spellbound ...

That woman, the woman he had encountered at the astrologer's house and again by the banks of the Arisilaru ... hadn't her face seemed familiar? Could it be that ...? No, this was madness! There was no way it could be! But why not? If it happened to be so, there could be no greater fool in the world than he! Nor as miserable an unfortunate wretch. He had behaved like a savage, a neanderthal with a queen whose praises were sung from Lanka to the Vindhyas. No, there was no way it could be! If it were, how would he show his face to her with the letter her brother had entrusted him to deliver?

As he put two and two together, forging links between all and sundry from the sky to the earth, Vandiyadevan found himself at Tiruvaiyaru, along the banks of the Kaveri. The beauty and prosperity of that town stole his heart. He asked around to make sure it was Tiruvaiyaru. All that he had heard about this astonishing place fell short of the truth, he thought. The description Gnana Sambandar had written in his Devaram was fitting. Three hundred years hadn't changed the place one bit. How green and healthy the trees along the Kaveri bank were! How enormous the jackfruits were! One could never see such things in Thondai Mandalam. Aha! One could bet that monkeys would sniff out any place that was lush with fruit and vegetation. What a lovely sight they made as they swung from branch to branch! What was it that Sambandar had said? Yes, he remembered!

Sambandar wrote that women danced in improvised halls at street corners. Hearing the song that accompanied the dance and the maddalam that kept the beat, the monkeys figured it was thunder and climbed to the topmost branches of the trees to see if it was about to rain. Adada! That was quite apt today! The monkeys were indeed climbing to the higher reaches of the trees. And that was not all. Vandiyadevan could hear the sweet notes of instruments that accompanied the dance performance. The sounds of the yazh, the flute and percussion instruments such as the muzhavu and thannumai were punctuated by the rhythm of the salangai anklets, the rhythm of dancing feet. These dancers were not the kuravai koothu performers of Kadambur Sambuvarayar's palace. These

were the pleasant songs that accompanied classical
dance, the sound of the salangai of those who danced
Bharatanatyam, steeped as it was in ancient culture.
The sound of the dance teacher's thattukkazhi, the
tiny wooden baton that he tapped against a wooden
plank, kept time.

> *Koloda kolvalaiyaar koothaada*
> *Kuvimulaiyaar mugathininru*
> *Sayloda silayaada seyizhaiyaar*
> *Nadamaadum Tiruvaiyare!*

> *O, Tiruvaiyare!*
> *Where, as dance teachers direct them with the kol,*
> *The ample-bosomed dancing women*
> *Dart their lovely, long, fish-shaped eyes about*
> *And move their bow-like eyebrows to portray emotion*

Aha! Sambandar was a Shiva bhakt. But he was an even
more ardent rasika. The Tiruvaiyaru of today was just
as he had described it all those centuries ago.

He ought to stay back for a day and make sure
he caught some of the dance programmes that were
reputed to be stunning and got a darshan of the
temple deities, Aiyaarappar and Aram Valartha Naayagi
Amman. Adada! How many devotees had seated
themselves in penance on the banks of the Kaveri!
How much devotion the sacred ash they smeared on
themselves inspired! At times, the sonorous 'Nama
Shivaya!' of their voices drowned out even the sounds

of music and dance. Why, someone was singing verses from Sambandar's Devaram! It was as if God had made this town exclusively for music and culture! There were no two ways about it—he must stay back for a day in Tiruvaiyaru.

What would be the point of hurrying to Thanjavur, anyway? What were the chances of his entering the fortress? And even if he contrived to do so, what were the chances of his being granted an audience with the maharaja? Apparently, the two Pazhuvettaraiyars had imprisoned Sundara Chozhar in a gilded cage. He must go to the northern bank of the Kaveri!

At the very moment Vandiyadevan arrived at this decision, an incident occurred. A palanquin appeared from the west, along the banks of the Kaveri. There were several bodyguards accompanying the palanquin, in addition to its bearers.

Vandiyadevan felt suspicious. Could it be that ...? He waited until the palanquin came near. It was as he had thought. The curtains screening the interior of the palanquin bore the palm tree emblem of Pazhuvettaraiyar. Aha! So it *was* the palanquin from Kadambur. While he had come through the Kudandai route, they had taken another. But Pazhuvettaraiyar was missing in action. Perhaps he had stayed back somewhere along the route?

The palanquin took a turn towards the southern bank, in the direction of Thanjavur. That was it. Vandiyadevan abandoned all plans to stay on in

Tiruvaiyaru. He decided to follow the palanquin. It was an impulsive decision, and he did not articulate properly even to himself at the time why he had made it. He was certain of one thing alone—the occupant of the palanquin was Madurantaka Devar. His revulsion for the man had only grown since he had first seen his face through the screen. But his intuition told him something good might come of his tailing the palanquin. An opportunity might present itself. The bearers might set it down for a while. Madurantakar might make an appearance from within. Vandiyadevan might perhaps be able to make his acquaintance. This could be handy in assuring him a passage into the Thanjavur fortress, and perhaps even an audience with the Chakravarti. He would have to come up with a ruse. Nothing could be achieved without some chicanery, particularly where matters of governance were concerned.

He allowed the palanquin and its entourage to go ahead, and then followed at some distance. However, none of the opportunities for which he had been hoping presented themselves. They had crossed four rivers since he had first sighted the palanquin on the banks of the Kaveri. Yet, the bearers did not set it down.

There! The town walls and entry to the Thanjavur fortress were already visible. If the palanquin disappeared into them, this entire journey would have been pointless. He would have to do something daring to stop it. What did he have to lose, anyway? No one would chop off his head. And even if they did, that would be a worthier end than to return without having fulfilled the task assigned to him.

For all this, Vandiyadevan was furious with Madurantaka Devar. His hands itched and his heart yearned to tear apart the curtain and expose the fact that its occupant was no woman, but a grown man.

As he was intensely contemplating how he would go about stopping the palanquin, a member of its entourage fell behind until he was in step with Vandiyadevan.

'Who are you, appa? Why have you been following us since Tiruvaiyaru?'

'I'm not following you, aiya! I'm going to Thanjavur. This is the road to Thanjavur, isn't it?'

'Yes, this road does lead to Thanjavur. But it is reserved for people of eminence. There is another road for the rest,' the bodyguard said.

'Is that so? But I'm a person of great eminence!'

His interlocutor smiled and asked, 'Why are you going to Thanjai?'

'My chiththappa[1] lives in Thanjai. I've learnt he is unwell, and so I'm going to see him,' Vandiyadevan said.

'What does your chiththappa do in Thanjai? Is he in the employ of the palace?'

'No, no; he's the supervisor of a chatram.[2]'

'Oho! Is that so? Then, why don't you go ahead of us? Why are you tailing us?'

'My horse is tired, aiya! That's why. What joy could I possibly derive from staring at your backs?'

Vandiyadevan had reached close to the palanquin even as the exchange took place. The idea for which he had been racking his brain presented itself to him. He pressed his feet against his horse, pulled the reins and then let it loose on the palanquin-bearers. They turned in shock, scared out of their wits.

At once, Vandiyadevan shouted, 'Maharaja! Maharaja! The palanquin-bearers have rammed into my horse! Aiyo! Aiyo!'

The curtain that screened the palanquin went 'sala-sala'.

22

THE VELAKKAARA ARMY

It was the palanquin's outer screen, which bore the palm tree insignia, that parted first. Next, the inner silk screen began to move. The same hand Vandiyadevan had seen once before, so white it was nearly pink, made its appearance. Vandiyadevan decided it wouldn't do to remain on his horse, and jumped down with a single, smooth leap.

He ran towards the palanquin, and crying, 'Prince! O Prince! The palanquin-bearers ...' he looked up.

He stared. And stared harder. He blinked once, and stared again. His eyes smarted. His tongue ran dry. His throat felt parched.

'No, no! You ... you're the *Princess* of Pazhuvoor! Your men's ... their horse hit my palanquin!' he blithered and blathered.

All this happened in the blink of an eye. The bodyguards who had accompanied the palanquin rushed to surround Vandiyadevan. His hand reached instinctively for his sword. But he couldn't tear his eyes from the Mohanangi—the woman of intoxicating beauty—whose moon-like face shone at him from the interior of the palanquin.

Yes. Contrary to Vandiyadevan's expectations, it was genuinely a woman's figure that occupied the palanquin. And what a woman she was! It had never occurred to him that there could be such a beauty on earth that the sight of her face alone might drive a man insane. Thankfully, a single nerve in his brain found itself able to work, even as the rest of him stood paralysed. He decided to put this nerve to use.

He took a deep breath, cleared his throat, summoned the power to speak and said, 'You must forgive me. You are the Ilaiya Rani of Pazhuvoor, aren't you? I came all this way only to see you!'

A gentle smile teased the lips of the Pazhuvoor Ilaiya Rani. The lotus bud that had been closed thus far unfurled its petals to reveal a hint of a row of pearly whites. The sight of that lovely smile stole away our young hero's capacity for speech. The bodyguards who surrounded him seemed to be waiting for their mistress's order. She made a sign with her hand, and they retreated to a polite distance. Two of them held the horse, which was still butting against the palanquin.

The queen looked at Vandiyadevan from her seat. It was as if two sharp spears had pierced his heart.

'Yes. I am the Ilaiya Rani of Pazhuvoor,' she said. Which intoxicant could have found a way to blend itself into her voice? Why must one feel giddy just to hear its notes?

'What was it you said just now? You had some sort of complaint? Against the palanquin-bearers?'

Could the softness of silk from Kashi, the soporific effect of alcohol, the sweetness of forest honey and the dazzle of lightning in monsoon skies wind their way through a woman's voice? In this case, it appeared they could.

'My palanquin-bearers ran my palanquin into your horse, you said ...?'

The smile that played on the Pazhuvoor queen's coral lips revealed her amusement at his claim. This emboldened Vandiyadevan.

'Yes, Maharani! That is just what they did. My horse was stunned,' he said.

'You are just as stunned. You'll need to have an exorcism done. Go to the Durgai Amman temple and ask them to drive away whatever is haunting you with neem leaves. May your fears vanish!'

By now, Vadiyadevan's fears had vanished without a trace. He was tempted to laugh.

Just then, the Pazhuvoor queen's expression changed. The smiling moon turned into an angry gust of wind.

'You can laugh later. Tell me the truth now! Why did you run your horse into my palanquin?'

He had to answer her question satisfactorily. If he did not ... Fortunately, he had already prepared a response.

He said, sotto voce, so only she could hear, 'Devi! Nandini Devi! Azhvarkadiyaar ... Tirumalaiappar, you know ... had requested that I meet you. That was why I came up with this idea. Please forgive me!' he said.

Even as he said this, he scrutinised the Pazhuvoor Rani's face. He wondered what response his reply might elicit. It was quite like hurling a stone at a tree heavy with fruit. What would happen next? Would a ripe fruit fall? Or an unripe one? Would the stone ricochet towards him again? Or would something totally unexpected occur? The Pazhuvoor queen's dark eyebrows rose ever so slightly. Surprise and suspicion played in her eyes. The next moment, it appeared the queen had made her decision.

'Right. It isn't prudent to speak in the middle of the road of such things. Come to our palace tomorrow! You can tell me everything in detail,' she said.

Vandiyadevan's heart felt full. It seemed his mission might turn successful. Yet, there was no point in successfully crossing only three-quarters of the river. He must cross the remaining quarter, too.

'Devi! Devi! They won't allow me into the fort, let alone the palace! What must I do?' said Vandiyadevan anxiously.

The Pazhuvoor Rani reached for a silk purse by her side and took out an ivory ring.

'Showing this to the guards will gain you entry into both the fort and the palace,' she said, as she handed it over to Vandiyadevan, who received it eagerly. For a moment, he studied the ring, with its insignia of palm leaves. He straightened up to thank the queen and greet her once more, only to see that the screen of the palanquin had been drawn shut. Aha! When the moon is eaten by Raahu, he consumes her bit by bit. But the screen of the palanquin had engulfed that beautiful talking moon in a fraction of a second!

'Now, at least, stop following me! You'll be in danger. Linger awhile, and go slowly to the city,' said a silky soft voice from behind the screen.

The palanquin moved forward, with its entourage of bodyguards.

Vandiyadevan held his horse's reins and paused by the side of the street. His eyes observed that the man who had fallen back in order to speak to him turned to glance at him several times. His eyes duly conveyed the observation to his brain. Yes, his outer mind couldn't stop thinking about the Pazhuvoor Rani's bewitching beauty. Was all he had seen and heard real? Or had it all been an illusion, a dream? Could such a ravishing woman, such a flawless figure, actually exist in this human world?

The puranas spoke of celestial maidens such as Rambha, Urvashi and Menaka. Their beauty could disrupt the penance of even ascetics who had forsaken material comforts. But in this world ... the gossip about Periya Pazhuvettaraiyar being slave to his new wife might well be true. If it were, it ought not to surprise anyone. All the signs of age—greying hair,

fading eyesight, sunken shoulders—and all the scars
of war had manifested themselves on him. She was a
sukumari, a stunner whose form defied description.
What would he not do to win the slightest smile from
her?

Having spent a fair bit of time standing by the
path and giving himself over to such reflection,
Vandiyadevan finally mounted his horse and began his
slow journey towards the Thanjai fort.

It was dusk when he reached the entrance to the
fort. The city's outer limit began some distance from
the fort walls. The town spread in circles from the city
walls. There were shops selling various commodities,
and streets on which townspeople engaged in various
professions lived in communities. Between those
hurrying along on the street and those bargaining with
shopkeepers, between the bullock carts and horse-
drawn chariots, the city wore an air of effervescent
activity. Vandiyadevan was tempted to saunter through
the streets and observe how the residents of Chozha
Naadu's new capital behaved. But he had no time to
indulge in such things. He had a mission to accomplish
first.

Having made his decision, Vandiyadevan approached
the grand entrance to the city. The enormous gates of
the fort were closed at the time. The guards were
herding the townsfolk away from the middle of
the street. The crowd obliged and retreated to the
pavements. It appeared they were waiting for some

sort of procession or event. Men, women, children and the elderly had assembled with an air of anticipation.

A space had been cleared at the entrance of the fort. Only the palace guards were allowed to inhabit this area. Vandiyadevan wondered what was going on. He didn't want to accost the guards when everyone else was meekly obeying commands. That could lead to a heated argument or an unpleasant confrontation. This wasn't the moment for such things—prudence would have to take precedence over bravado.

So he retreated to a spot from where he could observe the entrance of the fort. A heady floral fragrance suddenly teased his nostrils. He turned. A young man, bearing all the signs of a Shiva devotee, from a rudraksham to sacred ash, stood with a flower basket in each hand.

'Thambi, why is everyone assembled by the road? Is some sort of procession on its way?' he asked the young man.

'Are you not from these parts, aiya?'

'No, I'm from Thondai Mandalam.'

'That explains it. It would be wise for you to get off your horse.'

That would make it easier to talk to the young man, who was on foot. Vandiyadevan leapt off his horse.

'Thambi! Why did you ask me to dismount?' he asked.

'The Velakkaara Army has just had its daily darshan

of the king. They are about to emerge from the fort. That's why everyone has retreated to the sides of the road.'

'To watch the procession, right?'

'Yes.'

'So why can't I watch from my saddle?'

'You could. But if the Velakkaara Army soldiers were to spot you, you'll be in danger.'

'What danger? Will they whisk away my horse?'

'They will. They won't hesitate to whisk away even men, the brutes.'

'And they get away with whisking away horses and men? The townspeople do nothing about it?'

'What could we do but let them get away with it? The word of the Velakkaara Army is law here. No one can question their actions. Not even the Pazhuvettaraiyars poke their noses into the affairs of the Velakkaara Army.'

At that very moment, there was some commotion from within the fort walls. The nagara drums, the parai, bugles, conches and several hundred human voices made for a stentorian chorus.

Vandiyadevan was well aware of the Velakkaara armies. They were a veritable force, of great importance in the lore of the Tamil lands, particularly of Chozha Naadu. A 'velakkaara' was technically a bodyguard to the ruler of the time. However, there was a crucial difference between a velakkaara and an ordinary bodyguard. The velakkaaras had sworn to protect the life of their king, even at the cost of their own. If their carelessness, or even forces beyond their powers, had led to danger or calamity befalling the king, they would kneel at the sanctum sanctorum of Goddess Durga and decapitate themselves with their very own hands as punishment for the oversight. It was but natural for warriors who had taken such a terrible oath to be given concessions to which the common man had no recourse, wasn't it?

The two imposing gates of the entrance to the fort swung open with a 'padaar-padaar'. First, two horsemen emerged. Each held aloft a flag with his right hand. The flag bore a unique emblem. On a red background, a tiger glowered above a crown. Under the crown was a sacrificial slab, a disembodied head and a ceremonial sword. The emblem was formidable, even frightening.

The horsemen were followed by a huge bull who bore two perigai drums. The bull was accompanied by two drummers, one beating each perigai.

Next came a band of about fifty men beating the siruparai, perumparai and thambattam drums.

They were followed by another fifty trumpeters, who blew a 'baam-baam-ba-baam' on their curved instruments.

There might have been a thousand soldiers who came next. As they strode forward, they shouted the following war cries in thundering voices:

'Long live Parantaka Chozha Poomandala Chakravarti!'

'Vaazhga, vaazhga, long live, long live!'

'Long live King Sundara Chozha!'

'Vaazhga, vaazhga, long live, long live!'

'Long live Kozhi Vendar!'

'Vaazhga, vaazhga, long live, long live!'

'Long live the ruler of Thanjai!'

'Vaazhga, vaazhga, long live, long live!'

'Long live the god who toppled Veerapandiyan!'

'Vaazhga, vaazhga, long live, long live!'

'Long live the Ko Rajakesari who is the conqueror of Madurai and Eezham and Thondai Mandalam!'

'Vaazhga, vaazhga, long live, long live!'

'Long live the great dynasty of Karikaal Valavan!'

'Vaazhga, vaazhga, long live, long live!'

'Victory to Goddess Durga Mahakali Paratpari Parashakti!'

'Velga, velga, victory, victory!'

'Victory to the heroic tiger flag that will fly from every pole in all the world!'

'Velga, velga, victory, victory!'

'Vetrivel! May the spear be victorious!'

'Veeravel! May the spear realise heroic deeds!'

The resonating cries from hundreds of deep voices gave the listeners goosebumps. As the soldiers emerged from the entrance, their voices found echoes in the assembled gathering. Many of the townsfolk joined the chorus of war cries.

The readers might be aware that the Tamil God Murugan has 'Velakkaaran' for one of his names.

Scholars posit that the name has been attributed to him because he is considered a deity who has sworn an oath to protect his devotees.

As the Velakkaara Army made its way past the fort gates, and then the streets, the air was abuzz with a fevered excitement until they disappeared into the distance.

23

AMUDAN'S MOTHER

The Velakkaara Army made its way down the main market street of the city, its widest boulevard. The soldiers who brought up its tail decided to indulge in their divine leelas. One helped himself to a basketful of adhirasam from a sweet shop and proffered it to his fellow soldiers. He then ceremoniously upturned the empty basket upon the shopkeeper's head, the coronation drawing a merry 'Hahahahaha' from the soldiers as well as passers-by.

Another warrior grabbed a flower basket from an elderly woman. He threw the blooms in the air, and yelled, 'Look, it's poomaari, the rain of flowers!' The other soldiers tried to catch the flowers, and jumped on the fallen petals, laughing.

Yet another stopped a bullock cart, freed the bull and gave chase to the animal, which plunged into the crowd, disorientated. Several people lost their footing as the bull ran amok, prompting more raucous laughter from the Velakkaara Army.

Vandiyadevan, looking on, thought: *These men play the fool just like Pazhuvettaraiyar's men. But their antics amuse the townsfolk. Thank heavens, I managed to keep a low profile. If they had messed with me, a grand fight would have broken out, and my mission would have been a failure.*

He noted an important difference between the response the two bands of troublemakers elicited—the Velakkaara Army, for one, wasn't disliked; the residents seemed to enjoy their clowning about, cruel though it was. When he turned to question his interlocutor about this, he couldn't spot him. The young man had merged into the crowd. Perhaps he had gone to finish whatever task he had set out to do.

Vandiyadevan learnt that once the Velakkaara Army had left the palace in the evening, no visitors were permitted. The only people who had access to the fort any time of the day or night were members of the royal family, ministers and army commanders. The members of the Pazhuvettaraiyars' family were also treated as equals of those dignitaries, he understood. His plans to enter the palace before sunset now changed. He didn't want to put the ring he had been given as a token to the test just yet. It might be a better idea to stay the night outside the fort, do a recce of the city and then try his luck. Even if he were permitted inside that evening, there wasn't much he could do. He couldn't very well ask to meet the emperor and hand him the letter his son had secretly sent.

He sauntered through the streets that ran around the palace walls. His horse was exhausted from the many kaadhams it had travelled through the day. He would need to rest the animal soon, or the horse would prove useless if he needed to get away in a hurry the next day. He would have to find his lodging for the night as soon as he could.

Thanjai was a young city, thriving and expanding thanks to its sudden importance. As the day faded into dusk, torches flared in hundreds on the street, lighting the way for residents and tourists alike. Crowds thronged the thoroughfares. People from out of town were going about their various offices. One could spot those from the cities and villages of Chozha Naadu, as well as others from territories that had been recently brought under Chozha dominions. The new capital drew visitors from the Porunai River to the Palaru, from the eastern coast to the western. One might even spot the odd traveller who had journeyed from the north of the Vindhyas or overseas to Thanjavur.

Customers gathered like flies at the shops selling aappam and adhirasam. Mountains upon mountains of fruits drew those with healthier palates. One need hardly describe the flower shops. Mullai, jasmine, thiru aththi and shenbagam flowers were arranged like little hillocks. Women buzzed around these flowers like bees drawn to their nectar.

The flower shops reminded Vandiyadevan of the

young man he had met. How convenient it would be if he were to meet that boy again! He could ask him to suggest a place for the night. As if he had conjured him from his thoughts, the young man materialised in the distance. Vandiyadevan jumped off his horse and approached him.

'Thambi! Why, your baskets are empty! What happened to the flowers? Have you sold them all?' he asked.

'Oh, I didn't bring the flowers to sell them. They were for the puja at the temple. I've handed them over. I'm going back home now.'

'Which temple have you chosen for this floral offering?'

'Have you heard of the Thalikulaththaar Aalayam?'

'Oho! I have heard of the Thanjai Thalikulaththaar. Is this the temple to which you refer? Is it a grand one?'

'No, it's just a little temple. The Durgai Amman temple is the one which is famous in Thanjai. That is the one the royal family and the Pazhuvettaraiyars visit. The Thalikulaththaar temple isn't well known, and doesn't have many people waiting for darshan ...'

'Do you receive any remuneration for the flowers you bring to the temple?'

'My family has received a grant for this. It was endowed by Kandaraditya Chakravarti in my grandfather's time. Now, it is my mother and I who carry on the duty.'

'Is the Thalikulaththaar temple made of brick? Or have they fortified it with stone?' Vandiyadevan asked.

He had noticed on his way that several of the temples made of brick were now being rebuilt with stone.

'It is a brick temple for now. I've heard that it will soon be converted to stone. Pazhaiyarai Periya Piraatti wishes that the work begin right away, but ...' the youngster trailed off.

'But ... what?'

'What's the point of spreading rumours? I've heard it said that one must speak with caution by day, and never by night. And here we are, at the crossroads, surrounded by people ...'

'It is precisely in this kind of place that the deepest secrets may be discussed with the least fear of repercussions. In all this noise and commotion, no one will hear anything we say.'

'What deep secret do we have to discuss, anyway?' the young man said, looking somewhat askance at Vandiyadevan.

Aha! This was a bright kid. Befriending him might have its uses, Vandiyadevan thought. He might learn something that would come in handy. But there was no point in arousing his suspicions, and so Vandiyadevan said, 'Yes, what secret do we have, anyway? Nothing. Let that be, thambi. I need a place to sleep without disturbance for the night. I've travelled a long way, and am bone-tired. Could you direct me to a good inn for the night?'

'There's no shortage of places to stay. There are regular boarding houses, and then royal inns for travellers visiting from foreign shores. But if you would like to ...'

'Thambi! What is your name?' Vandiyadevan asked.

'Amudan. Senthan Amudan.'

'Adada! What a lovely name! "Senthan" sounds like "Senthen", red honey. And then Amudan, nectar. *The nectar of red honey.* The tastiest honey there is. I can taste the very nectar in my mouth when I hear your name. You were about to tell me that if I would like to, I could come and stay at your house, weren't you?'

'Yes, but how did you know?'

'I have all sorts of superpowers. Among them is the ability to read minds. Where do you live?'

'Our flower garden is within shouting distance of the city limits. Our house is inside the garden,' Amudan said.

'Aha! In that case, I will *have* to come stay at your place. I can't spend the night in this crowded city. Besides, I would like a darshan of the exalted woman who has birthed a son of such wonderful character.'

'She certainly is an exalted woman. But she is very unlucky, too.'

'Adada! What makes you say that? ... Is it that, perhaps, your father ...?'

'Yes, my father has indeed passed away. But that's not all. My mother was born unlucky. You'll see for yourself when you meet her. Come, let us go.'

A half-naazhigai's walk took them to the garden.
The heady fragrance of the flowers at twilight greeted
them. They could barely hear the commotion of the
city streets. A thatched house stood in the middle of
the garden. There were two little huts by it, occupied
by families that helped tend the garden. Amudan called
out to one of the men and instructed him to tie
Vandiyadevan's horse to a tree and bring some hay
for the animal.

Then, he ushered Vandiyadevan into his home.
The moment he met Amudan's mother, Vandiyadevan
realised why her son had spoken of her as unlucky.
The elderly woman was deaf-mute. Yet, her face shone
with compassion and love. She had bright eyes, and
her entire being glowed with intelligence. It was one
of nature's wonders that people who were denied the
use of one or two senses made up for it with their
other senses somehow being keener than average.

Amudan conveyed with a series of signs that
Vandiyadevan was a guest from another land. His
mother greeted their guest and welcomed him with
her expressive features, needing no interpretation from
her son. Before long, she had laid out a banana leaf.
She motioned for Vandiyadevan to sit, and began to
serve him. The meal began with idiyappam and sweet
coconut milk. Vandiyadevan had never tasted anything
so good. He wolfed down ten, perhaps twelve,
idiyappams and half a padi of coconut milk. This
was followed by tamarind curry and fried cornflour

dumplings, to which he did full justice. It wasn't
before he had demolished a quarter padi of rice and
half a padi of curd that he got up from his dinner.

Even as he ate, he learnt a few things from
Amudan. He asked who stayed at the fort aside from
Sundara Chozha Chakravarti and his retinue. The
Pazhuvettaraiyar brothers had built their own palaces
within the fort. The treasury and the granary were also
housed in the fort, and so the supervisors, guards and
accountants responsible for those departments lived
within its walls. The minister Aniruddha Brahmaraayar,
who enjoyed Sundara Chozhar's unstinting trust and
affection, and the royal scribe were residents as
well. The men who guarded the Thanjai fort under
Chinna Pazhuvettaraiyar's command and their families
were given accommodation inside. Goldsmiths and
silversmiths and gemstone dealers were among the
traders housed in the fort. The hundreds of officials
who worked in the tax department under Periya
Pazhuvettaraiyar also lived within those walls. The
Durgai Amman temple occupied one corner of the
grounds. The priests and others who served the temple
in various capacities had their homes nearby.

'Are all the ministers inside the fort now?'
Vandiyadevan asked, once he had learnt all this.

'How is that possible? They keep coming and
going, depending on the work they have. It's been
a while since Aniruddha Brahmaraayar was in the
city. I've heard he's gone to Chera Naadu. Periya

Pazhuvettaraiyar left four days ago. Apparently to the north of the Kollidam.'

'He could have returned, couldn't he? As if you won't know!'

'The Pazhuvoor Ilaiya Rani's palanquin arrived this evening. I saw it outside the fort with my own eyes. But Pazhuvettaraiyar wasn't part of the procession. Perhaps he stopped somewhere along the way, and will return tomorrow.'

'Thambi! Does Prince Madurantaka Devar live inside the fort, too?'

'Yes. His palace is right next to the Pazhuvettaraiyar palace. He is Chinna Pazhuvettaraiyar's son-in-law, isn't he?'

'Oho! Is that so? I had no idea!'

'Not many people know. Keeping Chakravarti's ill-health in mind, the wedding was a muted affair. It was deemed inappropriate to celebrate in a grand fashion.'

'Good, good. So Madurantakar is inside the fort now, isn't he?'

'He must be. But Madurantaka Devar does not usually come out. People are not able to see him either. One hears that he is an ardent Shiva devotee, who spends all his time in prayer and meditation and puja.'

'And yet, after all this time, he has got married?'

'Yes. That did come as a surprise. They also say he has had a change of heart since he got married ...

but why does that concern us? It's best not to discuss the nobility.'

Vandiyadevan was eager to ask Senthan Amudan about several other matters. But he had to be careful not to seem too keen and provoke the latter's suspicions. Something told him this timorous young man would prove to be a great help one day. He had also lucked out in finding a house like this in Thanjai. Why ruin all this?

Besides, he was so tired from his journey that his eyes began to droop even as he was speaking. Sleep made his lids heavy. Senthan Amudan noticed this, and got a bed ready for him.

In the haze of half-sleep, the last conscious memory Vandiyadevan had was a vision of the Pazhuvoor Ilaiya Rani's face. Appappa! What beauty! What radiance! The moment he had seen that bewitching face, it was as if he had been turned to stone—he couldn't move, not even to blink his eyes. His body's reaction triggered another memory.

In his childhood, he had once taken a path through the forest. Suddenly, he had noticed a cobra raise itself from the ground, expand its hood and hiss. Its beauty was something else, he had thought then, so attractive it drew you closer. The snake's hypnotic dance had had the same effect on his body. He had been frozen in place, unable to move. He couldn't so much as blink his eyes. The snake had kept up its dance as he stared, and then his own body had begun to move in sync with the snake. He would never know how this would have ended, for at that very moment, a mongoose had pounced on the snake and the two had begun a vicious fight. Vandiyadevan had made use of the opportunity to take to his heels.

Che-che! What sort of an analogy was this? Would anyone draw a comparison between the bhuvana mohini, a woman of such beauteous form whom he had had the great fortune of encountering that day, and a snake with its hood poised to strike? Just the sight of her innocent face could satiate one's hunger. And he was going to meet her the next day! Her voice carried such sweet notes. She truly was incredibly beautiful.

But that other woman, the woman he had met at the astrologer's house and then at the banks of the Arisilaru ... her face had shone with a lustrous glow, sparkling beauty. They were both lovely faces, and yet there was such a difference in their respective loveliness. One was stately and regal, with an air of generosity; the other was captivating and intoxicating, with an air of sensuality. Even as his heart was weighing the relative merits of the faces of these two women, a third woman intervened. The omnipotent sovereign of sleep, Nidra Devi, took complete and total control of Vandiyadevan.

24

THE CROW AND THE KOEL

Having slept like a log through the night, Vandiyadevan
rose well after the sun did the next morning. Even after
he woke, he was loath to get up, and lay dawdling.
The wind blew with a 'virrrr', stirring the trees,
plants, branches and leaves. They synced their way
to a 'cho' as they brushed against each other. In tune
with the shruti of this 'cho', a young man's voice sang
Sundaramurti Swamigal's Devaaram:

Ponnaar meniyane
Pulitholai araikasaithu
Minnaar senjadaimel
Milir konrai anindavane!

He of the golden skin
Who wears a tiger's skin at his waist
He of the lightning-like locks
Ornamented with a garland of konrai flowers

Vandiyadevan opened his eyes upon hearing these words. The sight of konnai trees heavy with their blossoms—the very konrai flowers evoked in the song—greeted him. Senthan Amudan, bearing a basket in one hand and a stick to pluck flowers in the other, was singing as he placed the konrai flowers in his basket. Amudan, who had bathed early in the morning and anointed himself with sacred ash, brought to mind the legendary Shiva devotee Markandeya. Vandiyadevan rose with the thought that the boy's mother didn't have the good fortune of hearing the sweet notes of her son's pleasing voice.

What stopped him from being like Amudan, he wondered. Why didn't he tend a garden and devote himself to the service of Lord Shiva, and pass his days in peace? What made him wander from town to town, sword and spear in hand, ready to kill or be killed? These thoughts dawned on him, only to be swept away by a change of heart in a bit. Was the world populated exclusively by Shiva devotees like Senthan Amudan? There were thieves and robbers and conmen and those who delighted in bullying the vulnerable. Governance was needed in order to control them and to ensure that justice and fairness prevailed. Governance mandated that kings and ministers oversee affairs. They needed protection, for which Velakkaara armies must be maintained. And then there were men like himself, who had to deliver letters to kings.

Yes! He absolutely had to meet Sundara Chozha

Chakravarti that very day. That window was open only for as long as Periya Pazhuvettaraiyar was away. Once he was back, the task may prove impossible.

Vandiyadevan bathed in the lotus pond near the flower garden, and dressed himself in his finest clothes and jewels. He couldn't very well wear everyday clothes and present himself to the emperor. We can't tell whether this was indeed his reason for taking particular care to look good that day, or whether it was also at the back of his mind that he was to meet the Pazhuvoor Ilaiya Rani again that day.

After breakfast, Senthan Amudan made his way to the temple for the noon puja, accompanied by Vandiyadevan on his mission to meet Sundara Chozhar. They went by foot. Vandiyadevan had already decided not to take his horse inside the fort. It was important that the animal was well-rested. For all he knew, he may need to make his escape from the city and take off at a gallop. It was best that he leave the horse in Amudan's garden. Before he reached the entrance of the fort, Vandiyadevan picked up a fair bit of information from a chat with Amudan.

'Don't you have any family other than your mother?' Vandiyadevan asked.

'I do. My mother is one of three siblings. Her sister is no more; her brother serves the Kuzhagar temple at Kodikkarai, supplying flowers for worship as we do. He is also in charge of tending to the lighthouse lamp at night. He has a son and daughter. The daughter …' he trailed off.

'What about the daughter?'

'Nothing. There's this bizarre thing about my family—some people are born mute. Others are blessed with beautiful voices, and they sing very well ...'

'Your uncle's daughter isn't mute, is she?' Vandiyadevan asked.

'No, no!'

'So you mean she sings well. Very well. Better than you?'

'Some question you've asked. You might as well have asked, "Does the koel sing better than the crow?" When Poonguzhali sings, the king of the ocean, Samudra Raja, stops crashing one wave against the next and listens quietly. The cattle and wild animals alike freeze in place and listen, forgetting to graze, forgetting themselves ...'

'Your uncle's daughter's name is Poonguzhali, is it? Beautiful name!'

'As if it is only her name that is beautiful!'

'She must be a beauty, too, or you wouldn't speak with such fervour, would you?'

'The deer and the peacock would have to beg her for a fraction of her beauty. Rathi and Indrani would have to do penance for several births to be blessed with her beauty.'

Vandiyadevan observed that Senthan Amudan's heart was not entirely dedicated to his worship of Shiva.

'So she's the right match for you, then! If she's your

mother's brother's daughter, she is your muraippennu, your bride-to-be, isn't she? When is the wedding?' Vandiyadevan asked.

'I would never say she's a match for me. I can in no way claim to be her equal. If they organised a swayamvaram for Poonguzhali as they did for princesses in the old days, the rulers of all fifty-six kingdoms would rush to win her hand! The devas might descend from the skies, as they once did in the hope of marrying Damayanti. But perhaps all this won't come to pass in Kalyug.'

'So you mean, even if she wished to marry you, you would turn her down?'

'Yeah, right. If God were to appear before me and ask, "Would you rather come to Kailash as Sundaramurti did in this corporeal form, or would you rather live on in this earth with Poonguzhali for your wife?", I would choose the latter without a moment's hesitation. But what's the point of my saying it?'

'Why do you say there's no point? As long as you're willing, the marriage is only a formality, isn't it? Does everyone wait for the woman's consent for marriage? Take the case of Periya Pazhuvettaraiyar, who has got married after turning sixty-five. Do you think the wedding would have taken place with the queen's consent?'

'Anna! This concerns a powerful house. Why must we talk of their personal affairs? Let me give you an important warning. You're about to enter the fort.

Don't speak about the Pazhuvettaraiyars inside. That would invite danger.'

'What is this, thambi, you're scaring the daylights out of me!'

'I'm not exaggerating. To tell the truth, it is the two Pazhuvettaraiyar brothers who are running the Chozha kingdom now. No one can override their authority.'

'Not even the Chakravarti?'

'The Chakravarti is ill. People say that he won't cross the lines chalked by the Pazhuvettaraiyars. They say not even his sons can get through to him.'

'Is that so? The Pazhuvettaraiyars' influence must be quite limitless then. I don't remember their having such great authority a couple of years ago?'

'No. To be precise, it was after the emperor moved to Thanjai that their authority crossed all limits. There is no one to even question their commands. One hears that Aniruddha Brahmaraayar has left for Pandiya Naadu from frustration and disgust at how things stand.'

'Why did the emperor move from Pazhaiyarai to Thanjavur? Do you know, thambi?'

'I'll tell you what I've heard. Three years ago, Veerapandiyan died in battle. Apparently, the Chozha Army went on a rampage in Pandiya Naadu around then. Those are the ways of warriors, aren't they? Madurai was brought under Chozha rule. But I believe some of Veerapandiyan's most loyal men have sworn to exact revenge and are hatching some sort of conspiracy. The Pazhuvettaraiyar brothers brought the emperor to Thanjai because they felt he couldn't be protected in Pazhaiyarai. The fort is impenetrable, and there is strength in the number of guards they have at their disposal. The physicians also said this place was better suited to the king's health than Pazhaiyarai.'

'Everyone speaks of Sundara Chozhar's health. But no one seems to know what ails him.'

'What do you mean? Of course, people know! The emperor suffered a stroke that rendered both his legs useless.'

'Adada! So he can't walk at all?'

'He can't walk. He can't ride an elephant or a horse. He is confined to his bed. The only way he can travel is by palanquin. And that, too, with great discomfort. So, he never leaves the palace. They say that, of late, his mind is not what it used to be either.'

'Aha! What a terrible pity! How very pathetic!'

'You shouldn't use words like "pity" and "pathetic", anna! The Pazhuvettaraiyars might punish you for treason.'

Pazhuvettaraiyar, Pazhuvettaraiyar!—everywhere he went, everyone he spoke to went on and on about the Pazhuvettaraiyars! So what if they were so very powerful and so very courageous? The emperor shouldn't have let things come to such a pass that they now controlled the entire infrastructure of the treasury, granary, security, defence and espionage!

It was only because he had ceded so much authority
to them that they had felt emboldened to conspire
against the emperor himself. How successful would
that conspiracy be? He must do all he could to ensure
that it failed. If the opportunity arose, he must warn
the emperor, too!

He had arrived at the entrance to the fort.
Senthan Amudan took leave of his newfound friend
and went towards the Thalikulaththaar temple. And
Vandiyadevan approached the palace, building his own
castles in the air.

25

INSIDE THE FORT

The ring that bore the palm leaf emblem turned out to be quite as powerful as the magical rings that populate folklore. Its omnipotence was in evidence at the entrance, where dairy farmers, flower vendors, vegetable and fruit sellers, craftsmen and artisans of various persuasions, clerks, accountants and several others were jostling against each other to get in. The guards made full use of the authority they had over this piece of earth, and insisted on letting them in one by one through a tiny gate embedded in the main gate. But the moment Vandiyadevan brandished the ring, they treated him with utmost respect, even deigning to open one of the main gates so that he could make a grand entrance, which he duly did.

Aha! What was it about the moment Vandiyadevan set foot inside the fort that set off such a series of significant events? This occurrence spawned great events, events that would change the course of the

Chozha Empire's history. We can't tell how the celestial bodies were aligned at the time, but the planets must have conspired to create such ramifications that a single moment turned out to be quite momentous.

For a while after he entered the fort, Vandiyadevan walked in a daze. Kanchi had been the capital of the ancient Pallava Empire. It had been subjected to enemy attacks over and over again. The forts and palaces and other old buildings had run to ruin, their walls coated in moss and mildew. The beautiful sculptures that adorned the walls had been defaced by time as much as by weapons. The few buildings that had been renovated or rebuilt since Aditya Karikalan had taken up residence there stood out like fresh flowers on a dying tree, and only served to further exacerbate the city's air of dilapidation by highlighting how old and brittle most of its buildings were.

Thanjai presented quite the contrast. Every fort, every palace and every grand residence was new.

Most were of white chunna, while some were of burnished red brick. To his eyes, the red brick structures appeared like rubies set among pearls and diamonds. Some of the palace gardens housed grown trees that had drawn their nutrients from the red soil and stretched out their lush foliage. Punnai, coconut, ashoka, peepul, aal, jackfruit and neem trees spread their leaves in various tints of green. It was balm to the eyes, invigorating to the mind. This city must have been designed by Mayasura, the architect gifted with magical powers! His heart felt full, and an inexplicable sense of pride infused his being.

The stringent security and ceaseless criteria for entry into the fort had led Vandiyadevan to think few people could have got past the gate, and that the world beyond the walls would be sparsely populated. He couldn't have been more wrong. The streets were bustling with people. Horses and horse-drawn chariots thundered past, their hooves making the earth shudder and quake. Looming black mountains approached—the elephants' slow, stately walk made the bells they wore tinkle, and the lilting sound carried through the air. The shouts of traders selling flowers, vegetables, fruits, milk and curd deafened the ears. The pealing of the bells that announced the hour was punctuated by the beats of the perigai drum. The pleasant instrumental music that rang through the city was complemented by the melodious singing voices of women. One would think the temple tiruvizha was on.

This truly was the pinnacle of civilisation. The capital of an empire that was expanding by the day ought to be like this, with its festive atmosphere, grand avenues and lofty architecture.

Vandiyadevan did not wish to make it obvious that he was new to the city. If he asked the way to the palace, he would be seen as a bumpkin from out of town. He must find his way to the emperor's palace without making enquiries. Surely this wasn't an impossible task?

Everywhere he looked, the buildings were crowned by makara thoranam—decorative brass arches—and flags. They fought the brisk westerly wind with a 'sadasada' and 'padapada'. Flags bearing the tiger emblem and the palm tree emblem outnumbered the rest. Dwarfing all others and rising to the skies was a particularly large tiger flag. *That must be the emperor's palace*, Vandiyadevan thought, and directed his steps towards the building.

First up, he would have to hand over the letter to Sundara Chozhar. He would also have to deliver the verbal message with which Aditya Karikalan had entrusted him. He could not meet the emperor without the permission of Chinna Pazhuvettaraiyar. How was he to obtain this permission? He had entered the fort thanks to divine intervention. But could he depend on the gods to show him the way and sit back until they did? No, he would have to come up with a ruse himself. *What ruse will work? My brain, inherited from generations of Vaanar scions, please do some thinking. Let your imagination come up with something. It is not only poets and writers of epics who have need of imagination. People like you, who have royal duties, need a strong kalpana, too. Let's see what you come up with!* Vandiyadevan said to himself.

He had already ascertained that Periya Pazhuvettaraiyar had not returned.

The moment he'd passed the entrance to the fort, he had asked the guard who stood right inside, 'Appa, has Pazhuvettaraiyar returned?'

'Whom are you asking after, thambi? Chinna Pazhuvettaraiyar is in the palace.'

'Like I don't know that! I was asking after the senior, who has journeyed to the midlands.'

'Oh! He has gone to the midlands, has he? I didn't know that. Ilaiya Rani's palanquin returned last evening. Periya Arasar has not returned yet. We've been told he is scheduled to return tonight,' the guard had said.

This was good news. He had to deliver the letter before Periya Pazhuvettaraiyar returned. How was he to go about it? A thought occurred to Vandiyadevan, and wiped the anxious frown off his face. He wore an impish smile and a cheerful air instead.

He didn't have much trouble finding the emperor's palace. He kept his eyes on the mammoth tiger flag, and soon found himself at the entrance. Aha! What a palace this was! It could rival that of Indra in Devalokam and that of Vikramaditya in Ujjaini. The sculptures at the entrance were mesmerising. Every pillar had been carved with a horse that stood on its hind legs, its forelegs kicking as if it were about to break out of its confines.

There were several gates that opened into the palace, each guarded by two horsemen and several foot soldiers. Many of those who had hoped to sneak into the palace turned back at the sight of them. Some others made so bold as to stare at the façade and admire the flag. If they overstayed their welcome, the guards would ensure a crowd didn't gather by signalling that they should leave. No one protested. Those who stood waiting didn't raise their voices; they whispered among themselves.

Vandiyadevan didn't dawdle like the others. He walked straight up to one of the gates and came face to face with the guards. The horsemen closed ranks so he could not enter, while the foot soldiers crossed spears.

Vandiyadevan brandished his magical ring. That was it; the soldiers seemed rather excited by it all. Three of them examined the ring closely.

'All right, give way!' one of them said at last.

Vandiyadevan walked past jauntily. And yet, what had he achieved? How many more spears and horses would block his path? Where could Chinna Pazhuvettaraiyar be? How would he find out? Whom could he ask? He could not meet the emperor without Chinna Pazhuvettaraiyar's permission. Who knew where the ailing king had been housed in this enormous palace? Where could he begin his search?

Suddenly sensing a group of men behind him, Vandiyadevan turned. Yes. A group of ten or fifteen had approached the guards, and stood before them now. They wore expensive silks, and sported pearl necklaces, brass ornaments and dangling earrings. Some had anointed their foreheads with the Vaishnavite mark, while others wore sandalwood paste or vermilion. Ah! They looked rather like poets. Yes, it was certain they were. Vandiyadevan was to have proof for this surmise in a moment.

One of the guards, likely their leader, said, 'The poets are here! Give way!' He then singled out a soldier and said, 'Chinna Pazhuvettaraiyar is in the astana mandapam. Take them to him!' He added, 'My dear poets—if you're given a reward, make sure you exit this way. If not, go through one of the other gates when you return,' prompting a burst of laughter from those who were listening.

The fruit has fallen into the milk all by itself, Vandiyadevan thought. If he were to join the group of poets, he would be taken to Chinna Pazhuvettaraiyar. Then, it was up to his smarts. And good fortune! With these thoughts, he joined the procession of poets.

26

'DANGER! DANGER!'

Vandiyadevan entered the astana mandapam—the royal hall—ahead of the poets. The man sitting authoritatively on a high throne must be Chinna Pazhuvettaraiyar, he surmised. Around him was an assembly of men with their arms folded and mouths covered by one hand in an unctuous display of respect. One of them held all the letters that had arrived that morning. The accountant waited his turn. The commanders of the security forces awaited instructions for the day from Chinna Pazhuvettaraiyar. Various servants stood about, ready to do their master's bidding. Two stood behind the throne, fanning Chinna Pazhuvettaraiyar with the yak hair fans that were a symbol of royalty. A man stood by with a box of betel leaves. Such was Chinna Pazhuvettaraiyar's aura that even Vandiyadevan, who was rarely awed by a show of pride and didn't lack for arrogance himself, felt compelled to approach the throne with some trepidation and timorousness. The younger brother appeared to outdo the older with his regal form.

He smiled upon seeing our hero and asked, 'Who are you, thambi? From where have you come?'

When he chanced upon well-built young men, Chinna Pazhuvettaraiyar's scowling countenance was prone to alter itself into a smile. He was keen to absorb every strapping young man who crossed his path into his security forces.

'Thalapathi![1] I have come from Kanchi! The prince has sent a missive!' Vandiyadevan replied, in a humble tone.

Chinna Pazhuvettaraiyar's face grew severe at the reference to Kanchipuram.

'What? What did you say?' he asked.

'I've come from Kanchi, with a missive from the prince!'

'Where is it? Hand it over!' Chinna Pazhuvettaraiyar said. Although he took care to sound nonchalant, even dismissive, his voice betrayed that he had been flustered by the statement.

Vandiyadevan took out the scroll, but said in a tone of great humility, 'Thalapathi! The missive is for the emperor!'

Ignoring the mild protest, Chinna Pazhuvettaraiyar took the scroll and looked at it with interest. Then, he asked the man standing by his side to read it aloud. Having heard it, he muttered as if to himself, 'There's nothing new in here.'

'Thalapathi! The missive I brought ...' Vandiyadevan began.

'What about it? I'll hand it over to the emperor!'

'No ... I've been instructed to hand it over to the emperor personally.'

'Oho! So I'm not to be trusted, is it? Is that what Prince Adityar has told you?' Even as he spoke the words, the face of the man who had charge of the Thanjai fort glowered with fury.

'It wasn't the prince who told me to hand it over personally. It was your brother who gave me the order.'

'What? What did you say? Where did you meet Periyavar?'

'I had stayed at Kadambur Sambuvarayar's house one night. That was where we met. He gave me this ring, too ...'

'Aha! Why did you not tell me this right away? You stayed the night at Kadambur? Who else was there?'

'There were dignitaries from Mazhanaadu, Nadunaadu, Tirumunaippaadi, and a host of other places ...'

'Wait, wait! We'll talk at leisure later. First, go deliver the letter personally to the emperor and come back here. Or the poets will arrive, and go on and on and on ... You, there! Take this boy to the emperor!' Chinna Pazhuvettaraiyar said, turning to a guard who stood nearby.

Vandiyadevan followed the guard further into the interior of the palace.

The throne of an empire that covered such a large swathe of land that one could hear the waves crashing against three different shores without leaving its domains had been serving as a sick bed for some time. Parantaka Chozha Chakravarti sat leaning against the back rest of the throne now. Although he had delegated his royal duties to others and was focused on the medical treatment that he was undergoing, there were certain important occasions that necessitated that the emperor meet certain important people. It was deemed crucial for the welfare of the kingdom that his ministers, army commanders and Velakkaara warriors saw him every day.

A veteran of numerous wars in which he had conducted himself with such valour as to have earned the epithet 'Asagaya Soorar'—the warrior who can take on any enemy with no assistance—and a man so handsome his only equal was Manmadha was now so frail that Vandiyadevan was stunned into silence upon seeing the emperor's stooped shoulders and skeletal frame. He felt his eyes brim with tears. He went close to the emperor, knelt at his feet, paid his obeisance and held out the letter with immense devotion.

As he took the scroll from him, the emperor asked in a reedy voice, 'Where have you come from? Who has sent this?'

'Prabhu! I came from Kanchi. Prince Adityar has

sent the scroll!' said Vandiyadevan, stammering from the shock of learning just how ill the king was.

The king's face brightened at once. Tirukkovaloor Malayaman's daughter, Chakravartini Vaanamahadevi, was seated by him. He turned to her and said, 'Devi! There is a scroll from your son!' He opened it eagerly. 'Aha! I believe the prince has built his golden palace in Kanchi, and wants us to come stay.' Even as he spoke the words, his face fell. 'Devi! You see what your son is up to? My forebear, Parantaka Chakravarti, whose praises were sung the world over, donated all the gold in the palace treasury to build a golden roof for the Tillai Ambalam and turn it into Ponnambalam. None of the great rulers who have preceded us has ever built a golden palace for himself. All of them considered temples far more important than palaces. But look at what Aditya Karikalan has gone and done! Aha! What penance could I possibly undertake to make up for such sacrilege!'

The Chakravartini, whose face had glowed with the delight of hearing from her son a moment ago, now looked even more morose than she had earlier.

Vandiyadevan impetuously summoned up the courage to venture, 'Prabhu! What your son has done is not quite so terrible, is it? He has, in fact, done something noble and praiseworthy. Is it wrong for a son to see his parents as his primary gods? Is it not natural that he build a palace of gold for his gods?'

Sundara Chozhar smiled and said, 'Thambi! I don't

know who you are, but you seem to be an intellectual as well as a sophist. Well, a mother and father may be gods to their son, but they are not to anyone else, are they? Shouldn't temples of gold be reserved for gods whom everyone can worship?'

'Prabhu! A son considers his father his god; and the people consider their king their god. The vedas and puranas say the ruler is God's representative on earth. So, whichever way you look at it, you must admit it's quite appropriate that you live in a golden palace,' said our hero.

Sundara Chozhar looked at Malayaman's daughter and said, 'Devi! Do you see how intelligent this boy is? If our Adityan has people like this young man around him, we need have no cause for worry on his account. His brashness and carelessness have made us so anxious, but we can draw comfort from the fact that he has such friends!'

He then turned to Vandiyadevan and said, 'Thambi! Whether building me a palace of gold was noble or ignoble, it is quite impossible for me to come to Kanchi. You have seen for yourself that I'm confined to my bed. I cannot dream of undertaking such a long journey. It is Adityan who must come here to see me. We do long to see him. Come here again tomorrow! I will have a reply ready for him!'

Just then, Vandiyadevan sensed a crowd approaching them. Aha! It must be the poets. Chinna Pazhuvettaraiyar might have chosen to accompany them, too. Vandiyadevan wouldn't be able to say what he had to if he let this moment pass! He would have to blurt it out as quickly as he could. Having unspooled this thread of thought and arrived at his conclusion, Vandiyadevan said, 'Chakravarti! Please permit me to say this. Have the kindness to hear me out! You must absolutely leave this Thanjai. You are surrounded by danger here! Abaayam! Abaayam! Danger! Danger!'

Even as he was saying these words, Chinna Pazhuvettaraiyar entered the king's chambers. The poets followed him.

The commander of the fort heard Vandiyadevan's last words. Flames of fury danced across his face.

27

THE POETS OF THE
ROYAL COURT

'Paraak! Paraak! Here come the illustrious poets! The crown jewels of the empire, the great composers! The blessed who have seen the shores of the great ocean that is Tamil! The descendants of Sage Agastya! They who have drunk the very essence of great treatises such as the *Tholkaappiyam*! They who have read the five iconic Tamil epics such as the *Silappadikaram* backwards and forwards and sideways, too! They who have conquered the very epitome of divine Tamil, the *Tirukkural*! They who know the grammar that informs literature! They who know the literature that conforms to grammar! They who are adept at composing their own lyrics, too! Each and every one of them has filled enough scrolls with poetry to ensure that crores and crores of termites may survive for several years on those alone!'

The distinguished poets arrived in a mob at the altar of Sundara Chozha Chakravarti.

'Vaazhga! Vaazhga! Long live, long live! Long live
Sundara Chozha Mahachakravarti who has brought all
the seven worlds under a single flag! Long live the lord
who felled the Pandiya king! Long live the guardian of
poets! Long live the compassionate patron who is the
very refuge of laureates! May the blessed grandson of
Pandita Vatsalar Parantaka Chakravarti live for a very,
very long time!' said the poets by way of greeting.

Sundara Chozhar was not a fan of such exuberance
and oleaginousness. But he kept this to himself and,
forgetting his indisposition, attempted to stand to
greet the poets.

Chinna Pazhuvettaraiyar came up to him at once
and said, 'Prabhu, the poets are here for a darshan
of Your Highness, and to pay their respects, not to
inconvenience you in any manner. I pray that you not
trouble yourself!'

'Yes, yes! O, king of kings! Lord of emperors! We
do not wish to inconvenience you in the least!' said
the general of this army of poets, Nallan Saatanaar.

'It gives me great joy to meet you all after such
a long gap. Please take your seats. You must recite
some poetry before you go!' said the emperor, who
had great love for the language of his land, Tamil.

Everyone sat on the opulent rugs that had been
arranged on the floor. Sensing an opportunity, our
hero Vandiyadevan took his seat among the poets as
well. He had no mind to leave without saying all he
had to say to the emperor. He sat down in the hope

that he would get the chance to finish what he had started.

Chinna Pazhuvettaraiyar noted that Vandiyadevan had made himself comfortable in the poets' midst. His cheek twitched, taking his moustache with it. He wondered whether he should order him out. Then, he concluded it was best the young man remain under his nose. So, he chose to ignore him. Once the poets left, he would take him aside and interrogate him so he learnt what exactly the emperor had been told. He could still hear the urgent whisper, 'Abaayam! Abaayam! Danger! Danger!'

'Esteemed poets, it has been a long time since I heard a Tamil composition. My ears ache for the sound of our beautiful language. Has anyone among you brought a new composition for me today?' Sundara Chozha Chakravarti asked.

At this, one of the illustrious crown jewels stood up and said, 'Prabhu! I come from the great Palli that has been endowed your name—the Sundara Chozha Perumpalli of Ulagapuram. The fact that a Shiva devotee such as you has bestowed grants for the constructions of Buddhist temples has moved the Buddhists across Tamizhagam, and they sing your praises. But upon learning of your ill health, they have been frenzied with worry and are praying for your recovery. You must permit me to sing one of these prayer songs!'

'Please do go ahead; I'm waiting eagerly to hear it,' said the emperor.

The poet sang the following lines:

Bodhiya tirunizhal punida! Nirparavudum
Medagu Nandapuri mannar Sundara
Chozhar vanmayum vanappum
Thinmayum ulagir siranduvaazhgenave!

The divine shade and shelter
To the followers of Buddhism,
May His Excellency, the King of Nandapuri[1]
Sundara Chozhar grow in prosperity, beauty and strength
Unparalleled in this world!'

The other poets chorused, 'Wonderful! Excellent!' once he was done.

'It comes as a surprise that the Buddhists have so much gratitude,' said one devout Shaivite among the poets.

'Yes. It is indeed a surprise. My service to the Ulagapuram Buddha temple is so meagre that it is hardly deserving of praise!' said the king.

'Which person who has been on the receiving end of the Chakravarti's largesse could resist singing his praises, if for nothing else then as a paltry expression of immense gratitude? Why, Indra, Surya and Shiva Peruman themselves have had the experience of benefiting from your generosity!' said another gem among the poets.

A smile playing on his lips, Sundara Chozhar said, 'What is this now? Indra, Surya and Shiva Peruman, too? Why must they feel immense gratitude to me?'

'You must permit me to recite a poem,' the poet in question said.

'As you wish,' said the emperor.

The poet brandished the scroll he had brought, rolled it open and began to read:

> *Indiran era kari aliththaar*
> *Pari ezhaliththaar*
> *Senthiru meni Dinakarku*
> *Sivanaar manaththu*
> *Paindugilera pallakaliththaar*
> *Pazhaiyarai Nagar*
> *Sundara Chozharai yaavaroppar thonnilaththe!*

> *He gave Indra an elephant,*
> *Seven horses*
> *For the golden-hued Sun to mount,*
> *A palanquin for Shiva's wedding procession.*
> *Who in this world could be*
> *The equal of Sundara Chozhar of Pazhaiyarai Nagar?*

The response to this poem was befitting of its unctuousness. The other poets applauded and sighed and gasped and chorused, 'Aha!' and 'Wonderful!' and 'Excellent!'

Sundara Chozhar laughed and said, 'Could someone explain what this poem means?'

Several of the poets stood up at once. Eventually, everyone except Nallan Saatanaar sat back down, and he began to explain the import of the lines:

'Once upon a time, Devendra[2] and Vritrasura were engaged in a fierce battle. Indra's mount Airavata died fighting, and Indra was searching for an elephant that could replace the celestial one. Where could he possibly find an equal, he wondered. He finally approached Sundara Chozhar of Pazhaiyarai Nagar and asked if he had an elephant that could match Airavata's prowess. 'I have none that can match Airavata,' the emperor said. 'I'm afraid I only have elephants that could outdo your late celestial mount.' He then led Indra to the elephant stables, where Indra stared in awe at the thousands of magnificent animals, each as large as a mountain, and wondered which he should pick. Sundara Chozhar noticed his bewilderment, and picked an elephant for the Lord of the Devas. *How am I going to tame this monster?* Indra wondered. *Not even my Vajrayudha, my thunderbolt, would be effective!* Reading his mind, Sundara Chozhar gave Indra a bull hook that was even more powerful than the thunderbolt.

'Another time, Surya Bhagavan who spreads his golden rays and lights up the world got into an epic fight with the asura Raahu. Raahu tried to swallow the sun whole, but he wasn't able to, so powerful were Surya's rays. But the seven horses that pulled the Sun God's chariot fell victim to the kalakuta venom of the demon. As Surya was wondering how he would travel across the skies without his steeds, Sundara Chozhar donated seven of his own stallions to Surya Bhagavan, who was now beholden to the emperor for his timely help. It was also a matter of great pride to Surya that this aid had been rendered by a scion of the Suryavansh, his own clan.

'As for the third story, Shiva Peruman and Parvati Devi were to be married in Kailash. The bride's family had brought a dazzling array of gifts as dowry. But they failed to include a palanquin. When they arrived, they realised the only mount available to the couple for the wedding procession was the bull. The bride's family was now worried. The moment Sundara Chozha Chakravarti got wind of the situation, he ordered that his pearl palanquin be brought from the Pazhaiyarai Palace. The king then gifted it to Shiva Peruman with great devotion, as his wedding present.

'Is there anyone in this wide world, any soul living on any land mass surrounded by its oceans, who can claim to be the equal of Sundara Chozha Chakravarti, then?'

Sundara Chozha Chakravarti, having heard him out, now burst into laughter. Hearing her husband, whose illness had robbed him of laughter and her ears of its pleasant resonance, his devoted wife, the daughter of Malayaman, felt invigorated by his energy. The royal physicians found themselves open to hope, and the various servants standing around were cheered by the emperor's mirth.

The guardian of the fort, Chinna Pazhuvettaraiyar, who had stood silent all this time, now bowed low to the emperor and folded his hands to ask for forgiveness.

'Prabhu!' he said. 'I am guilty of a grievous error. I beg that you be so kind as to give me clemency.'

'Ah! Is it the Thalapathi who speaks? What grievous error have you committed? Why all this talk of clemency? Perhaps you have seized the elephant I gave Indra and the seven stallions I gave Surya, and brought them back to the stables? Or dragged the palanquin away from Shiva? You're not incapable of such deeds!' said Sundara Chozhar, and began to laugh again. The poets laughed, too. Vandiyadevan laughed louder than anyone else.

Chinna Pazhuvettaraiyar made note of this and threw him a fierce glare. And then, he turned to the emperor and said:

'King among kings! This is the error I have committed—all these days, I have prevented illustrious poets such as these men from coming to meet you. I did as the royal physician ordered. But I now see I was in the wrong. The arrival of these poets has enlivened you. Their words have rejuvenated you. Their songs have made you laugh out loud. The sound of your laughter has made Udaya Piraatti's[3] face glow, and thrilled everyone else in the room. I am overjoyed. It was truly a crime, was it not, to have denied these people who can bring you so much cheer access to your chambers?'

'Well said! You have finally realised the error of your ways, haven't you? You see why I would so often ask you to ignore the physician's orders and tell you not to prevent the poets from visiting, don't you?' said the Chakravarti.

The royal physician got up, bent low, put a hand over his mouth in a show of humility and launched into some sort of explanation or apology. Sundara Chozhar ignored him and addressed the poets instead. 'Does any of you know who composed this wonderful poem? Please do tell me if you know.'

Nallan Saatanaar said, 'O king among kings! I'm afraid none of us does. We have been trying to find out. We would like to bestow the title "Kavi Chakravarti" on him, and carry his palanquin on our shoulders for some distance as a mark of our admiration for him. But our efforts have not borne fruit thus far.'

'This does not surprise me. A poet who has packed so many lies into four short lines would never want to step forward and announce himself to the world, would he?' said the Maharaja.

The poets' faces were a sight now. They were too stunned to think of a reply.

At this moment, our Vandiyadevan had the gumption to jump up and say, 'Prabhu! It isn't right to dismiss all of this as lies. If a commoner came up with a narration that was entirely fictional, yes, it could be deemed a lie. If those in charge of governance were to do so, that is chicanery of Chanakya's school of thought. If poets were to do so, it is creativity, a decorative literary device that enhances the truth, *ani alangaaram, ilporul uvamai*—an analogy that imagines the nonexistent ...'

The poets turned to him as one and chorused, 'Well said!'

The emperor, too, looked at Vandiyadevan sharply, and said, 'Oh! You're the one who brought the scroll from Kanchi, aren't you? You clever, clever boy! You've managed to outwit me!' He then turned to the others and said, 'Esteemed poets! However wonderful the verse might seem to you, there is no need to trouble yourself looking for the poet or bestowing titles upon him. I know the poet who came up with these lines. His head is already burdened by the unbearably heavy crown of the Chozha Empire. This king among poets must also carry the titles of *Bhuvi Chakravarti, Tribhuvana Chakravarti, Ezhulaga Chakravarti*—the king of the world, of the three worlds, of the seven worlds—against his will.'

If I were to say here that the entire body of poets now flailed about in an ocean of surprise, the readers must not claim I am lying. They must see it as creativity, a decorative literary device that enhances the truth, *ani alangaaram, ilporul uvamai*—an analogy that imagines the nonexistent!

28

AN IRON GRIP

Once the first flood of the shock had receded, Nallan Saatanaar said, 'Prabhu! You mean that the poet who composed this verse ... is ...' and trailed off.

'None other than the Bhuvi Chakravarti who lies on his sick bed before you, having lost all use of his legs,' said Sundara Chozhar.

Exclamations of surprise and wonderment rippled through the assembly of poets. Some of them, not sure how to express their inner voices, shook their heads and shuddered. Others, not even sure what their inner voices were saying, stood as if turned to stone.

Sundara Chozhar said, 'Esteemed poets! Once upon a time, poets and composers would come to visit me at Pazhaiyarai. Some among you must have been in those groups. They would often sing the praises of the Chozha clan, and particularly of me. *He endowed so-and-so with this, He bestowed that upon so-and-so*, that's how the songs went. Ilaiya Piraatti, who was a child back then, was by my side on one such occasion. Once the poets had received their gifts and left, the princess began to sing *their* praises. I told her I could compose a better paean to myself than the poets had. And I made up this verse as a joke. I asked Kundavai for a reward. My little girl jumped up on to my back, said, "Here's your reward!" and gave me two sharp slaps on the cheek. I remember it like it was yesterday, but it happened more than eight years ago.'

'What a wonder, a wonder!' 'Amazing, amazing!' The poets, as was their wont, were overjoyed by this royal anecdote.

The very name 'Kundavai' sent tremors through Vandiyadevan's body. He had heard ever so much about the beauty and wisdom and intelligence of this Chozha princess without parallel. Sundara Chozhar was the man who had the fortune of being the father of that wondrous woman; and her mother was the elderly lady before him. What pride and joy it gave Sundara Chozhar to speak of his daughter! His very voice had been infused with warmth and tenderness.

Vandiyadevan ran his right hand over the silk cloth he had tied around his waist. That was where he had hidden away the scroll he was to hand over to Kundavai Piraatti. His hand froze. His heart stopped. Aiyo! What was this? The scroll was missing! Where had it gone? Had it fallen somewhere along the way? Perhaps it had been pulled out accidentally when he had reached for the scroll he had handed over to the emperor? Where could it have fallen? Perhaps in the royal court? In that case, what if Chinna Pazhuvettaraiyar were to get his hands on it? If that came to pass, what dangers would it pose? Adada! What a terrible blunder this was! What an enormous mistake! How was he to come out of this?

Once he realised the scroll he was to deliver to Kundavai Devi was missing, Vandiyadevan couldn't bear to stay on. He barely heard the repartee that followed. Even when he did hear the words, he didn't register them.

Sundara Chozhar looked at the poets flailing in the aforementioned ocean of surprise and said, 'Kundavai must have recited the poem I made up as a joke to someone. Perhaps to Eesaanya Bhattacharyar of the Pazhaiyarai Tirumetrali temple. He must have gone to town with it and made me the laughingstock of the land.'

'Prabhu! So what if you wrote the verse yourself? It is a wonderful poem! There is no doubt about it. You're not just Bhuvi Chakravarti, you're Kavi Chakravarti, too!' said Nallan Saatanaar.

'And yet, if I had written it now, I would have added another one to the great exploits of Sundara Chozhar. I wouldn't have stopped with the largesse of an elephant to Indra and stallions to Surya and palanquin to Shiva. When Yama came for Markandeya, Shiva kicked him away, didn't he? Yama ran for his life, but his poor buffalo died from the vicious kick. Seeing

Yama suffer without his mount, Pazhaiyarai Sundara
Chozhar gave the God of Death a fresh buffalo. I would
have imagined this scene, too. And as poetic irony, we
have this—it is on that very buffalo that Yama now
comes for me. Not even our commander, Chinna
Pazhuvettaraiyar, can deny Yama and his buffalo entry
into the Thanjai fort, can he?'

Hearing these words, tears welled up in the eyes
of his wife. The poets began to sob and wail.

Chinna Pazhuvettaraiyar alone stood steadfast.

'Prabhu, I am ready to fight even Yama in your
service!' he said.

'I have no doubt you will, Thalapathi. And yet no
human can defeat Yama in battle. All we can do is
pray that we don't live in fear of him. O poets! Didn't
one of our great poets sing a verse that went *Namanai
anjom—We don't fear Yama*—?'

One of the poets stood up and recited:

Naamaarkkum kudiyallom
Namanai anjom
Naragaththil idarpadom
Nadalaiyallom
Emaappom piniyariyom

We shall be slaves to no one
We shall have no fear of Yama
Hell shall not discomfit us
We shall not turn to deceit or treachery
We shall never know the pain of affliction

The emperor interrupted at this point to say, 'Aha! Who could have sung with such courage but a great soul who has had the good fortune of seeing God in the flesh! The saint Appar had severe arthritis and rheumatism. He was cured by the grace of God. This is why he sings, "We shall never know the pain of affliction." Esteemed poets! Please stop singing of me and of my largesse, and sing the praise of God instead. Appar, Sambandar and Sundaramoorti have sung thousands of devotional verses in Tamil. How wonderful it would be if we could compile all of them! One lifetime will not suffice to read those verses and learn them and sing them and sense the joy of hearing those words ...'

'King among kings! If you permit us, we will start this divine pursuit right away!'

'No, this task of compilation cannot possibly be completed in my time. Perhaps when I'm no more ...' Sundara Chozhar trailed off as his eyes took on a faraway look. He was in deep contemplation when the royal physician approached Chinna Pazhuvettaraiyar and whispered in his ear. Seeing this, Sundara Chozhar opened his eyes wide with a start and stared at the assembly. He appeared as a man who had suddenly returned from another world, from the jaws of death, from under Yama's nose.

'Prabhu! You had said you would like to listen to a poem from the Sangam era. Perhaps once they have fulfilled that wish, the poets may leave?' Chinna Pazhuvettaraiyar asked.

'Yes, yes. I had forgotten all about it. It seems it isn't simply my body that has lost possession of itself, but my mind, too. Who will recite the Sangam poem for me?' the king said.

Chinna Pazhuvettaraiyar signalled discreetly to Nallan Saatanaar, who stood at once and said, 'O king! Karikaal Peruvalaththaar was the most illustrious of your ancestors. He was the great warrior who erected the tiger flag of the Chozhas in every region, right up to the Himalayas. In his time, Poompuhar—Kaverippattinam—was the capital of the Chozha Empire. All kinds of goods from countries all over the world would be sent by sea for sale here. One of the Sangam poets who describes the wealth and prosperity of Poompuhar details the various products that were brought to this land. This is what he says:

> *Vadamalai piranda maniyum ponnum*
> *Kudamalai piranda vaaramum akhilum*
> *Thenkadal muththum gunakadal tugirum*
> *Gangai vaariyum kaveri payanum*
> *Eezhaththu unavu kaazhaga thaakkamum ...*
>
> *The gold and jewels of the northern hills,*
> *Sandalwood and akhil perfume from the western ghats,*
> *Pearls from the southern sea*
> *Coral from the eastern sea*
> *Grains from the shores of the Ganga and Kaveri*
> *Food from Eezham, dyed cloth from ...*

At this point, at a signal from Sundara Chozhar, the poet paused.

'Thalapathi! This poem says food was sent from Eezham to Tamizhagam in the era of Karikaal Valavar. It is for this to be conveyed to me that you have arranged for the poets to visit, is it not?'

'Yes, sire,' said the commander of the fort, in a tone that bordered on the sheepish.

'It has been conveyed to me. Now, you can reward the poets and send them on their way,' the king said.

The poets cried, 'Vaazhi!' and having wished for the long life of their sovereign went on their way.

Vandiyadevan, who was perturbed from having lost the scroll intended for Kundavai Devi's eyes, thought it might be prudent to make his escape with the poets. He slipped into their midst.

But his plans fell through. As he reached the threshold, a strong iron grip took firm hold of his wrist. Vandiyadevan was powerfully built. And yet the strength of the hand that seized him was such that it was as if an electric shock had rattled him from the top of his head to the tips of his toes. He found himself paralysed into stillness.

He looked up, only to realise that the iron grip that had so shaken him was that of Chinna Pazhuvettaraiyar.

The poets left the chamber.

NOTES

1. AADI TIRUNAAL

1. Tirunaal literally means 'The Holy Day'. It refers to the eighteenth day of the Tamil month of Aadi, when the river Kaveri—the Ponni of the title—breaches her banks.
2. This line was written in 1950.
3. An ancient unit of measurement, equivalent to seven and a half naazhigaivazhi, approximately ten miles.
4. Kummi and Sindhu are genres of Tamil folk song.
5. The '-e' at the end is a call to the addressee, something like an 'O'. Pangiyar is the term used for the women among the farmerfolk.
6. Thozhiyar is the term used for female friends.
7. Pangiyar is the term used for a dear friend who shares one's life.
8. Literally means 'younger brother', but is used to address any young man or boy.
9. Respectful address to an older man, something like 'sir'.
10. 'Periya' is 'large', 'big' or 'old'.
11. 'Chinna' is 'small' or 'young'.

2. AZHVARKADIYAAN NAMBI

1 Lady Kundavai.

2 The day when the idol is bathed and anointed with various liquid or floral offerings.

3 Lord Vishnu.

4 (The wearer of) a bun at the forefront of the head.

5 Lout or thug.

6 'Appan' literally means 'father', but can be used sarcastically or seriously to call out to any man, or even—under certain circumstances—a male child.

7 Lord Krishna.

8 A reference to a legend where King Arimarthana Pandiyan calls for each family among his subjects to send one person to help build a dam across the Vaigai River, which was in spate and causing devastation downstream. Vandi, an old woman who sold the rice flour dish puttu for a living, had no family and felt she had failed to contribute to the dam. In response to her prayers, Shiva appeared as an able young man called Chokkan, and offered to stand in for a family member in return for a meal of puttu. Chokkan carried the mud for a while, and then dozed off. The king arrived for an inspection, saw the sleeping man and whacked him on the back with his navaratna staff. Chokkan woke, finished the work, appeared in his true form and gave moksha to Vandi. He also demonstrated his goodwill by stopping the floods on the Vaigai through a divine order.

9 The abode of Vishnu, according to Hindu mythology.

10 A corporeal measure, denoting the distance between the tip of one's thumb and one's elbow.

11 'Pillai' means 'boy'. Pillaai, with an extended -aai sound implies that the person is being addressed or importuned, as with '-e'. This would translate roughly into, 'Ei, you boy!' or 'Watch out, boy!'

12 The traditional Tamil spelling of 'Hari' is 'Ari', since the Tamil letter for 'h' was a relatively recent invention inspired by Sanskrit.

13 Ariyaadavar means 'Those who don't know'. The 'r' sound here is stronger than in 'Ari', similar to the Spanish 'rr'.

14 Are you evil?

15 Are you atheists?

16 The greatest of warriors.

17 Glorious in courage.

18 A man with arms so long his fingers can touch his knees. It is said this physical attribute speaks to the high birth of the man, who might be a god, saint, king or warrior.

3. THE VINNAGARA TEMPLE

1 A corruption of 'kuthirai', the grammatically correct word for horse, prevalent in the south of Tamil Nadu and some parts of Sri Lanka.

2 'Ilakkana aaraaichi' would be the correct phrase for 'grammatical analysis' or 'syntactical analysis'. In one of his many delightful uses of irony in the text, Kalki Krishnamurthy uses the corruption 'ilakkona' with an extended 'o' sound, which tells us that the grammar of the man who mocks the grammatical analysis could do with some editing.

3 A prop used in a folk dance, where the dancer wears the shell of a horse.

4 A mild curse word in Tamil, equating one with the ill luck Shani brings.

5 Sanctum sanctorum.

6 Seva or service to the deity of the temple.

7 Birth star of the Tamil poet and Krishna devotee, Andal.

8 Verses in praise of a god, which lend themselves to various tunes.

9 The Kopparakesari who conquered Madurai and Eezham; 'kesari' means lion, and 'para' could denote either 'clan' or 'enemy', depending on which word it is the stem of. And so, this title, which is exclusively given to Chozha kings, could either mean, 'The king who is a lion to the enemy', or 'The lion of the clan of kings'.

10 Boodham is often used to refer to ghosts, in the same way as 'bhoot' is used. But it may also be said to refer to spirits or forms. Here, Nammazhvar speaks of devotees as manifestations of their god.

11 The word means 'he who contains' or 'he who has'. While some believe the title means 'owner of two worlds', it could also mean 'he who contains the soul of his disciples', where all Vaishnavites could be considered his disciples.

4. THE KADAMBUR PALACE

1 An ancient measure of time, estimated to be around twenty-four minutes.

2 The young master, or the junior master.

3 The festival of Soorasamharam commemorates the legend of Muruga killing the asura Soorapadman and his race. Subramanian is another name for Muruga.

4   This Captain Haddock-like phrase is a faithful translation
    from the Tamil 'ulakkai kozhundhu'. The ulakkai
    is a pestle or rice-pounder used to pulverise crop.
    'Kozhundhu' refers to any tender plant or sapling.

5. THE KURAVAI KOOTHU

1   The practice of winding a richly embroidered cloth
    around the head of a guest, like a turban.

6. MIDNIGHT CONFERENCE

1   The Goddess of Sleep.
2   Someone in disguise, a pretender.

7. RIDICULE AND RAGE

1   While the term 'Piraatti' is the Tamil equivalent of
    the title 'Lady', 'Periya' could mean 'elder' as it does
    in this context, or 'grand', or 'big' too. 'Ilaiya' means
    'young' or 'junior'.
2   This is a reference to the Kallanai Dam built by the
    king across the Kaveri River.
3   Palm leaves on which letters and messages were
    traditionally written.
4   'Tantram' means 'strategy', with the connotation that
    it involves some cunning and chicanery.
5   Aunt; it literally means 'older mother', and could refer
    either to the mother's older sister, or the wife of the
    father's older brother.
6   Scripture.
7   Alli was a legendary queen of the Sangam era, who
    apparently had her own Amazonian kingdom. The
    army was entirely composed of women, as was the
    council of ministers; everyone with any power was

female. The men were merely servants. While the kingdom of Alli flourished, and there is a version of the story in which the Pandava Arjuna was so drawn to Alli for her bravery that he put his life at risk to break into her palace and meet her, 'Alli Rajyam' is always used with negative connotations, as if to suggest governance by women must necessarily be ridiculous.

8. WHO IS IN THE PALANQUIN?

1 The law of Manu, a reference to the *Manusmriti*.
2 The god of love, often erroneously equated with Cupid; Manmadha is a full-grown youth of unequalled beauty, who carries around a bow and five arrows that purportedly induce love.
3 This literally means 'Victorious Spear, Courageous Spear!' Usually associated with the exploits of Lord Muruga, this evolved at some point in history into a war cry.

9. A CHAT EN ROUTE

1 The giant brother of King Ravana; he is said to have slept six months of the year, and entire armies could not wake him up.

10. THE ASTROLOGER OF KUDANDAI

1 This is sung by Madhavi in the *Silappadikaram*. The husband referred to here is the master of the Kaveri River, the Chozha king. She says the king's rule is just, with his sceptre never bending to favour a side, and that he is a great conqueror wielding his spear, because he and the Kaveri draw their strength from each other. This is a verse sung to her lover Kovalan,

suggesting that the two of them, too, feed off each other's strength.

2   Although 'amma' technically means 'mother', it is also a form of endearment, used when one is speaking fondly or sometimes—as in this case—in frustration,

3   'Josiyar' means 'astrologer'. The addition of the 'e' is due to the fact that she is addressing him.

4   'Thaai' is 'mother', but also used as a respectful form of address to any woman.

5   A form of address to a young woman.

6   Princess or royal maiden.

11. GRAND ENTRANCE

1   A term of endearment.

12. NANDINI

1   In Tamil, 'Nama Shivaya' is five letters, and 'Om Namo Narayanaya' or 'Narayana, Narayana'—the two calls devotees use for Lord Vishnu—is eight letters.

2   Appar, Sundarar and Tiru Gnana Sambandar are often referred to as the 'Moovar' (Trinity), the three most prominent Shaivite saints

3   This is nine hundred and eighty years before 1950.

4   A kind of tilaka worn by Vaishnavites on various parts of their bodies, each corresponding to a particular one of Vishnu's names.

13. THE WAXING MOON

1   A sixteenth fraction.

2   Staff, in this context.

3   Kingdom, in this context.

4   Horns, in this context.

5   An ancient measure, amounting to about two-thirds of a sovereign, or 5.4 grams of gold.

15. VANATHI'S SORCERY

1   A demoness from the Ramayana, whose chief preoccupation was to disturb ascetics during penance and desecrate their pujas.

16. ARULMOZHI VARMAR

1   This was written in 1950.
2   The Tamil original says 'twelve years', but this seems to be an error since Madurantakar was a year old at the time.
3   Perhaps closest in connotation to 'nutcase'.

17. THE HORSE REARED!

1   Literally meaning 'female thief', it is an affectionate term for anyone who is mischievous or clever.

18. IDUMBANKAARI

1   A memorial temple erected in honour of kings who had lost their lives valorously on the battlefield.

19. THE FOREST BATTLEFIELD

1   This suggests the two men were built like Bheemasena of the Pandavas.

21. THE SCREEN WENT 'SALA-SALA'

1   An uncle. This could either be one's father's younger brother, or the husband of one's mother's younger sister.
2   This could refer either to a temporary resting place

for travellers, or—if used in a religious context—the sanctum sanctorum of a temple.

26. 'DANGER! DANGER!'

1   This literally means 'general' and refers to the general of the army. But it can also be used loosely to mean 'leader'.

27. THE POETS OF THE ROYAL COURT

1   In the old days, when it was under Pallava rule, Pazhaiyarai was known as 'Nandapuri'.

2   Indra. This name is an agglutinative form of 'Deva' and 'Indra'.

3   This was the customary address for the chief consort of the emperor.

The story continues in

BOOK 2
TROUBLED WATERS

An Extract

'DO YOU REMEMBER ...?'

Nandini went to the garden entrance of the lata mandapam and clapped thrice.

We can't say whether her face had clouded over from fear, or from the dark shadows cast by the trees.

For some distance, ancient trees with enormous trunks and creepers winding their ways up those gnarled trunks made gaunt shapes in the fading light. Beyond, there was only the inky black of night.

Clawing through the inky black and tearing the creepers apart, the mantravadi—the sorcerer—made his appearance from behind a tree.

Nandini returned to her flower bed. Her lovely features wore a sense of calm now.

The mantravadi entered the lata mandapam. The light of the golden lamp fell on his face.

This is a familiar face! Who is he? Oh, yes! He is one of the men from the group that held a secret conference at the Tiruppurambiyam pallipadai. He is the one who emptied his bag and made a heap of gold coins on the forest floor. He is the man who instructed the others to 'kill Azhvarkadiyaan the moment you see him, at the very place you spot him'—Ravidasan.

Even as he arrived, his face simmered with rage. When he saw Nandini reclining against the floral bed, the very embodiment of peace and contentment, his cat eyes glared gimlets at her. The very air around him turned hot and dry from the fires of fury that blazed from within his powerful frame.

Seating himself on the wooden bench before Nandini's bed, he began to chant, 'Hoom! Hreem! Hraam! Bhagavati! Shakti! Chandikeshwari!'

'Enough, stop it! That damned servant woman has gone and fallen asleep on the doorstep. Tell me what you came here to say, quickly! *He* has entered the fort,' Nandini said.

'Adi paadagi! You traitor!' Ravidasan hissed, in a voice that resonated with all the venom of a cobra poised to strike.

'Whom are you talking about?' Nandini asked calmly.

'I'm talking about none other than Nandini the Ingrate; none other than the Ilaiya Rani of Pazhuvoor! None other than you!' said Ravidasan, pointing his index finger dramatically at her.

Nandini made no reply.

'Woman! It appears you have forgotten certain incidents that ought to have been etched on your memory. Let me remind you of them,' said Ravidasan.

'Why dig up the past now?' said Nandini.

'Why now, you ask? I'll tell you. Let me remind you, and then I'll tell you,' Ravidasan said.

Nandini sighed as if she knew there was little point in trying to stop him, and then turned away.

'Rani! Listen! One fine day three years ago, in the middle of the night, a funeral pyre blazed by the banks of the Vaigai River. This was no send-off with final rites officiated by a priest according to the shastras. The pyre had been built from dry branches and twigs and leaves foraged from the forest floor. A corpse that had been hidden behind the trees was then brought and laid on the wood before the pyre was lit. The dry branches and twigs and leaves crackled and the flames rose high into the air. Some people spotted you skulking in the dark and brought you there. Your hands and legs were tied. Your mouth was stuffed with cloth. The hair that is so beautifully arranged in a bun and decorated with flowers was loose, dragging raggedly against the forest floor. Those people wanted to burn you alive in the pyre.

'"Let the fire burn some more," one of them said.

'Those men threw you to the ground and then swore a terrible oath. You were listening. They had gagged you, but hadn't bothered blindfolding you or covering your ears. And so, you kept those eyes and ears open. Having taken their oaths, they came towards you. You, who had stayed silent until then, tried desperately to make some sort of sign with your bound hands. You opened your eyes wide, knitted your eyebrows together and made all sorts of tormented faces.

'One of your captors said, "She wants to say something!"

'Another said, "Must be the same old story. Throw her into the pyre!"

'Yet another said, "No, no! Let's hear what it is she wants to say before we toss her in. Get the cloth out of her mouth!"

'Since he was their leader, they took the cloth out of your mouth. Do you remember what you said then, woman?' Ravidasan asked and paused.

Nandini neither replied, nor turned to face him. The revulsion and terror in her heart were writ large on her countenance, as was the resolve of a truly terrible divine pact. Each of her black eyes played host to a single teardrop that trembled at its corner.

'Woman! You refuse to speak! All right! Don't. Let me remind you of that too. You said you too, like all those men, had sworn to exact revenge. You swore that you had more reason to take that oath than any of them. You said you would use your beauty and intelligence entirely in the service of that oath. You promised to help them to the best of your ability. You averred that you had already decided to take your own life once that oath was fulfilled. None of the others believed you. But I did. I believed you, and I stopped them from throwing you into the fire. I saved your life. Do you remember all this?' Ravidasan asked, and fell silent.

Nandini inclined her body so she was facing him and said, 'You ask if I remember this. All of this is written in indelible letters, forged as if by fire, branded into my heart.'

'Later, we were walking by the shores of the Kaveri, along the forest path. Suddenly, we heard the approach of horsemen. We decided to separate and hide in the forest, each in a different spot. But you alone went against that decision and stood your ground, in broad daylight. Those men took you captive. Their leader Pazhuvettaraiyan was intoxicated by your loveliness, and fell into your honey trap. You married him. The rest of the group told me I had been had. I did not give up on you. I contrived to catch you alone. I wanted to put a dagger through your treacherous heart and kill you. But you begged me to spare your life yet again. You said you had orchestrated all this so we could fulfil our vow. You swore you would help us from the inside, even while living in this palace. Is all this true or not?' Ravidasan demanded.

'All this is true. Who has claimed otherwise? Why are you recounting the story over and over again? Tell me what you're here for!' Nandini said.

'No, woman! You don't remember. You've forgotten everything. You've plunged yourself into the luxury of the Pazhuvoor Palace, and have forgotten your oath! You feast on meals that celebrate all six flavours, ornament yourself in jewellery, drape yourself in fine cloth, sleep on silks and flower beds, and travel

in an ivory palanquin! You are the queen of Pazhuvoor!
Why would old memories carry any meaning?'

'Chhi! Who wants these beds and silks and clothes
and jewellery? Do you think I'm slave to these material
things? Not at all!'

'Or perhaps you have fallen for the handsome
face of the young man who crossed your path? An old
oath could have been subsumed in the fervour of new
romance, couldn't it?'

For the fraction of a second, Nandini was startled.
She made an immediate recovery and said at once,
'Lies! All lies!'

'If it is all lies, why didn't you send your servant
girl to the usual place although I'd sent word ahead
that I'd be coming here today?'

'I did send her. But someone else got in using the
ladder meant for you. That fool of a girl mistook him
for you, and ushered him in. How is that my fault?'

'What does it matter whose fault it was? My very
life was in danger. The fort guards who were looking
for that youth were about to catch me. I jumped
into the pond in the woods by this palace, and stayed
underwater until I was all but out of breath. I surfaced
only after those men had left. That is why I'm even
alive. I was dripping wet ...'

'You deserve it. You have washed off the sin of
suspecting me of treason.'

'Woman! Swear to this! Are you not intoxicated
by that young man's looks?'

'Chhi! What kind of talk is this! Does anyone talk of the good looks of men? It is only in this shameless Chozha Naadu that they celebrate the king's handsomeness. Male beauty must be measured by the battle scars on a man's body, shouldn't it?'

'Well said. Assuming you speak the truth, why did that young man come here?'

'I told you earlier, Vasuki mistook him for you and brought him here.'

'Why did you give him the signet ring that you've refused to give even me?'

'To bring him here so I could speak to him. Now that I've done that, I'm going to take the ring back from him ...'

'Why did you bring him here? What were you yapping about with him all this while?'

'I was *yapping* with him keeping a crucial prospective advantage in mind. He will cause things to turn in our favour.'

'Adi paadagi! You've shown your pennbudhi in the end, the stupidity of the woman you are! You've gone and revealed our secret to a stranger whom ...'

'Why are you panicking? There's no reason for you to rant and rave. I haven't revealed a thing to him. On the contrary, I extracted a secret from him. I inferred a great deal.'

'What did you *infer*?'

'He's taking a scroll from Kanchi to Pazhaiyarai. He's taking it to the tigress in Pazhaiyarai. He showed it to me. I was telling him he would have to show me the reply she wrote, when you landed up.'

'The scroll be damned, and the stylus be damned. Of what use is all that to us?'

'Your brain has reached its saturation point. We have sworn to wipe out the tiger clan. But the lot of you think only of the male tigers. You forget that the dynasty can grow from the tigress too. And that's not all. Who do you think pulls the strings in this Chozha Empire? The old man who has lost all his strength, lost even the ability to move, and lies in his sick bed? The princes in Kanchi and Lanka?'

'No! The man who has had the good fortune of winning you for his queen, the Dhanadhikari Pazhuvettaraiyar. The whole world knows it!'

'That's wrong too. The world believes that to be the case. The old man too has been fooled into thinking that is the case. And you too have been fooled. In reality, it is the tigress in Pazhaiyarai who is running the show. That arrogant woman sits in her palace and pulls all the strings. She believes she can control all the puppets. I'm going to put her in her place. And I'm going to use this young man to do that ...'

Ravidasan's face showed signs of surprise and respect. 'Some skill, you have. I must admit that. But how do I know any of this is true? How do I trust you?'

'I'll hand that young man over to you. You take him through the subterranean passage out of the fort.

Blindfold him when you take him. Then lie in wait near Pazhaiyarai. Bring him back here with the scroll on which Kundavai writes her reply. If he tries to escape, or tries to trick you, do away with him at once.'

'No, no! You and he can go to hell. Chinna Pazhuvettaraiyar's men are scouring the fort for him now. If I went anywhere with him, I'd be putting myself at risk. No. Just tell me what I came to hear.'

'You haven't told me what that is yet ...'

'Preparations have been made for men to go to Kanchi and Lanka. The ones who are going to Lanka have a tough task ahead of them. They'll have to conduct themselves with great expediency ...'

'What do you want me to do about that? You want more gold? Is there no limit to the lust for gold of you lot?'

'The gold is not for our personal use. It is to finish the task we have undertaken. Why else have we allowed you to sit here? The men who are going to Lanka will have no use for the gold coins of Chozha Naadu. It is Lankan gold coins that we need ...'

'Why take so long to say something so simple? I'd kept it ready even before you asked,' Nandini said, and bent under the cot. She reached for a bag, and handed it over to Ravidasan. 'Here's a bagful of Lankan gold. Take it and leave! He will be here any moment!' she said.

As Ravidasan took the bag and made to leave, she

said, 'Hold on! At least show that young man out of the fort. Let him go his own way after. I have no wish to show him the secret passage.'

She rose and peered at the palace, cloaked in dusk.

She couldn't see a thing. She made a sign with her fingers. She clapped softly. It was of no use.

She and Ravidasan walked some distance through the passage that led from the imposing mansion to the exit. They went nearly up to the threshold.

But there was no sign of Vandiyadevan. In all four directions, near and far, there was simply no sign of him!